"You're brilliant."

Christopher complimented Ellen. Then he kissed her. One solid kiss on the lips before he shot her that dimpled grin. That grin that made her stomach flip-flop. That grin that made her realize just how much she liked having him kiss her.

That craving again.

Leaning across the table, she kissed him back.

Christopher's reaction was much more impressive than hers had been. Before she could back away he'd driven his fingers into her hair, locking her against him so he could kiss her once more. A real kiss.

His tongue plunged into her mouth, stealing her breath. Her insides swooped again and her thighs tingled. The only thing she could say was that kissing him back sparked her craving as if she'd tossed a lighted match into a puddle of gas.

Their tongues tangled with urgency. She grew dizzier and giddier as the tabletop cut into her rib cage. Or perhaps it was only his kiss that crushed the breath from her lungs. Either way, Ellen knew she had to have him…*now.*

Dear Reader,

I lived half my life quite happily north of the Mason-Dixon Line and even have the accent to prove it, which most people catch when I ask for a cup of coffee. Then I moved south and discovered that while I may be a Yankee by birth, I'm a Southern belle at heart. Something about the Deep South just captivates me...and writing *One-Night Man*, Blaze #42, set in the Big Easy, only sparked my desire to write a romance that took me into the sultry bayous south of New Orleans.

Enter Ellen and Christopher. Ellen is a romance editor who doesn't believe heroes exist off the written page. Christopher Sinclair is a savvy businessman...a real-live hero who is determined to prove her wrong. To make his case, he has developed a strategy that breaks all the rules, a strategy he calls *red-hot pursuit....*

Blaze is the place to explore spicy romance, a place where you'll find steamy journeys to happily ever after. I hope *How To Host a Seduction* brings you to happily-ever-after, too. Let me know. Drop me a line in care of Harlequin Books, 225 Duncan Mill Road, Don Mills, Ontario M3B 3K9, Canada, or visit my Web site at www.jeanielondon.com.

Very truly yours,

Jeanie London

Books by Jeanie London

HARLEQUIN BLAZE

HOW TO HOST
A SEDUCTION

Jeanie London

TORONTO • NEW YORK • LONDON
AMSTERDAM • PARIS • SYDNEY • HAMBURG
STOCKHOLM • ATHENS • TOKYO • MILAN • MADRID
PRAGUE • WARSAW • BUDAPEST • AUCKLAND

For the gypsy.

ISBN 0-373-79084-8

HOW TO HOST A SEDUCTION

Prologue

SEX HAD ONLY CLINCHED THE DEAL.

Making love to Ellen Talbot had just proven what Christopher Sinclair had suspected since first meeting this remarkable romance editor at a friend's wedding—no woman had ever affected him like she did. No woman had ever come close.

Ellen left his heart thundering, his muscles vibrating so hard that he collapsed against the sheets, unable to do much more than press his shell-shocked erection into the cradle of her warm thighs and try to catch his breath. His thoughts raced with the singularity of the event and just how shattering making love to her had been. Their first time. *Damn.*

Locking his arms around her, Christopher savored the feel of her bare curves, her long, long legs tangled with his, their skin clinging in a thin sheen of sweat. He'd never even realized he could feel the way he felt when he was with her.

The lack had nothing to do with experience. He'd just celebrated his thirty-third birthday and could honestly say he'd *lived* most of those years, had explored the challenges life tossed his way and added a few variations of his own. He'd experienced his share of incredible lovemaking and mind-blowing orgasms with some very lovely ladies.

Not one of those women had ever left him like this, so demolished he could only hang on tight until he recovered.

And he needed to recover to gauge the effect he'd had on Ellen.

Pulling her closer, he inhaled the fresh scent of her hair, a shiny sheet of sable that cascaded over his arm and the pillow, cool silk to the touch. Her full breasts pressed against his chest, the tips he'd explored so thoroughly earlier sealed to his skin as if an extension of him. The lines had blurred. Christopher wasn't quite sure where he ended and Ellen began.

"Mmm." She breathed the sound on a sigh.

Even annihilated from the most awesome sex he'd ever had, Christopher managed a smile at the pleasure in her voice.

"Mmm, yourself," he said.

Forcing his fingers from where they'd been idly threading through her hair, he hooked a knuckle beneath her chin and coaxed her to look at him.

She lifted her gaze…and his heart pounded impossibly harder. Her hazel eyes reminded him of a forest in autumn, a sultry, mysterious place where woodsy greens, browns and golds met in a striking clash of color he'd thought about often in the months since they'd started dating.

But now he found himself staring into eyes he didn't recognize, eyes that seemed more golden than before, more mysterious. Eyes that reflected how contented Ellen was. And damn if he didn't have the ridiculous urge to pound his chest in pride that he'd leveled her with their sex as much as she'd leveled him.

This was another singular sensation, and Christopher found himself grinning as her lashes feathered over those incredible eyes and she rested her cheek on his shoulder with another sigh, a breath that expelled across his skin in a soft burst.

He pressed a kiss to her brow, wanted to drift off with

the scent of her filling his nostrils, to the whisper of her breathing. "Go to sleep. I want to wake you up with my mouth and make love to you while you're still half asleep."

Just the thought of this drowsy eyed beauty unfolding beneath him, of sinking into her moist heat in the quiet of late night, made his blood surge in a valiant effort at recovery.

But Ellen went rigid. The melting softness of her warm curves suddenly vanished, and before his orgasm-soaked brain could even register what was happening, she slid out of the bed.

"I *never* spend the night with anyone."

In one fluid move she stood, every glorious naked inch of her bathed in the silvery moonlight streaming through windows that overlooked the Upper East Side of Manhattan.

The sight of her, almost unreal with her long slim curves and pale loveliness, distracted him. By the time he'd thought to grab her, she was halfway across the room.

Christopher shook his head to clear it, then forced himself up on an elbow to watch her snag her hose from where he'd draped them over the armoire after he'd savored the pleasure of peeling them off her shapely legs.

"Really?" Here was an interesting turn of events. "Never?"

"Never," she shot back.

Flipping her hair over her shoulder, she sent it flowing down her back, then scooped up her cocktail dress from a chair. The black beads caught a moonbeam, glinted in the darkness. Every perfunctory motion belied the repletion she'd just demonstrated in his arms.

He recognized what was happening—Ellen was tossing

up invisible walls and putting miles of distance between them.

"Why don't you ever spend the night with anyone,
love?"

Plucking her bra from where it had landed on the floor,
she glanced up at him from beneath that incredible fall of
hair and said, "Relationship rule number one—*Senators'
daughters do not get caught sneaking out of anyone's bed
the morning after.*"

Christopher watched her sashay toward the bathroom,
an awesome display of moon-glazed skin and lithe motion,
before she disappeared inside. The door closed. The lock
clicked with a note of finality that echoed through his bedroom. Through *him*.

He sank back against the pillows, smiled. "Well, Ms.
Talbot, damn good thing I'm not just anyone."

And he wasn't. He was a man who knew what he
wanted.

Ellen.

As Senator Talbot's youngest daughter, she had to
weigh consequences more carefully than a woman from a
less visible family. He understood and respected her situation, which had meant easing into their relationship
slowly. No problem. Ellen was definitely worth the wait.
And three months of dating, and waiting, had only heightened the chemistry between them, had let them become
acquainted through very imaginative foreplay.

But Christopher was also a man who'd made a career
of seeing possibilities where others saw dead ends, of turning impossibilities into successes. The solution to this
problem was a no-brainer. Just like always, he'd meet a
challenge with a challenge, play the odds, take the risks
and get what he wanted.

Ellen.

When she emerged from the bathroom, completely dressed and coolly distant, he was ready.

"Marry me."

She stopped short in the doorway, lifted her gaze, those fascinating eyes still glimmering with golden lights.

"Marry me, love."

She blinked as though he must be some sort of mirage and she couldn't believe what she was hearing. "Marry you?"

"Yes."

She continued to stare, a frown slipping beneath her composure, the slightest crease between arched brows—a slip she'd never have made if not truly shocked by his proposal. "We've only been dating three months…we've only slept together *once.*"

"I'm ready to peel off that dress and go for round two."

That seemed to wake her up again. "Christopher!"

"We're right together." Covering the distance between them, he reached out to trace her lower lip, was pleased when she shivered in reply. "Do you doubt that after tonight?"

For an instant, she looked as if the wind had been knocked out of her, but then she backed away so fast she stumbled. He reached out to steady her, but she shrugged him off.

"You're crazy. No one gets married after sleeping together once. That's against all the rules."

He stared hard into those beautiful eyes, hoped she recognized how determined he was. "I'm not just anyone, love. And we need to establish right here and now that rules were meant to be broken."

1

CRADLING THE CELL PHONE between her shoulder and ear, Ellen Talbot hitched up the hem of her beaded cocktail dress—a dress she hadn't worn since *he'd* stripped it off her the night they'd made love. Of course, that had also been the night she'd received his marriage proposal and ended their relationship.

One very eventful evening.

But as she'd left *him* two thousand miles away in New York, Ellen deemed it safe to wear the dress again. Protecting her hose from snagging the beaded fabric, she sank into a chair in the bar of the Château Royal, the historic hotel in New Orleans's French Quarter that was hosting the annual romance writers' convention.

"Thanks for checking in with me." She spoke into the receiver. "Have a safe trip home."

She said goodbye to her mother, disconnected and flipped her phone shut. It might be three in the morning in this time zone, but her mother was currently in Bosnia, where she'd just concluded a breakfast with the Goodwill delegates from several foreign countries. As her mother wasn't only a loving parent who stayed in touch with all four of her grown children but a United States Senator, phone calls often came at odd hours.

Ellen didn't mind. She hadn't been sleeping. Far from

it, as she'd just broken free of a post-award ceremony party where both the winners and the nominees had gathered to celebrate. But now the party was over and, for the first time since she'd arrived in New Orleans, Ellen was practically alone. She checked to make sure her battery wasn't running low, returned the phone to her purse and willed herself to relax.

The muted glow of chandeliers sparked off the floor-to-ceiling windows that reflected the city beyond, shadowed by a black velvet night. Only a few guests still milled through the bar and the adjoining front lobby—stragglers from the award ceremony, she guessed by their formal wear. Ellen closed her eyes and let the calming hush filter through her. She could finally lose this smile that had been plastered on her face since she'd left her hotel room at 7:57 a.m. *yesterday* morning.

Exhaling slowly, she allowed her smile to fade, felt the tightness in her cheeks begin to ease.

Ah…

As an editor for the Brant Publishing Group, a corporation that published mass-market romance novels, the thick single-title historicals that readers devoured, Ellen's workdays didn't usually involve the spotlight or never-ending smiles. Her days involved meetings with the editorial, marketing and art departments. When she wasn't in meetings, she spent time on the telephone with any one of her thirty authors. Or reading through manuscripts that demanded her skill at recognizing story potential and writing pithy cover copy to entice readers into picking up a book from an already crowded shelf and buying it.

But during these industry conventions, smiling was as fundamental as breathing, because Ellen was a hot commodity—a romance editor with buying power. She spent her days conducting appointments with eager writers, presenting publishing-related topics to rooms filled to capacity, and socializing with people she only recognized by their name tags.

She preferred life out of the spotlight, so this moment alone was welcomed, would have been perfect if not for the thoughts of *him* that kept intruding on her overworked brain. She sighed. Maybe she shouldn't have worn this dress, after all.

Hindsight is twenty-twenty, her mother was fond of saying.

Ellen heartily agreed. Had she had clearer vision about him, she'd have turned down his first invitation for a date and saved herself a lot of heartache.

Marriage.

Ellen had thought he'd been kidding. He hadn't been, so he'd been history. At best, the man was a daredevil who lived life to test limits. At worst, he was certifiable. No person in her high-visibility situation would ever consider marriage after three months of dating, a lot of foreplay and one night of incredible sex. No matter how incredible the sex had been.

And it had been beyond anything she'd ever experienced.

She'd had to get away from him fast. Before his too-blue eyes, dimpled grins and steamy kisses had melted all her defenses. She wasn't willing to live with the sort of consequences that happened whenever she let her guard slip....

"Here you go."

Ellen opened her eyes to find a steaming mug of latte on the table. She glanced up at Lennon Eastman, one of her authors and a very close friend, despite the fact that she and her nutty great-aunt were the reasons Ellen kept winding up in the Big Easy, where she'd first met *him.*

She couldn't hold that against Lennon, especially not when her friend looked so happy. Even after a long night in heels that by all rights should have crippled her, Lennon looked ready to go for another round of schmoozing.

"Thanks. I so needed this," Ellen said. "I think my jaw is locked. I can't seem to stop smiling."

"Just let me know if you need to see my dentist." Lennon had settled into a wing chair opposite and shot her a less-than-sympathetic glance.

"I just might. Suffering is not on my vacation itinerary."

"Then we shouldn't be drinking espresso at three o'clock in the morning. We'll pay for this sleep deprivation tomorrow."

"Are you kidding?" Ellen rubbed her jaw to ease the stiffness. "I won't make it across the courtyard without the caffeine. The bellhop will find me asleep behind a potted palm."

"You can always ask him to load you onto his luggage cart and haul you up to your room."

"Then I'd wind up *in* a potted palm because I can't tip him. I gave you the last of my cash for these lattes."

Lennon laughed. "Maybe we should sit right here and pound espresso while the sun comes up. I've got that Regency writers' panel at eight. Don't you have plans to meet your new author for breakfast at Café du Monde?"

"I do." But Ellen couldn't tackle the thought of another day filled with marathon smiling just yet. Even when there were beignets involved. A favorite.

She raised her mug in a toast, instead. "Saluté. You deserved this year's RAVE Award for *Milord Spy*. The publicity should shoot your sales through the roof. The book distributors love that award. And you were very gracious when you accepted."

"Thank you, but winning hasn't even hit me yet. I'm still stuck on the fact that you actually let me keep my title."

"No offense, Lennon, but you're not title gifted."

"You say that to all your authors. I know, I've heard."

"No, only to you and Stephanie. Did she tell you what the working title of her latest book is?"

"*Lord of the Ravished.* I know, pretty dreadful. Tell me mine are never that bad." When Ellen didn't reply, Lennon relented with a sigh. "I'll be satisfied that my gift lies in writing orgasms."

"No argument there, but take credit where it's due. You picked a great title this time, born out by your award."

Lennon beamed. This award was just one more good thing to happen in a run of good things, starting with Lennon marrying her handsome new husband. Ellen knew of no one more deserving.

"Congratulations to you, as well." Lennon tipped her mug in salute. "Couldn't have done it without your exceptional editing ability. You were very eloquent while accepting your accolades. I thought we were an impressive team. And we looked so good."

"Thankfully, because I guarantee you the picture of our acceptance is going to make the cover of next month's *Romance Industry Review Magazine.* The RAVE is big, big news."

Not only for Lennon, but for her, too. A RAVE-winning author meant another feather in her cap, and collecting feathers happened to be one of Ellen's pastimes. She was currently collecting enough feathers to earn the position of senior editor at Brant Publishing, the goal she'd been working toward since accepting a job as an editorial assistant in college.

"Is the RAVE big enough to get me some perks?" Lennon asked. "Like a renowned cover model or a reprint?"

Lennon might be a creative wonder, a rising star who knew how to write women's fantasies to the delight of her readers, but she was also a businesswoman who didn't miss a trick.

Ellen scowled. "I'll see what I can do. Just don't forget I was the one who battled the marketing department to print your name bigger than the title on your covers."

"You know I appreciate it immensely, but that was two books ago. How long do you expect me to let you rest on your laurels?"

Ellen laughed, a heartfelt sound that took her by surprise. By all rights she should be too sleep deprived to feel anything but exhaustion right now, yet she felt more relaxed, more content than she'd been in a long time. Too long.

Lifting her mug, Ellen savored another swallow. It felt so good to be away from home, away from the office, away from *him*. She was a woman on the fast track—although her family didn't consider her career to be in the same league as those of her lawyer siblings, chief justice aunt, campaign manager uncle, political analyst and lobbyist cousins...

Or her Senator mother and former Cabinet-member father.

In a clan that boasted enough high-power careers to rival those of the Kennedys, Ellen's decision to go into publishing—albeit with a Fortune 500 company—still had the ability to make all of her relations scratch their heads in bewilderment.

She deserved a break from the hectic pace, the constant pressure...from thinking about—

"Look, it's Lennon and her gorgeous editor!"

Glancing up, Ellen couldn't miss the group that had just entered the front lobby, returning from a night of reveling on Bourbon Street, if their costumes were any indication.

"Oh, bloody hell. It's Mr. Muscle-Butt and his entourage. Oh, Lennon, look at him, he's wearing a cape."

"Be nice," Lennon admonished. "He's trying to impress you."

"By looking like Zorro?"

"By looking like a romance hero. You're a romance editor—see the connection?"

Ellen saw, all right. Was *not* interested. Romance heroes didn't exist outside of books and even if they did, she'd had her fill of men recently, thank you very much. This one swept through the lobby with a dramatic flourish that demanded the attention of every person in the place, including the sleepy-eyed desk clerks.

His brown hair fell to his waist and the black cape flew out behind him as if he were striding off a windswept moor. Not to mention his thoughtlessness—his entourage, a gaggle of model-thin women dressed in outlandishly sexy costumes, was forced to gallop to keep up with his long-legged strides.

"Oh, no. He's not wearing his name tag. Who is he again? I can't very well call him Mr. Muscle-Butt."

"Vittorio," Lennon whispered beneath her breath while standing to greet the new arrivals. "Congratulate him on winning first place in the cover model competition tonight. He'll be crushed if he thinks you didn't notice."

"Got it." Ellen set her mug on the table, slapped on her professional smile again and followed Lennon's lead. "Good evening, Vittorio. Congratulations on your win."

He extended his hand, and she had no choice but to offer hers, while he smiled what had to be a smile even more professional than her own. She had the unkind thought that he'd probably devoted days to practicing that smile in front of a mirror. *Going for charming...dashing...roguish—* ugh!

"My lovely Ellen." He bowed and his mouth grazed her knuckles gallantly, while she struggled to keep a straight face. Lennon rolled her eyes in her periphery. "Congratulations on your success this evening, as well."

He reluctantly let her hand slip away before turning to kiss Lennon on both cheeks.

"Where's Josh? Surely your new husband isn't neglecting you on your special night."

She waved a hand dismissively. "He came for the award ceremony and offered to stay, but I could tell he was antsy. Too much estrogen flying around for his taste."

A frown drew Vittorio's brows together. "*Too much estrogen?*" He swept an expansive glance at the groupies who'd settled into silence behind him. "No such thing."

No doubt. Ellen wasn't sure whether he referred to her or his entourage, but when he flashed another smile—definitely aimed at her—she suspected the former and bit back a groan.

"Lovely Ellen—tell me you're not planning to run off right after the convention. I want to tour you around the Big Easy. Show you all the secret places only the locals know."

He may have said *secret* but he meant *intimate,* and his suggestive tone made her swallow back yet another groan. "I'm not running off. Not right away," she said.

"My good fortune, then." Another roguish smile, this time accompanied by a slight flaring of his nostrils that just screamed testosterone. "You'll make time for me."

No question. No politely asking. Just a you-*will*-make-time-for-me declaration that jump-started her half-sleeping synapses.

"I'm sorry, Vittorio. We're going to need a day planner to keep up with all we've got scheduled," she said, lying so easily it was scary. "Lennon's Auntie Q has this murder-mystery thing planned. We'll be leaving New Orleans on Wednesday."

That wasn't a lie. She'd committed to some corporate-training-murder-mystery event for Miss Q's—Miss Quinevere McDarby's—latest business venture. Ellen still wasn't clear on the details, but Lennon and a few of her other authors would be attending, and she figured solving mysteries would provide an interesting diversion.

She needed a good diversion right now.

A quizzical lift of dark brows hinted that Vittorio wasn't turned down very often. Ellen would have felt bad, but the man appeared to have enough women fawning over him. So technically she was saving him from disappointment—because she didn't fawn. Ever.

"Right. Okay." He eyed her as though something had taken place and he hadn't yet figured out what.

His groupies obviously recognized the power shift, though, and stopped glaring long enough to console him, enveloping him in a press of bodies and a cloud of expensive perfume. Vittorio took his cue to leave, with a dashing smile and a jauntily delivered "Good night."

Ellen watched him go, marveled that not one of those women had objected to him asking her out in their presence. No, they'd glared at *her,* instead, like she'd forced him to flirt.

"Why me?" she asked.

The question had been rhetorical, but Lennon obliged her, anyway. "It's your hair. That swingy new style." Her gaze shot straight to the hairstyle in question. "I love it."

"My stylist gets the credit." Ellen sat back down and reached for her mug. "He promised me something different.'' She shook her head, still enjoying the way her shorter, fuller style swung around her face when she moved.

''What made you decide to cut all your hair off?''

''A change to celebrate my upcoming thirtieth birthday.''

She wouldn't admit that *he'd* been attracted to her long hair, but a line from an old song echoed in her memory.

I'm gonna wash that man right outta my hair....

Well, Ellen had *cut* him right out of hers.

''Your new style makes your face softer somehow,'' Lennon said. ''And it's amazing how the change draws attention to your skin. You've got this whole creamy Snow White thing going on. No wonder Vittorio is smitten.''

''I hope I didn't put you in an awkward position,'' Ellen said, though she didn't feel the least bit repentant.

''He doesn't need my help to get a date. Besides, his ego is rock solid. I don't think he even realized he was in over his head.'' Lennon sank back into her chair and grabbed her latte. ''So what didn't you like about him?''

''You know my family. Can you see me bringing home a man who uses more cream rinse than I do?''

Lennon burst into laughter, drawing the attention of a nearby bartender. ''That's not difficult with your new hairstyle. But you're selling Vittorio short. He may have an ego the size of the Southern Hemisphere but he's got a heart of pure gold.''

A heart of pure gold would *not* make the difference. Her family was already tolerant enough of her foibles. Bringing home a man with whom the media would have a field day would cast doubt on her sanity. She could already see the headline: *Senator's Daughter Plays Fantasy Games with a Hero From a Trashy Romance Novel.*

Her mother, of course, in an effort to help, would likely

direct her wayward youngest to the nearest psychiatric facility.

It's for the best, Ellen, really. Let's give you a chance to take a deep breath and clear your head, reassess your priorities and reexamine the objective. We'll tell the press you're suffering stress from your bohemian career....

All for Mr. Muscle-Butt?

She'd pass, thank you.

Sometimes Ellen thought that as an infant she must have been left in a basket on the front doorstep. In a family of high achievers, she always seemed to be a step behind. Her siblings had all gone into law, yet she'd chosen publishing. They were all still scratching their heads over that one. Perhaps if she edited more literary fare, or even better, nonfiction...

Her parents had assured her long ago that she hadn't been a foundling they'd taken in as a charitable publicity stunt for some campaign. And given that she resembled other family members, Ellen was forced to take them at their word.

But she still didn't feel like she'd ever make the cut.

None of her siblings had ever been questioned about whether they were the "right fit" for the fancy private schools the Talbot children had attended while growing up. But Ellen had.

She's very creative, the administrators had said, *not sufficiently goal-oriented. Perhaps she'd be better suited to a school with a less ambitious curriculum.*

With the clarity of that twenty-twenty hindsight, Ellen thought the administrators might have been right. Especially after the summer debacle when her older sister Leah had been chosen student ambassador for their school. Their parents had decided the family should accompany Leah on her tour of the continent to support her in her new duties. A great plan that the whole family had quickly embraced.

Until Ellen's report card had arrived.

Her grades had nosedived so much during the previous two semesters that the school had considered retaining her. Of course, her grades had only nosedived because she'd been struggling so hard to grasp pre-algebra and she'd only gotten so far behind because she'd been determined to solve the problem herself....

The choices had been to leave Ellen home with her grandparents for a stint in summer school or to hire a tutor to travel with the family. Believing in always keeping a united front, her parents had opted for the latter solution and amended their travel arrangements to afford Ellen time to study in the hotel rooms during the mornings.

That was just one example. Unfortunately, the list went on and on. And after this latest episode with *him*...

Lennon peered at her over the rim of her mug. "I want you to have fun while you're in town. What was it Mr. Bingley said to Mr. Darcy in *Pride and Prejudice?* 'I wouldn't be as fastidious as you are for a kingdom'?"

"Humph." Ellen dismissed her with a laugh. "Spoken by a woman who just married a hero straight off the cover of one of her books."

"A man you said existed only in books, incidentally."

"So you found the only one who didn't, lucky girl." Ellen managed to keep a straight face. Josh Eastman was a doll, definitely the perfect man for Lennon—but a hero? Well, Lennon thought so and that was all that counted.

Lennon's smile faded. Leaning forward intently, she tapped her manicured nails on the tabletop, and her sudden intensity put Ellen on red alert.

The subject of romance heroes and whether such beasts

actually existed off the written page was a topic much debated, and one that would logically lead to...

"Auntie Q found you a hero, too, but you threw him back," Lennon said, right on cue.

Ah, here they were, at the place Ellen had been side-stepping for three months. Only, this time she couldn't hang up the phone. She would finally have to face the subject of *him*.

Rule number one of Ellen's sound business strategies: *A strong offense was more effective than a strong defense.*

"The real question here is, why did your great-aunt feel compelled to set me up with a man at all?"

"You'll have to ask Auntie Q yourself. I can't speak for her, and trying to second-guess her is always risky business."

Truer words had never been spoken. Lennon's diminutive great-aunt, the woman Ellen had come to know as Miss Q, was definitely an odd duck. A woman who believed in passion and crusaded for everyone else to believe, too. Ellen might have smiled if the memory of *him* hadn't been quite so fresh.

"Christopher Sinclair is a romance hero incarnate," Lennon said. "And he was perfect for you. Executive-level management. A talented businessman who's sharp enough to appreciate a strong independent woman without being pushed around or intimidated. He's from a respectable Southern family. Not to mention that he's financially successful enough to keep up with your rather upscale interests."

Ellen arched a skeptical brow. Okay, so it was no secret she preferred slumber parties at the Plaza Hotel to those in tents, art painted on canvas as opposed to lithographs, but that didn't necessarily mean she was an expensive date....

"I also happen to know Christopher isn't the kind of man to fawn or cling or crowd you, and he's absolutely gorgeous," Lennon continued. "His parents loved you, and not only did your family approve of him, Ellen, they liked him. Your mom told me so."

Yes, her family had liked him, which had translated into awkward explanations. She wouldn't share her real reason for breaking up with him and have them question her judgment, *again.*

"So what happened?" Lennon was saying. "I'm not buying that lame excuse you gave me. I've waited to hear the truth in person because I care about you, but be forewarned, Auntie Q wants answers, so you'd better have them handy. You'll be a captive audience during this murder-mystery training. Think four days and five nights in an antebellum plantation with no escape."

There usually wasn't any escape when it came to Miss Q. Not even her own great-niece had managed to outrun the little schemer's matchmaking. Her efforts to bring Lennon and her new husband together could have made a RAVE-winning book.

"It's old news now. We dated…"

Three months where he could make me tingle with the slightest touch…and that one red-hot night.

"…and realized we were heading in opposite directions. We have different goals…"

Marriage? After three months? Was the man crazy?

"…so we went our separate ways."

I ran screaming because he wouldn't play by the rules.

A lifetime of dealing with the high-profile baggage she brought to a relationship had taught her the hard way to be careful. She'd learned to walk the straight and narrow. And to force her creative brain into remembering the rules, she'd devised a method of making lists just to keep them straight in her head.

Her latest rule for survival: *No dating impulsive men.*

Lennon frowned as though she wasn't quite buying this explanation. "What do you mean 'opposite goals'?"

"He wanted to get married."

Lennon dissolved before her very eyes into one of those melting oh-how-romantic expressions Ellen was very familiar with after eight years of working with romance authors.

"And you turned him down?"

"Of course I turned him down, Lennon. Honestly."

"But why? You were crazy about him."

That was before she'd found out *he* was crazy. "Listen, Lennon, he's past history and I'm looking to the future." Plastering her smile back on, Ellen tried to look reassuring. Her cheeks stretched. Her jaw creaked. "I'm waiting to meet *the one,* and when I do, you'll be the first to know."

"The one?"

"The man who'll love me for who I am, with no questions. The man who'll respect my situation enough to play by my rules."

Lennon looked thoughtful. "Unconditional love. Are you sure you believe that exists?"

"Of course. I couldn't edit romances if I didn't. But I'm not going to sit around waiting for it to happen. I've got things to accomplish and goals to reach. Worrying about whether or not a man fits into the equation is simply not something I'll do. If I meet *the one,* so be it. If not, well, so be it."

"You're sure Christopher isn't *the one?*"

"Completely."

"What convinced you?" Lennon insisted. "A man that intense and that gorgeous has to be amazing in bed."

"I am not sharing the details of my sex life, so don't bother badgering me. You and Miss Q might discuss how much and how good over dinner, but I prefer to keep my sex life private, thank you. That's the second rule of the Talbot family code of conduct—no discussing sex at the dinner table."

"Note to self—" Lennon grimaced "—have a handy excuse to decline the next Talbot family dinner invitation. Just out of curiosity, what's the first rule?"

Ellen patted her purse. "Always be accessible, which means the cell phone stays on."

Talbot family code of conduct rule number four: *Don't pry.* Ellen could almost hear her mother explaining, *Prying shows a decided lack of manners, and unless you're interested in answering similarly private questions...*

She wasn't.

Unfortunately, Lennon wasn't versed on Talbot family code of conduct rule number four. She sighed so heavily that Ellen knew she was in for a lecture about making time to have fun. Another conversation they'd had before.

She switched gears, fast. "I will tell you it'll be a frosty Friday before I involve myself with another impulsive man."

Lennon set her mug down on the table with a *thunk*, leaned back in her chair and smiled. And kept smiling.

"What's so funny?"

"Finally." She made a visible effort to curb her amusement, though not much of one, judging by her smothered laughter. "You are the most stubborn person I know."

"I'm not stubborn. I just like stability and constants. He's an adrenaline junkie who lives life to test fate. The press would have a field day, and that wouldn't be fair to him. Or me, for that matter. I can't handle living my life worrying about what sort of stunt he's going to pull next and what the fallout will be. Marriage! We'd only dated three months.''

''I accepted Josh's marriage proposal after three *days*.''

''Your decisions aren't subject to public scrutiny. If I accept a marriage proposal after three days or even three *months,* my mother's parenting skills come under fire. Her party spins my acceptance to mean she raised a confident daughter. The opposing party spins it to mean she has no control over her wild child. I prefer not to start the debate. I don't enjoy the spotlight in my face, and the media loves writing about guys who flaunt the rules.''

''Christopher is one of the neighborhood kids, Ellen. I've known him since I was ten years old.''

She might have laughed at Lennon's casual description of ''neighborhood kids,'' which brought to mind a motley gang riding bikes or playing ice hockey on frozen ponds in the winter. But like Ellen's own, Lennon's upbringing hadn't exactly been traditional. She'd been raised in the exclusive Garden District of New Orleans, where kids lived in mansions and toured the continent during summer breaks.

''What's your point?''

''My point is that I've known him a long time. Christopher may enjoy adventurous hobbies, but he's no adrenaline junkie. He just likes to have fun—which is something you could use a little help with, I don't mind saying.''

She should have known Lennon would drag her back here despite evasive maneuvers. ''You call driving a car in circles at a hundred miles an hour *fun?*''

''He plays hard, but that's only because he works so hard. He's incredibly driven. Just like someone else I know.''

Her pointed stare left no doubt that she considered Ellen guilty of the same crime.

"Well, I don't spend my weekends jumping out of airplanes, or scuba diving for sunken treasure."

"I don't always go into the Gulf with Josh on his week-long fishing excursions—and we make out just fine. A couple can enjoy individual interests. What's wrong with that?"

"I don't equate the risk factor of deep-sea fishing with rappelling down a mountainside in the Rockies."

"It could be dangerous if Josh was caught in a hurricane."

"Josh won't be caught in a hurricane unless he's an idiot. They have meteorological satellites that track storms."

Lennon was still battling that smile when Ellen slugged back the last of her latte and set the mug on the table.

"He thrives on breaking the rules," she said. "I was just his challenge *du jour.*"

"You don't believe Christopher cares about you?" That wiped away the last of Lennon's humor. "Ellen, the guy's crazy about you. I know because he told me."

He told me, too.

With a sigh, she decided to make the argument she'd intended to reserve for herself. "If he was so crazy about me, then why couldn't he compromise and do things the right way? Why did he just let me go? He made a few token phone calls and that was it. I haven't heard from him in three months."

"You wanted him to chase you?"

Ellen winced at how petty that reasoning sounded. And yes, she would even consider that her need to know he was *the one* might be petty in some regards. But she'd spent most of her life trying to prove herself—to her family, to the press, to her supervisors, to *herself.* Was it really so much to ask to be reassured that the man she married would always, *always* believe in her, no matter how rough-and-tumble life got? No matter how much baggage she came with?

"If he'd been *the one,* he would have been willing to compromise, Lennon, willing to find some way of accommodating both our needs. He wasn't."

It was her most fundamental rule of sound business: *Choose your battles and only fight for what you believe in.*

She obviously hadn't been worth fighting for.

2

"THERE YOU ARE," a familiar female voice called across the lobby, shattering the tense moment and buying Ellen a welcome reprieve. "You guys should have come with us. We had a blast."

Blast appeared to be the equivalent of a rip-roaring time on the town, judging by the size of the tumblers the trio of women held. Hurricanes, if Ellen correctly identified the color through the plastic.

"Looks like we should get the waiter to bring espresso," Lennon whispered as the women started toward them.

"It'll only wake them up and make them even louder."

Lennon grimaced. "Can't you control them? They're your authors."

"They're your friends."

"I'd never have met them if you hadn't taken us all out to that show at the Reno convention."

Ellen's rebuttal was lost when the trio descended, plunking down sweating plastic tumblers and dragging chairs around the table amid a chorus of hellos.

Susanna St. John, Tracy Owens and Stephanie Kondas were all successful romance authors at very different stages in their careers. Industry-savvy women, when they weren't indulging in mobile Hurricanes, they hosted a Web community with Lennon, a place where readers could chat on bulletin boards, enter various contests and generally keep tabs on author news between book releases. Ellen enjoyed working with each of them.

"Oh, Stephanie pinched some man's ass. I am *so* telling her husband," Tracy, a die-hard glamour girl, informed them as she swept around the table, as dramatic as ever in a pale gold chiffon that swirled around her ankles.

Stephanie, the newest author of the group, was a slim, athletic-looking woman who admirably held her own with the three more experienced authors she'd embraced as friends. She plopped down with a scowl. "You dared me. I do not back down on a dare."

Tracy winked slyly. "She had a death grip on his biscuit."

"Well, he had some mighty fine biscuits. What can I say?"

"Save it for the husband."

Ellen chuckled at the thought of sweet Stephanie trying to explain her antics to her equally sweet husband and kids.

"We've been drinking," Susanna stated unnecessarily while arranging her black taffeta gown and maneuvering unsteadily into a chair. "Hope we're not intruding."

Screwing her smile back into place, Ellen ignored the way her jaw ached and decided she'd make out better by just leaving the smile on until the convention ended. "Of course not. Shall we order coffee?"

"And ruin this divine buzz?" Tracy asked incredulously. "I'll just keep sipping my too-sweet alcoholic beverage, if you don't mind." Then she swept an unfocused gaze around the table. "Do you all realize this is the first chance we've had to talk privately? Between the publisher's functions and the awards ceremony tonight, I've moderated three author discussions. Can you believe it?"

Actually, Ellen could. "Don't you know how to say no?"

"Say no? You're kidding, right?" Susanna shook her head. "Tracy's been schmoozing the convention committee for months to be invited to fill these slots. She's a glutton for attention."

"My name looks good printed on the program."

Lennon laughed. "With all your promotional efforts, I don't know when you find the time to write. You put us all to shame."

"That's my job, dear." Tracy glanced at her manicured nails, preening.

Ellen laughed, another one of those heartfelt, liberating chuckles that she hadn't enjoyed nearly often enough of late. That was, of course, until she found herself the recipient of Susanna's button-black stare.

Susanna St. John had been in the romance industry for years, writing for various publishing houses before becoming Ellen's author. She routinely enjoyed a place on the *New York Times* bestseller list, and Ellen considered having acquired her a major feather in her cap.

But Susanna was also older than Ellen by almost a decade, had been in the business longer and possessed an unsettling knack for calling a spade a spade.

She wore one of those no-nonsense looks now. "What's been up with you lately?"

An innocuous question in itself, but there was something less than offhand in her tone that caught Ellen's attention. "Nothing much. Swamped as usual."

Silence. A trio of tipsy gazes fixed on her, waiting…

"You'd tell me if I wasn't living up to expectations, wouldn't you?" Stephanie asked, a not-so-innocuous question.

As she was currently revising her third contracted book,

Stephanie's curiosity about her editor's expectations was natural. But this question came out of left field, reinforcing Ellen's impression that this conversation was headed somewhere.

"Of course I would. But wretched title aside, your latest book is coming along beautifully. You're not letting these jaded old hacks worry you with their war stories, are you?"

Tracy huffed. "Watch who you're calling old there, Ms. I'm-getting-ready-to-turn-thirty."

"You're right behind me, Ms. I'm-getting-ready-to-turn-thirty-a-month-after-me." Ellen forced a laugh, but she caught Lennon's frown across the table.

"What else did you do on Bourbon Street tonight, *besides* pound Hurricanes?" Lennon neatly diverted the conversation.

"Visited a few sex toy stores to get ideas for our books," Tracy said.

"And pinched a few cute butts." Stephanie grinned.

"The usual Saturday night fare for horny women," Susanna added. "You've been so busy that we haven't had a chance to chat. How's the family? Parents, siblings, all those aunts, uncles and cousins doing okay?"

Ellen nodded. "Everyone's fine. How's Joey making out?"

Susanna's son had recently started summer session here in New Orleans at Tulane University, leaving Susanna, a divorcée of many years, with an unusually quiet house in Shreveport.

"Great. Except that life without mom-the-maid is coming as a shock. For me, too. I'm astounded at how much I'm *not* running the washing machine."

Susanna laughed, but Lennon eyed her narrowly. "Don't let her fool you, Ellen. I happen to know she just dropped big bucks on a laptop so she can still work when the urge to hop in her car and visit Joey strikes.''

Ellen guessed this might have something to do with Lennon's invitation for Susanna to participate in Miss Q's murder-mystery training. "A laptop is a good idea with your tight schedule.''

"My schedule,'' Susanna said, "wouldn't be nearly so tight if I hadn't forgotten how to write a decent hero. But alas…'' She heaved a dramatic sigh. "I have, which means I've been riding my deadlines because I'm rewriting half my books.''

"You, too?'' Tracy chimed in, peering at Susanna with what had to be feigned astonishment. "I've forgotten how to write a decent hero, too. I don't know what's going on. If I'd turned thirty already, I might worry about senility, but as I'm still in my twenties—''

"Oh, thank goodness!'' Stephanie covered her eyes with a shaky hand. "I thought I was the only one having this problem. The rewrites on this book have been so extensive that I'm completely off schedule with my other projects. And if I miss my deadline, I'll never sell another book.''

"Try not to let revisions undermine your confidence,'' Susanna suggested pragmatically. "Revisions are just part of the process. Right, Ellen?''

Ellen stared at the three tipsy faces, recognized high drama at its finest, and knew this scene had been staged, rehearsed and fortified with alcohol.

"Okay, ladies.'' She steepled her fingers before her and assumed a professional mien. "What's on your minds?''

"Heroes,'' Susanna said.

Not surprised that Susanna had been appointed the spokesperson of the group, Ellen asked, "What about them?''

"Our normally brilliant and insightful editor doesn't seem to like them anymore."

The woman didn't pull any punches, but it wasn't her delivery that blew Ellen away, but her allegation. "What on earth makes you think I dislike heroes?"

The trio stared at her, but they suddenly didn't seem so tipsy.

"The fact that you hated my last one," Susanna said.

Tracy nodded. "And mine."

"And mine, too," Stephanie added.

Ellen stared, expression carefully schooled as her mind raced to assess the accuracy of this accusation.

Susanna's last hero...the medieval bastard—no, baron—who kept abandoning the heroine to run off to battle.

Hmm, Ellen remembered him well and Susanna was right, he'd required some serious revision. She wouldn't say exactly half a book's worth, but abandoning the heroine was not a quality she or the romance readers considered heroic.

Who wanted a man who would leave at the drop of a hat, a man who wouldn't hang around long enough to fight for his heroine when the going got tough?

Tracy's last hero...the Elizabethan nobleman who'd gone to court as a spy and made love to the heroine without revealing his true identity.

Lying to any woman suggested a character flaw that was tough to tackle successfully in any commercial book-length novel. But lying was especially dastardly when it involved an affair of the heart. It was never easy for a woman to let her guard down, to trust a man enough to become vulnerable, especially knowing she might wind up heartbroken.

Stephanie's last hero...the Scottish lord whose heroine

had been kidnapped by a rebel clan. His lame attempts to rescue her had spanned several chapters.

If Ellen had been Stephanie's heroine she'd have been disappointed in a hero who couldn't manage a decent rescue in a timely fashion. Any hero who left the heroine alone for so long was lucky his woman didn't run off with the villain. A true hero would have pursued his heroine at all costs, *quickly....*

Okay, so she'd had some problems with their heroes. Valid problems? Ellen had thought so. But writing was a subjective business, a creative business. Even at their most professional, her authors were still artists, emotionally attached to their work. Editing often required performing a delicate balancing act of compliment and critique, to get the job done.

Okay, she saw where they were coming from, knew they wouldn't have approached her unless sure their concerns were valid.

She glanced at Lennon, who'd risen, hightailing it toward the bar. The coward. She'd known this conversation would invariably circle around to her latest hero.

...The Regency smuggler who was more interested in his wants and needs than his heroine's.

A true hero would have found a way to satisfy both. And even all those scrumptious orgasms in some very steamy cave scenes didn't make up for the lack.

Uh-oh.

Ellen stared into the trio of worried faces whose careers were currently riding on her ability to be as brilliant and insightful, and reasonable, as they believed her to be.

And they must have seen something encouraging in her expression because Susanna threw a hand across her forehead in true Sarah Bernhardt fashion and sighed breathlessly.

"Woe is me, I've forgotten how to write a hero and now my publishing house will stop buying my books. My agent will have to hit the streets, scrambling for new offers—"

"At least you'll get offers." Tracy shot her a dubious look. "You're a *New York Times* bestselling author. Publishing houses will be fighting over you. Even with all my promotional efforts, I'm still only in the mid-list with seven books."

"But at least you've got numbers." Then Stephanie met Ellen's gaze with a look of entreaty. "My third book isn't even out yet. I'm completely at your mercy."

Folding her arms across her chest, Ellen tried to smile at their theatrics, but not so surprisingly, the smile that had seemed etched on her face had done a disappearing act, because a terrible, *terrible* thought had just occurred to her.

If these ladies were right about her lack of objectivity—and Ellen had the sinking suspicion they might be—there could only be one explanation....

He was interfering with her work, too.

Félicie Allée—three days later

THOUGH THE PLANTATION wasn't quite an hour south of New Orleans, Félicie Allée might have been on a deserted island. The shady oak-lined alley leading to the circle drive and majestic front entrance transported Ellen from the reality of well-traveled highways baking beneath the sun to a shadowy fantasy place cooled by the bayou breeze.

Sunlight streamed through the leaves overhead to play shadow-and-lace games along the columns and metalwork enclosing the double-tiered balconies around the plantation.

She'd first visited Félicie Allée after Lennon's wedding.

Perhaps her second visit was even more breathtaking, because this time Ellen knew what to expect. Her awe was tempered with simple appreciation for the way the plantation had been built to bring a touch of elegance and civilization to the wildly lush setting. Crepe myrtles, azaleas and camellias all burst in bright bloom on the grounds, and to a woman like Ellen, reared beneath the often leaden skies of Manhattan and Long Island, the scene resembled a living oil painting.

"Leave it to your great-aunt to turn boring old corporate training into a game," Ellen said, as Lennon steered her sport utility vehicle down the oak-lined drive leading to the plantation. "Corporate training and murder-mystery events. Who'd ever have thought of combining the two?"

Lennon shot her a sidelong glance. "No one has ever accused Auntie Q of lacking imagination."

Ellen couldn't help but smile. Lennon's great-aunt believed in having a good time and didn't make apologies, an odd attitude to Ellen, whose family operated in such a different manner. Chatting with Miss Q always proved refreshing, very different from the in-depth business strategy sessions she had with various relations during family functions.

"So who's my partner?" she asked Lennon, who slowed her SUV in front of the entrance. "Did you put a bug in your great-aunt's ear to give me Susanna? Nothing against Tracy but she doesn't travel light. I won't stand a chance if I have to room with her. And you know how weird I am about sharing my space."

"I know, but Auntie Q had already made the arrangements. She promised you'd be comfortable, though." Lennon paused with her hand above the door handle. "You okay?"

Okay? No, she wouldn't go straight to okay. Not when

the first few days of her vacation had gone bust because all she could think about was *him*. The man had a power over her that was nothing short of scary. Whether involved with him or not, he consumed her thoughts, influenced her actions, sneaked right past the barriers she worked so hard to maintain in her life.

But all was not lost yet. She still had almost a week of vacation to let the fantasy of murder and mayhem clear her head so she could return to reality with some brilliant idea about how to put all thoughts of *him* firmly behind her.

"I've just spent the last three days listening to you preach about how I don't make enough time to have fun," Ellen said. "May I enjoy the rest of my vacation, please? Without any mention of work, or *him*."

"You got it." Lennon shoved her door wide and climbed out. "No more reality, as long as you promise to turn off your stinking cell phone. You can survive a few days without it. We'll do fantasy this weekend and— Oh, how timely. Here comes the queen of make-believe herself. You can ask her who you're rooming with."

Miss Q strode across the gallery toward them, looking as if she'd stepped off the pages of a historic costume book in an oversize plaid dress with leg-o'-mutton puffed sleeves.

"Welcome to Félicie Allée, my dears." She captured each by an arm when they reached the top of the steps and maneuvered them around toward the door. "I'm so pleased you're a part of our opening event."

After kissing Lennon on the cheek, she clasped Ellen's hands in a paper-thin grasp. "Thank you for accepting my invitation. I wanted Southern Charm Mysteries' grand opening to be a special event among friends."

"Everything coming together?" Lennon asked.

"All the clues have been placed. The red herrings planted," Miss Q said. "The cast is in character, and you're all going to have a grand time playing the detectives to solve the mystery."

"I'm sure we will, Auntie."

"Of course," Ellen said, distracted by their entrance into the grand hall.

The octagonal rotunda extended three stories of sheer visual majesty with curving staircases and intricately carved balustrades. Evidence of the plantation's new ownership could be seen in woodwork that had been refinished to a gleaming luster and plank flooring so highly polished that light from the cut-crystal chandelier sparkled off it.

"It's even more beautiful than I remember," she said, recalling her first visit after Lennon and Josh's wedding.

Miss Q beamed. "Just wait until you see everything we've done with the place."

"We?"

"Quite a few of us have been involved in pulling together Southern Charm Mysteries."

"Is Josh here yet?" Lennon asked.

Miss Q nodded. "I've installed him in the sky suite. I thought he'd be more comfortable with a floor all to himself, even if you did have to hoof it up three flights."

"Who am I rooming with, Miss Q?" Ellen asked.

"Your roommate is a surprise, dear, but I will tell you this—you're staying in the garden suite, the loveliest of all our accommodations. And you won't have to hike up any stairs because it's right here on the ground floor. So come along."

A surprise? The thought of a Miss Q surprise was enough to make the bravest soul quake in her sandals. She exchanged a curious glance with Lennon, but was cut off from further questions when Miss Q motioned them through the hall.

"You're the last to arrive and everyone is getting into their costumes. We'll meet for cocktails on the lower gallery at seven, before heading into the parlor for the introduction. Dinner will be served afterward and you'll have a chance to meet the other guests and begin your investigations. I believe I've given you time to unpack, meet your partners and get settled. Oh, and your wardrobes have been filled with the appropriate costumes and everything you'll need to get into character."

Without pausing to inhale, Miss Q drew a chain from her bodice and peered down at the gold timepiece attached. "Now I've got to run. The cast is assembling in the library so I can make last-minute addresses. Lennon, up to the third floor. Ellen, you head down the west wing." She pointed to a nearby hallway. "The suites have nameplates so you'll know which is yours. Ta-ta, dears."

Lennon rolled her eyes. "I'll catch up with you later."

Before Ellen had a chance to reply, Miss Q shooed them off. "Go. I want you to see your suites." Then, with a swish of her huge plaid skirts, she hurried off in the opposite direction.

Easily locating the garden suite, Ellen knocked tentatively, reluctant to meet whoever was inside. Lennon had explained that this grand opening training session hosted Josh's company, Eastman Investigations, where two of his investigators were in serious need of teamwork training. Knowing Miss Q, Ellen might very well wind up rooming with a total stranger.

After receiving no response, she tried the handle, and found the room unlocked and her luggage already in the entry.

"Hello, anyone home?"

No answer.

From the doorway, she could see a sitting room with two sets of French doors opening onto a garden. Through the windowpanes, wisteria bloomed, lush against the backdrop of an ivy-covered wall that enclosed the garden to a courtyard.

The sitting room was simply furnished with several antique pieces in a deep gold upholstery, a sofa, a small dining table, a desk and a set of artfully arranged chairs in front of the fireplace. A spacious area that made her feel a little better about sharing her space.

The suite passed muster. Would the surprise roommate? "Hello?"

Still no answer.

Smooth strains of a familiar jazz piece emitted from within the bedroom, and while Ellen silently complimented her new roommate's musical tastes, she recognized the sound of the shower running in the bathroom. Great. Should she call out to let her roommate know she wasn't alone? Or close the door?

Ellen hated awkward situations almost as much as she hated surprises. She'd just decided on the closed door, when a pair of Top-Siders beside the bed caught her eye.

Top-Siders?

What woman wore Top-Siders? The thought stopped Ellen cold. The last time she'd accepted Miss Q's hospitality after Lennon's wedding, she'd been set up....

Heading into the bedroom, she took in the toiletries on the dresser and the garment bag hanging from the closet door in one glance. She stopped in front of the shoes.

My, what big feet you have, my dear.

Ellen knelt to inspect them, staring at the well-worn shoes as if they might actually launch into dialogue to explain who they belonged to. But in keeping with the theme of solving mysteries, Ellen had already divined two telling clues.

One, that slightly gamey aroma suggested their owner wore them frequently without socks, and two, her new roommate was a man.

Why on earth would Miss Q ensconce her in a one-bed suite with a...

An awful, *awful* thought struck her when she remembered Mr. Muscle-Butt from the convention. Surely Lennon wouldn't have colluded with Miss Q when she'd known Ellen wasn't interested.

I want you to have fun while you're visiting.

Staring at those shoes, Ellen wished they could talk, because she needed to know if she'd been set up *again*.

The shower spray shut off, and a quick glance revealed the bathroom door wide open. Whoever was in there—and she desperately hoped it wasn't who she thought it was—would step out of the shower—*naked*—and see her.

Ellen had this wild urge to drop the shoes and race out of Félicie Allée, not stopping until she hit the highway. But she just knelt there, shoes in hand, *panicked,* like a squirrel staring down a two-ton SUV.

The shower door skidded across the track and a hand—definitely male—reached out to grab a towel from a nearby rack.

Then her roommate stepped from the shower.

One gorgeously muscular leg appeared at a time, silky dark hairs shimmering with water, dripping onto the mat. He unwittingly flashed her glimpses of flexing thighs, toned abs and strong biceps as he wrapped the towel around his waist to cover a very nice butt.

He shook his jet-black hair—not waist-length hair that

needed more cream rinse than her own, but neatly short hair—sent more droplets flying and turned toward her....

Ellen's breath and her heartbeat collided.

It wasn't Mr. Muscle-Butt.

It was *him*.

3

The Garden Suite

ELLEN HADN'T SEEN HIM in three months, yet her soul drank in the sight of this tall, athletic man as though she'd thirsted for this glimpse. His broad shoulders, the silky hairs nestled in that strong chest, the rippled lines of his stomach.

Though he enjoyed sports—he was an avid ice hockey player—Christopher Sinclair spent an equal amount of time indoors and outdoors. His skin flushed healthily, neither pale nor tanned, a combination that made him look so incredible in a tux that he'd have been an easy contender for Vittorio's cover model prize.

If she actually believed heroes existed anywhere except in her authors' stories, Ellen might just be convinced Christopher was one. At least looking at him didn't break the rules, which was a good thing since his polished good looks and striking coloring—black, black hair and blue, blue eyes—still tied her in knots. His piercing gaze had an amazing ability to sear through her.

His gaze seared through her right now.

She let her eyes flutter closed in self-defense and forced herself to breathe, to stand, to whisper. "Oh, please. Don't tell me you're my roommate."

The very idea was appalling, ludicrous; _exactly_ the type of surprise Miss Q might spring on her. But Lennon?

She couldn't reason this through, couldn't get past the fact that *he* was standing just a few feet away—practically naked—clear across the country from where she'd left him.

What was he doing here?

Someone needed to explain they were over. Finished. She forced herself to face him, found him staring at...*her hair.*

Suddenly she remembered the feel of his hands skimming along her scalp as clearly as if he'd just touched her. She remembered how he'd threaded his fingers through the long strands when they'd kissed, how he'd fanned it out over the pillows, over their naked skin on the night they'd made love. How he'd suddenly flipped her on top of him when she'd least expected it, cocooning them inside the drape of her hair, shutting out all stimuli, he'd said, to create a place where only the two of them existed.

In a last-ditch attempt to exorcise this man from her system and obey the rules she'd never break again, Ellen had cut her hair, refashioned her appearance as a cathartic exercise to transform herself into a new woman who wasn't hung up on Christopher Sinclair. It had been working.

Until she stared into those too-blue eyes...

All she could do was stand there, unable to breathe, waiting for him to say something. *Anything.*

And hoping, damn it. Hoping he liked what he saw.

All she could see was surprise. She knew she should say something, *do* something to take control of the moment, to stop this horrible vulnerability that was bridging the distance she'd worked so hard to put between this man and her emotions.

This man was against all the rules.

She should send him packing. Couldn't. And Christopher remained silent, moving toward her. Then he reached out....

Ellen watched as he threaded his fingers into her hair, just like he'd done so long ago, tipped her face toward his.

He took in her hair, his eyes caressing her with a look of such tenderness, as if he'd waited forever to see her.

And just like that, the months melted away, along with any will to resist him.

His mouth came down on hers, hard.

Ellen had the fleeting thought that even he seemed surprised by the intensity between them, the sudden rush of longing that swelled in their first exchange of shared breaths. But that was before his grip tightened. He tilted her head and held her firmly, revealing without words just how much he approved of her hair, how much he approved of *her*. In the process making a total lie out of her belief that any haircut would exorcise him from her system.

Without asking permission, without so much as a question about whether she wanted his kiss, he flaunted every rule of civilized behavior by plunging his tongue into her mouth as if he had the right to kiss her.

Experience told her she should shove him back. Experience told her that being with him would end in disaster. Experience told her to slap his face.

She kissed him, instead.

Reason scattered. How could she remember the rules when her tension liquefied into a heat that flooded her like a wave, warmed her blood and made her pulse with awareness and awakening.

Ellen recognized this sensation, grew amazed that she'd survived so long without it, that she'd convinced herself this dizzying rush she only knew with Christopher hadn't been real.

It was all too real.

How could she have forgotten this intensity, the almost violent swell of need that made thinking impossible, that made the careful deliberation she prided herself on diffuse like snowflakes in a blizzard? What was it about this man that dragged her down to an elemental, *primitive* level, where instincts ruled common sense?

He wasn't *the one*. No matter how much she'd wanted him to be. He was a wild guy who meant trouble. No question. And she'd taken the reckless road before. Reckless roads usually led to mistakes that left her feeling as if she'd disappointed everyone again, most of all herself.

But when his hands were on her, Ellen's entire world pared down to what felt good and what didn't. Christopher's hands anchoring her face close, his approval, and the longing he didn't even try to hide, all felt too good.

She slipped her arms around his waist.

Her actions weren't a concession. They simply were. A necessity. A fact. The chemistry between them was too potent to ignore. No point in even trying, although Christopher had always found this easier to acknowledge than she had. Perhaps because he'd simply been looking for a woman who challenged him. He hadn't been looking for *the one*.

At this moment, Ellen wasn't, either.

Dragging her fingers along his damp skin, she explored the contours, recalled the sleek strength of trim muscles, the way his waist veed into the broad lines of his back. She remembered this man. The feel of him. The scent of him. The taste of him.

Her tongue sought his and she answered his demand with a demand of her own. *Kiss me. Touch me. Want me.* Not an admission of how much she'd missed him, not a surrendering to his boldness, but simply a kiss that explored their desire.

His hands trailed from her hair, following the lines of her face, his touch gentle and searching, as though he was refreshing his memory or perhaps proving to himself she was real. She was very real. And she savored the feel of his fingertips against her skin, the hot minty taste of his mouth, her body's explosive reaction to him, his explosive reaction to her.

Christopher had always reveled in the chemistry between them, had held his hunger up as proof of how great they were together. She'd been the one overwhelmed by her need. Trying not to break the rules and sleep with him before enough time had passed had been a balancing act of anticipation and longing, where she could too easily lose all control in his arms.

She'd been sure this sort of passion meant he was *the one*.

He wasn't. But when his hands rounded the curve of her neck, tipped her chin just enough to deepen their kiss, Ellen forgot the past, forgot the rules. She knew only excitement when he crowded her back against the sturdy post of the tester bed, sealed their bodies together. Inch upon inch of hard, damp muscle crushed her, awakening all sorts of hunger.

Her hands raked his shoulders and trailed down his back, recalling the smooth flexing of muscle when he'd thrust on top of her, beneath her, from behind her.

Her sex began to clench with hot little aches.

And when he drove his thigh between hers, hard muscle into yielding skin, Ellen knew, oh, she knew exactly what Christopher wanted. He wasn't going to stop with a kiss. He wasn't going to waste their first meeting in so long— not when he was almost naked. Apparently time hadn't lessened their chemistry.

Lifting her, he anchored her along his hard thigh. Her

filmy skirt was only a whisper of protection separating skin from skin, nothing against the need making her sigh against his lips.

He caught the sound with his kiss and she felt his mouth curve upward, tasted his smile. He had the upper hand and he knew it, as he always had. Three months hadn't changed that.

Sanity cried out, a mental scream reminding her that she'd left this man for a good reason. The right reason. But reason didn't exist when he touched her. Nor did rules. Apparently time hadn't changed that, either.

But she wasn't the only one who lost her mind when they were together. Ellen may have sighed. She may have melted against him. She may have spread her legs to ride his thigh, the pressure kneading just the spot to feed that pleasure inside.

But Christopher's breaths were as ragged as hers.

His fingers dug deep as they dragged the curve of her shoulders, her silk tank top only inviting him to caress the length of bared arms, to slip below and reacquaint himself with her breasts. He did. A gentle weighing of her fullness that was at once appreciative and reverent.

And so needy. He was as caught up in this moment as she, clearly unable to resist the pull of their bodies or burying a hard-as-steel erection against her stomach.

His hot shaft was an insistent, demanding pressure, greedy for her attention, straining against the flimsy barrier that barely separated them, promised such ecstasy....

A promise Ellen couldn't ignore. Not when his hands traveled through sheer silk with such skill. Not when her breasts filled with an eager heaviness that made her swell into his palms, made her so sensitive she gasped when he flicked his thumbs across the tips.

Not when she hadn't had sex in so long, when she'd *never* had sex like she'd had with him.

But wasn't she already two steps ahead in the game since she knew he wasn't *the one?* Wouldn't knowing that protect her when she had to leave him all over again?

Damn Miss Q.

Damn her own disobedient body for this desperate ache that wouldn't consider denial, even though everything about him wrought havoc on her emotions.

And Christopher knew—damn *him*—pressing his advantage by trailing his mouth along her jaw, down her neck, nibbling, sucking, tasting her skin as though he planned to savor every inch of her at his leisure.

Tingles chased behind his kisses, the steady flicking of his thumbs over her nipples making her tension coil tighter.

He bent low, nipped her shoulder with exactly the right pressure to make her tremble. The sight of his dark head poised over her brought her emotions so close to the surface, made her recall with almost painful clarity how much she'd enjoyed having her world blocked out by the breadth of his wide shoulders, his dark head, his laughing kisses.

Slipping her hands beneath his towel, she dislodged it, and he assisted by shifting his hips to bare himself to her.

Skimming her hands along his skin, Ellen explored, cupping the tight curves of his butt, drawing him closer, his hot erection branding her through the sheer silk of her skirt.

He shivered, a vibration that ran from head to toe, and his teeth flashed white as he nibbled her nipple through her blouse.

She gasped.

He lifted his gaze, those blue eyes meeting hers with his

mouth parted over her breast, over the faintest trace of wetness on silk.

All she saw in his darkly handsome face was desire.

Christopher wanted her.

No matter that he'd let her go with only a few token phone calls and no fight. No matter that they'd lived in the same city and he'd never shown up at her office, or her apartment, never suggested a compromise that could satisfy his impulses and her needs. No matter that he hadn't followed the rules.

Christopher wanted her, and right now she wanted him.

So what if Miss Q had manipulated her—and most likely him—into this situation? They were together, the weekend's training session provided the perfect cover to protect her from the media's attention. Here they could play in privacy and safety.

There was a bed. And they weren't expected in the parlor until seven.

All hurt faded beneath the strength of their attraction. Nothing mattered beyond how explosive they were together. Every inch of her skin tingled, made her want to peel away her clothes and melt against him.

Letting her eyes flutter shut, Ellen pressed a kiss to the top of his silken head.

It was all the permission he needed.

Drawing the hem of her blouse up and over, Christopher peeled away her bra before his arms came around her, pulling her close. She melted into the strong circle of his embrace, breasts crushing his chest, bare skin against bare skin.

Then his mouth found hers again, his kiss urgent, as if he had something to prove. To her. Maybe even to himself.

Driving his fingers into her hair, Christopher cupped her head and braced her entire body upright, his free hand sliding down her hip, dragging her skirt up around her waist.

She'd worn only a thong, the temperature making even the thought of panty hose unbearable. But the sultry bayou heat was nothing compared to the fire raging inside her as Christopher sank his free hand between her thighs. He brushed aside the skimpy panties. His fingertips curled into the folds of her skin, separating, testing, finding her moist, ready for him.

With one bold stroke he slipped a finger inside.

Ellen's world narrowed to that fiery thrust. Her sex greedily tried to hold him steady, but Christopher controlled the moment, pressed his palm against her core of nerve endings, stroked her tenderly, knowingly, just the right pressure to coax her hips into motion.

Running her hands up his back, Ellen pulled him close and deepened their kiss. She rode his hand, each roll of her hips feeding the friction, coiling her tension tight.

Another finger circled lazily, intimately stoking new sensations to life, feeding her pleasure until she was wild with need, convincing her that Christopher did have something to prove. He would prove he could take her apart at the seams, unglue her until she was a mass of sensation.

Her body played right into his hands.

Ellen exploded, her moan swelling softly between them. He broke their kiss, stared down at her with eyes half hooded by pleasure, as though watching her climax was a wish granted. He held her entire body balanced with only a hand in her hair and another wedged between her thighs as he rode out the echoes of her orgasm with smooth knowing strokes and a big smile.

Only when she'd regained her senses enough to focus again did she follow his gaze to a very unique feature of the room that she hadn't noticed before.

A mirror. The reflection of Christopher standing dark and tall over her, her body arched erotically against his, her skirt wadded up around her waist to expose her parted thighs. Not one reflection, but many, each a little smaller, receding into infinity. She glanced in the opposite direction to see an identical mirror positioned on the other wall.

Ellen had seen vis-à-vis mirrors before, with Christopher in fact, when they'd toured an art exhibit at a New York museum. The interesting effect of multiple reflections had fascinated her at the time, but couldn't compare to the sight of their bodies twined together, as exotic as a living sculpture.

The reflection of the two of them together, forever.

Before she had a chance to react, Christopher drew his hand away, hiked one of her legs around his waist. She followed their reflection in the mirror with her gaze, the way his muscles shifted powerfully as he positioned himself.

The breath stalled in her throat as she watched him arch his hips purposefully, felt his erection searing, stretching as he pressed in, his throaty growl colliding with her gasp as their bodies joined.

Their gazes met in the mirror, his reflecting a longing that surprised her and her own heavy with desire, drugged by the feel of him inside her, the power he commanded over her.

Without one word spoken between them, Christopher proved their bodies recognized each other no matter how much time and space Ellen had put between them. His muscles flexed as he pulled back and thrust again, a deep beautiful stroke that dragged his name from her lips.

She had no balance save what he allowed her, with his hand cupping her head and her leg wrapped around him, but she could arch her hips to meet his thrusts. She lent her efforts to the cause, because each of his ragged breaths, every drumbeat of his heart meant she savaged his composure as he savaged hers.

With each driving stroke he lifted her, until her sex clenched in huge drawing pulls. His legs began to tremble and then…she was airborne.

In one powerful motion, he lifted her off the floor. He dragged her other leg around his waist, circled the bed and sank to the mattress on top of her, his erection still fast inside, his tongue never slowing a wild exploration of her mouth.

"Oh, Christopher," she whispered against his lips as his weight pressed her into the mattress. A sound of longing that acknowledged how his body filled hers in all the right places, how his broad shoulders blocked out her view of the world.

She'd forgotten how agile he was despite his size. All those years playing hockey. Speed and quick reflexes while sporting heavy equipment had developed his natural athleticism, a graceful strength that startled her. She wasn't particularly tall, but she wasn't short, either, and something about the way he could physically maneuver her lent an edge of excitement to their lovemaking.

When he smiled, a dashing grin that drove pinpoint dimples into his cheeks, emphasized the smooth definition of his freshly shaven jaw, Ellen could only smile back. Nothing mattered except this man. This moment.

And he knew. That flash in his lightning-blue eyes, that devastating grin proved he enjoyed her wildfire responses, that he'd anticipated her reaction to him completely.

Her first orgasm had only been an appetizer, a prelude to the one building. Three months of deprivation welled up inside her, made each thrust more poignant than the last, made her savor each taste of her mouth on his shoulder, his neck, his jaw, his freshly scrubbed skin, luscious on her tongue.

And when he rolled to his side, propped up on an elbow to stare down at her while he lazily continued to thrust, Ellen knew he liked the power he had over her, enjoyed this opportunity to wield it again.

She'd have to take him down a little, shift the balance back in her favor, but right now, she let him grin, too caught up in the feel of him inside her. There was no escaping the sensual indulgence of his hands on her skin, the strength of that smooth erection stretching, filling, driving deep, blinding her with the strength of her need.

Hiking one muscular thigh over hers, he anchored her hips against him, reared back until he almost completely withdrew. Then he plunged in. A thrust that made her gulp air, made her skin tingle. She'd played into his hands…and she didn't care. She'd been gifted with another chance to experience this man and the magic they made together, no matter how high the price she'd pay later. And she'd definitely pay.

He wasn't *the one.*

But as her muscles gathered and tightened again, her sex throbbing in time with his thrusts, Ellen could only hang on as another orgasm swelled inside. She went over the edge again with a throaty moan.

Christopher smiled, clearly very, *very* pleased.

Ellen closed her eyes, unable to face him, not with her sex gripping him greedily in the aftermath of orgasm, not with her chest heaving and her breasts quivering and her skin hot and wet from exertion. He still felt magnificently erect inside her, and she wanted him to say something— *anything*—to give her an anchor to latch on to.

But he didn't say a word. Maybe he didn't want to invite reality in on the moment. Or maybe his silence implied that what they shared was beyond description. Ellen didn't know. She only knew that his touch was oh so tender when he brushed away the damp hairs from her temple.

Damn him, he wasn't *the one*. Why wasn't he *the one?*

The disappointment that had dogged her for so long reared up inside, and she wrestled it down. Christopher might take apart her senses. He might eradicate her will when his hands were on her, but she wouldn't let him take apart her emotions. Not after the long months of beating them under control.

She wouldn't give him that. Not when he was playing her, holding himself back just to watch her go to pieces. And she was annihilated, barely able to lift an eyelid, while he toyed with her nipple and waited for her to catch her breath.

She remembered this feeling from their night together, too, and didn't have to open her eyes to know he looked all smiley and happy as though everything was just dandy in his world. But she was going to wipe that smug look from his face to prove he wasn't the only one with power here.

She opened her eyes and one glimpse into his smoldering expression told her he'd been counting on her to do exactly that. And seeing that look, knowing Christopher's need was as great as her own, was all it took to infuse her with new energy.

In an inspired motion, Ellen disconnected their bodies and shimmied away. Christopher groaned as his erection bobbed wildly, but she bit back her smile, shielded her expression beneath the fall of swingy hair as she rose to her knees and surveyed the tangle of fabric around her waist.

A visit to her dry cleaner would definitely be in order

before wearing this skirt again. But she decided making love to Christopher was worth any expense.

The emotional cost would be another matter entirely.

Dragging a pillow beneath his head, Christopher settled back, his body spread out before her, his erection draped across his abdomen, primed and ready. Ellen wondered if a skirt and panties were enough to make a good show, and decided she'd find a way to make a Broadway-worthy performance of nothing but earrings and a wristwatch if it meant earning that hungry look in his eyes.

Tossing her shoulders back, she reached around for the clasp of her skirt and twisted it around. Her back arched, breasts lifted high for his pleasure, and the motion made them sway heavily, eagerly, taut with her arousal and still swollen from his touch.

Working the clasp at her waist, she unfastened the zipper slowly, *slowly,* letting the fabric fall open to reveal more bare skin as she rocked her hips back and forth to the soothing jazz music. The skirt slid over her hips and fell into a filmy puddle around her knees.

Sinking back to the mattress, she drew the skirt along her calves and past her feet, leaving her clad in only a thong.

It wasn't much of a prop, but it was all Ellen had to work with and she was determined to make it go a long way. Rolling to her side, she slid off the bed, rose in an easy motion. The sultry air caressed her skin. Her short, full hair swung jauntily around her neck.

Keeping her shoulders arched, she turned just enough to give Christopher a shot of her in profile as she hooked her thumbs into the strings of her panties, began a leisurely swaying of her bottom to drag them down…down. With her own arousal damp between her legs, she moved languorously, her every motion, her every breath designed to hold his attention.

His hungry gaze followed her as she stretched out the moments, savored the feel of his gaze, arousal pumping a flush of heat into her skin, making her sex tingle with the memory of his hard thrusts, inspiring her to new boldness.

And when that little scrap of fabric fell to her feet, Ellen breathed deeply…and bent over to grab it.

Once upon a time, her long hair would have shielded much of her body during a move like this, played a sexy game of peekaboo she thought he would have enjoyed. But now her hair just swung forward onto her cheeks, leaving her exposed to his view—his *pleasure,* if the breath he sucked in was any indicator.

Grabbing her panties, she slung them off her finger like a slingshot aimed at his head. Quick as ever, he caught them, shooting her a wicked grin as he brought the scrap of lacy white fabric to his chest, pressed it directly over…his heart.

Damn him!

Everything inside her melted like winter's first snow-flakes hitting the pavement. Why did he try to turn a sexy game into something more? He was the one who couldn't play by the rules, who'd been perfectly content to let her get away. No coming after her. No fighting to keep her.

This was just sex, damn it.

Diving for him, she straddled his hips before the surprise faded from his face. Slipping her fingers around that hot erection, she took aim…and sank down, taking him all the way inside her moist body in a sleek stroke. Gratified by his loud grunt and the way he bucked hard at their joining, she arched her back and rode him.

Of course he wasn't content to let her control the game. Fastening on to a nipple, he drew her into the rough-velvet recesses of his mouth with a hot pull. She moaned, her whole body shuddering in reply.

This man and the effect he had on her was undeniable and utterly amazing, and she pressed a kiss to the top of his silky dark head, a stupidly tender urge she shouldn't have given in to.

She couldn't help herself. Not when his mouth drew on her nipple, first one and then the other, unfurling crazy ribbons of sensation inside. Not when he lifted his hips to meet her strokes, his heat branding her, making her drive down a little harder, a little faster to increase the friction.

And when he drew away from her breasts, leaving her nipples peaked and wet and tingling, he slipped his hands under her bottom, drove his fingers deep with his eagerness to quicken her pace. His thighs began to vibrate. His hips came up off the mattress, and he speared into her with a force that sent pleasure straight to her core.

His ridiculously thick lashes shuttered over those piercing eyes as he sucked in a hard breath and pressed his head back into the pillows. Ellen watched, unable to lift her gaze from the sight of his features sharpening with pleasure, that strong jaw clenching tight, the thick cords in his neck compressing as his body bucked hard.

He reached his own fulfillment with a low growl, and the sight and sound and feel of him coaxed another impossible climax from her, a liberation of senses that should have been depleted but were almost painfully intense.

Then Ellen collapsed on top of him, lay draped across his body, clinging, remembering the feel of his heartbeat throbbing against hers, the way her face fit perfectly into the curve of his neck, the way he smelled of their passion on his damp skin.

Why, oh why, couldn't he have been *the one?*

And when he ran his strong hands over her body as if

memorizing her, as though he'd been deprived for too long, she acknowledged that he'd broken her heart, that she'd wanted him like she'd never wanted another man in her life.

He wasn't *the one*.

When he pressed gentle kisses into her hair, Ellen knew the time had come to make her escape. Before she went to pieces right here. But Christopher wouldn't let her. He held her close and toyed with her hair, her breasts, her sex.

When she resisted, he moved in for another assault, pinning her on the mattress and raining hot kisses over every inch of her skin, proving that he hadn't forgotten any of the sensitive spots he'd discovered during months of foreplay.

When she tried to regain her senses, he simply pulled out the big guns. Wedging his shoulders between her thighs, he reacquainted himself with her most intimate places, his mouth and tongue curling into her heat sensuously, decadently, making her cry out with such heady attention.

The light faded beyond the French doors. The music continued to play, a sultry combination of songs that filled the quiet, worked into her subconscious. Christopher's touch blurred sound and sight and taste and pleasure in a way only he had ever done. He inspired her to unrealized boldness. He devastated her with his tender touches and caring kisses.

And when she couldn't possibly take any more, when it seemed he might actually kill her if he tried to wring one more orgasm from her overwhelmed body, Ellen pulled away from him, refused to let him see the tears that were suddenly blinding her.

"Don't go."

His voice filtered through the darkness, penetrated her

senses, so rich and deep with just the faintest hint of the Deep South, a sound she hadn't realized she'd missed so much until hearing it again.

Pulling her back to him, he curved his body around hers, locked his arm around her waist, cradled his sex against her bottom. He settled his chin on the top of her head, and she heard him inhale deeply, felt the corresponding rise and fall of his chest.

Ellen couldn't think clearly. She was too inundated with emotion and sensation even to try. Her body still trembled with the fading echoes of climax, the warmth of satiation, the boneless descent of an awesome adrenaline rush.

His breath tickled her ear. He held her so close their bodies were seamless, bound by a thin sheen of sweat.

In that moment, a moment when everything seemed right in her world for the first time in forever, Ellen didn't think about her ironclad rules for relationships. She didn't analyze the consequences of giving in to his request. She didn't think about making mistakes.

She just closed her eyes.

4
___

IN THE STILLNESS of the very late night, Christopher cradled Ellen close, savored the feel of her sleek legs tangled with his, her soft breaths breaking against his chest. Physically, he should be exhausted, but the singularity of holding her again precluded any need for sleep.

Just as she had on that night three months ago, Ellen had blown him away. He'd meant to engage her in the fantasy of a role-playing event in a place where she could feel safe from the restrictions guiding her complicated life. He'd wound up unable to keep his hands off her and made them miss all the opening night events, instead—an occurrence she'd have something to say about when she awoke. His only defense was that he'd lost himself in the challenge of coaxing sighs from her lips, slipping past those walls she so ably tossed up between them.

Those walls were what had done him in. She built them quicker than he could tear them down, her cool composure distancing him as efficiently as if she'd thrown an ocean between them. Christopher had been tired of distance last night.

Three months without her had been three months too long.

The fault was all his, of course. He'd made a judgment error, something he didn't do often. Ellen's refusal to sleep all night in his bed should have warned him to tread slowly, but unfortunately, treading slowly was not one of his strengths.

Gut instinct and the ability to make fast decisions marked his career. And for the hundredth time since Ellen had stormed out his door without a backward glance, Christopher told himself that a senior vice president of sales with forty-seven global divisions under his supervision should have had a firmer handle on his presentation.

Given Ellen's high-profile family, he'd believed proposing marriage was the logical solution to their problem of being together. He'd believed that commitment would bridge the distance she kept between them and prove he wanted to spend his life with her. Made sense.

Not to Ellen.

He hadn't factored in those damn walls she retreated behind whenever life slipped out of her grasp. He hadn't counted on her determination to play by her damn rules, either, which had resulted in him overplaying his hand badly. All he could claim was that love had made him lose his mind.

But, damn, what a feeling.

Closing his eyes, he luxuriated in the brush of her hair against his cheek, the delicate scent of her touched by the fragrant breeze wafting in through the open courtyard doors. The sense of completion he felt was like nothing he'd ever known before.

Except when he was with her.

She'd inspired him to pick up the phone in the middle of a workday just to hear her voice. He reveled in the challenge of peeling away the coolly composed layers to the passionate woman below, a woman he'd missed during these past months.

He wanted another chance.

As though she sensed the bent of his thoughts, she rolled

out of his arms with a sigh. Christopher didn't take it personally. Ellen clearly wasn't used to sharing her bed, and he'd been chasing her around ever since she'd fallen asleep. Every time she slipped away, he rolled with her and wrapped himself around her again.

But this time he slipped out of bed, dragged on jeans and a shirt, stepped into his favorite Top-Siders. After glancing at Ellen to make sure she still slept, he left the bedroom. He had business to conduct. Business that couldn't wait.

Heading into the sitting room, he looked for…there it was, on an end table right beside the bedroom door. Within earshot. Always.

Retrieving Ellen's purse, he flipped it open with no remorse for privacy invasion, grabbed her cell phone and pressed the power button.

Off.

Only luck had kept her phone from ringing while they'd made love, and Christopher was grateful. If that phone had rung, Ellen would have ejected from his bed like a shot.

Her life boiled down to a phone that remained on *always*. It was the connection that called the Talbot family together from anywhere and everywhere when the Senator needed her family by her side to present a united front to the press. In fact, Ellen had almost missed Josh and Lennon's wedding because of a family duty call during her mother's most recent campaign.

He understood that the Talbots needed to rally behind the Senator, but he didn't understand why Ellen lived her life on hold while waiting for these duty calls. He'd asked her, but she'd only said that her parents had certain expectations of their children and she had some catching up to do to meet them. Given what an intelligent and accomplished woman Ellen was, he'd had a hard time imagining where she'd fallen short. But she wouldn't discuss the subject. He added this to his list of things that intrigued him about her.

Heading out of the suite, Christopher recalled the very first time he'd laid eyes on Ellen—a vivid moment that still stood out in his memory.

June. Louis Armstrong Airport. Metairie, Louisiana.

With all the pre-wedding fittings and festivities, Christopher, a groomsman, had been recruited to make the airport run to retrieve a bridesmaid who'd changed her travel plans at the last minute, arriving only in time for the rehearsal.

A simple request he'd been happy to carry out. Since both made their homes in Manhattan and obviously shared the commonality of a busy schedule, Christopher had figured they would have something to talk about on the ride back into New Orleans.

He hadn't smelled a setup until Ellen emerged from the gate.

She was one cool beauty with her almost waist-length dark hair and willowy body. Beautiful in a very classic way, creamy skin and elegant features that brought to mind a porcelain doll on a collector's shelf. She had a smile that lit up the terminal like a spotlight and a mysterious self-possession that suggested she would remain unruffled in the middle of an avalanche.

It was that quality that had first caught his attention.

And continued alternately to fascinate and frustrate him. Shaking his head, Christopher left the garden suite and tucked the memory safely away. That image, along with others he'd collected during the time they'd dated, had been all he'd had of Ellen for three long months. He wasn't about to let them go until he saw how his plans for the next few days transpired.

Hence, he had to get about his business.

The light shining through the glass office door surprised him. He gave a quick knock and entered, only to find Miss Q sitting behind a desk, a cup of tea at her elbow and stacks of papers in front of her.

"Just the person I needed to see," he said. "I was going to leave you a note. I thought you'd be sleeping."

Miss Q gazed over the rims of her reading glasses with bright eyes that the passage of time hadn't dimmed. "I figure I'll have plenty of time to sleep when I'm dead, dear. Right now, I've got things to do."

She stopped Christopher in his tracks with her easy reference to the inevitable, and he quickly understood that Miss Q planned to face death in the same manner she faced life. With an appreciation for a new experience. Christopher supposed when one looked at death that way it became another adventure.

He filed that idea away for future reference, thinking he might like to handle matters with that same sort of aplomb.

"I'm not disturbing you, am I?"

"Of course not. But given that you and Ellen never showed up for the introduction, I was hoping you were engaged in something a little more exciting than talking to an old lady."

"No comment."

"Playing the gentleman, are you? Well, then, keep the details to yourself and just tell me how it went. You're still vertical and I don't see any blood, so I'll assume you and Ellen worked out some sort of compromise for the training."

"In a manner of speaking."

Technically he and Ellen hadn't discussed the training. He wouldn't have that pleasure until she awoke and realized they'd missed the introduction. Hopefully, there wouldn't be a splatter trail to mark the occasion.

"I see" was all Miss Q said.

And Christopher knew she did. Miss Q was one of the few people who had understood the significance of his marriage proposal. Not only had she lived with the love of her life for well over fifty years—a man who'd been close friends with Christopher's grandfather—but she'd also known him all his life. And she knew Ellen. Hell, she'd been the one to send him off to the airport to pick up the errant bridesmaid in the first place.

And the ensuing months had been...well, *awesome*.

For what seemed like the hundredth time since first meeting Ellen, Christopher thought that a man who made his living supervising client relations all over the globe should be more articulate. But Ellen had affected so many changes in him, this lack of articulation not the least among them.

"After seeing Ellen tonight, I'm convinced I've got a good shot at getting her to give me another chance."

A good shot. He sampled the effect of the words on his tongue, decided he disliked the taste of potential defeat—a feeling he hadn't experienced much in his life. "That's what I came to tell you."

"You're convinced she still loves you."

"Yes."

Only a beat of silence passed before Miss Q took him at his word. "Good, because I want everything to go your way, dear. You've gone through a great deal of trouble and expense to arrange this get-together and I must tell you how impressed I am with your ingenuity and imagination. If anyone can prove himself to our fiercely independent Ellen, you're the man."

"Thank you for helping me pull this off."

"My pleasure. It's been a good time, and I'm delighted that Olaf has taken to this place the way he has. He hasn't had so much fun in ages, and he deserves some after working so hard to organize the Eastman Gallery." She referred to the erotic art gallery she'd recently opened as a memorial to her late lover. "I want you to have fun, too. I think you'll be pleased with the script we've cooked up."

"I'm sure I will be."

"Then, smile, dear. You're an innovative businessman, the senior vice-president of sales in that fancy company, for goodness' sake. You can sell yourself to Ellen."

If only selling himself were as simple as wheeling and dealing for controlling interest in a Black Sea vacation resort or an antebellum plantation. But Miss Q did have a point, and he wasn't embarrassed to admit that her opinion mattered. He'd known Miss Q his whole life and he respected her. Knowing she returned the sentiment went a long way toward dispelling the lingering sense of defeat he'd been grappling with since Ellen ended their relationship and refused his calls.

"I've already taken the up-front approach, and she wasn't impressed. She's a very strong woman, so chasing after her was never an option. Ingenuity and imagination are all I have."

"Ellen's a tough sell. No doubt." Miss Q sounded thoughtful. "But then, so were you. Finding a woman to catch your eye hasn't been easy. Trust me."

"She has me between a rock and a hard place."

"Your favorite place to be."

"Admittedly. But I normally have more options."

"Even better," she shot back. "You like challenges."

"The more challenging the better. *Usually*." Taking a deep breath, Christopher steeled himself to admit the truth. "I don't want to lose her."

Miss Q sighed, and Christopher shook off the grim effects of his admission to manage another smile. This woman was a true romantic.

"Ellen's an intelligent girl and you two are perfect for each other. I know. I brought you together, and I don't make mistakes about grand passion."

"With luck I'll convince her, too."

Miss Q grinned a grin that lit up her wizened features, hinted at the gorgeous daredevil she'd been in her youth. "Luck has nothing to do with it. You just be your dashing self and let her heart do the rest. She's a smart girl."

"Who chooses to play it safe. She won't allow herself to get too close or too vulnerable, and right now she's convinced being involved with me is the worst possible move she could make. But one thing I do know is that beneath her cool exterior beats the heart of an idealist. She may hide it well, but editing those romances feeds her soul. She's very influenced by heroes, fantasies and happy endings, whether she admits it or not. It so happens I'm targeting idealistic souls this weekend."

"You'll be a wonderful hero, dear. It's in your blood. Just look at your parents. They're the love match of their generation."

No argument there. His parents brought to life the cliché *two peas in a pod,* as infatuated with each other today as they had been when Christopher was a child. Which had caused him considerable embarrassment in his youth. He used to roll his eyes and spend as much time with his grandfather as he could manage, but that was before he'd matured enough to appreciate how rare and special was the love his parents shared.

"You and Ellen are grand passion personified." Miss Q sighed again, with such drama that Christopher knew he'd come to the right place when he'd asked for her help.

True, hooking up with the little old matchmaker had been an unconventional approach to the problem, but he'd analyzed his options, assessed the success-to-failure ratio. Lovesickness aside, Christopher hadn't worked his way into executive management with a multinational holding corporation without the ability to read people and trust his gut instinct.

Miss Q was his best bet for success.

He would not overplay his hand again. Not remembering how he'd felt sitting in his Manhattan office, staring fifty stories down at the busy street. People rushing around the city, playing, working and living their lives. Ellen didn't work far away and could have been any one of them, hurrying out to meet with an agent at one of the city's fancy eateries or squeezing in some shopping on her lunch hour.

But from where Christopher had sat, he couldn't see her.

It was a feeling he didn't plan to experience again.

IF THE GLARE BURNING through Ellen's still-closed eyelids was any clue, sunlight was streaming into the room. The provocative jazz of the night before had yielded to silence. The shadows of lengthening dusk had melted away beneath bright Louisiana sunshine that singed her eyes and spotlighted dreamlike images of arms and legs twined, a strong body realigning itself around her whenever she'd moved.

Ellen didn't wake up easily on the best of days, and on a day like today, when her entire body felt tender and achy, disoriented but so very contented…

That thought brought her to full consciousness in less time than it took to blink.

Christopher.

Bolting upright, Ellen almost gave herself whiplash

looking for him, but he was nowhere to be seen. And she'd just about convinced herself he'd been nothing more than an erotic dream when she heard the sound of the shower running.

Tossing off the covers, she forced her feet over the side of the bed. Every part of her body, from her lips south, felt hypersensitive from his sexy attention. Her thighs trembled. Her muscles groaned from unaccustomed exercise. Her sex gave a needy throb—a warning, perhaps, that last night had reawakened an appetite she'd be hard-pressed to rein under control again.

Damn him. No wonder she'd been having such trouble getting him out of her head. Christopher was hands-down lethal in the lovemaking department and he irresponsibly shared his gift without consideration for the repercussions to his partners.

Pushing to her feet, Ellen yanked a sheet away from the tangle of covers—not difficult, considering the bed looked as though a battle had been fought there—wrapped it around herself and made her way across the room.

He'd left the French doors open, but she only spared a passing glance at the private courtyard where a swimming pool sat amidst a garden of lush greenery, Spanish moss and brightly blooming flowers. Gardenia scented the air, her absolute favorite, but Ellen didn't pause to savor the scent before striding through the bathroom door, across the tiled floor, and planting herself in front of the shower stall.

He tipped his head back under the spray, eyes closed against the shampoo sluicing down his face and over broad shoulders, along muscles that rippled beneath sheets of frothy lather, caressing him as possessively as she had last night.

Ellen slid the door open so hard the glass rattled.

"Don't go?" She repeated his words of the previous

night—his *only* words. Ignoring the gravelly sound of her morning voice, she met his surprised gaze head-on. "We haven't spoken in three months and all you can say is 'Don't go'? Couldn't resist the challenge of getting me to sleep all night with you, could you, even though you know how I feel. And I was a total pushover. Of all the low blows—"

Ellen suddenly found herself struggling to remain upright as he dragged her inside the shower stall. Hot water shot over her as the spray bounced off his head, leaving her sputtering and clutching the sheet, although she was getting soaked. Indeed, half still trailed through the open shower door, but Christopher didn't seem to care about the mess they were making....

Planting a foot on the hem, he crowded her back against the tile wall, forced the sheet from her grasp.

"Christopher!" She gallantly hung on.

He wrestled it away without bothering to meet her gaze, kicked the drenched fabric into a bundle outside the stall and pulled the door shut. Only then did he lift that too-blue stare.

"Good morning, love," he said cheerily, as though everything was as right as rain in his world. "I thought we should get the 'spending the night together' business out of the way since we'll be roommates. And you needed your rest."

Needed her rest? She glared, refusing to rise to the bait. Of course she'd needed her rest. He'd nearly killed her with what Lennon always referred to as "death by orgasm."

Clearly misinterpreting her silence as meaning everything was as right as rain in her world, too, he asked, "Sleep well?"

Sleep well? Oh, sure, she'd slept just dandy for a woman

who'd broken her cardinal rule for relationships: *Senators' daughters do not get caught sneaking out of anyone's bed the morning after.*

Sequestered as they were at Félicie Allée, the chances of being caught by anyone who'd alert the media were slim. She supposed that counted for something.

"I slept fine." There, she'd managed to sound reasonably composed, despite her froggy voice.

"I've missed you."

That potent blue gaze slipped to her lips, gleamed with a lightning fire that brought to mind all the intimacies they'd shared. And when he brought a hand to her mouth, traced her lower lip with a gentle caress of his thumb, Christopher made a huge dent in her composure. One touch and he dared her to tremble, to sigh, to pull away in indignation…*any* reaction would have sufficed, would have proven he still commanded the same power over her that he'd wielded so skillfully last night.

Through sheer dint of will, Ellen held his gaze, steeled herself as he trailed his wet fingertips along her jaw, over her chin, exploring every angle and curve through touch.

She wanted to deny that she'd missed him, but she'd gone to pieces in his arms. She knew it. He knew it. The only thing to do now was step back, reassess the situation and come up with a new game plan to handle this man's reappearance in her life.

When the answer isn't clear, step back and take another look at the question, her mother was fond of saying.

But stepping back proved impossible, literally. The tile wall came up behind her and Christopher's big-bodied self crowded her against it. Skimming his fingers down her neck, he traced each hollow as though he'd never before had the pleasure. Then his gaze flicked to her hair and his expression softened. That same look of approval that had undone her last night.

How could she have forgotten how his beautiful features mirrored his emotions?

Maybe she hadn't forgotten at all, rather had managed to bury the memory deep, in self-defense.

But denial was no longer her luxury. Not when Christopher stood there, water flowing, steam curling around them, misting the glass, softening the edges of the world with the incredible chemistry they created together....

For one rebellious moment, Ellen felt that same needy sense of hope she had felt last night, a soul-deep longing that urged her to toss aside reason for emotion, to follow her heart no matter where it may lead.

She squelched the feeling brutally. She recalled having felt this way before, and every time she threw caution to the wind, she wound up disappointing everyone.

"Why did you cut your hair?" he asked.

Because it seemed symbolic of ending our relationship. "I was in the mood for a change."

"I like it."

"I'm glad you approve."

He ignored her sarcasm. "Oh, I do." His face lowered and his mouth brushed her skin, that oh-so-sensitive juncture where her pulse rushed like wildfire through her veins. "I don't think I ever fully appreciated what a lovely neck you have."

Every inch of her grew heated by his big body and the spray sealing their skin together in a silky haze. All those places still achy from his lovemaking began to burn.

Ellen should push him away. Rule number one of survival was to be smart, which translated into knowing when she was in over her head. She was definitely in over her head with Christopher.

"What are you doing?" she demanded. "What are *we* doing?" She wouldn't give him the satisfaction of knowing how much he affected her.

"We're enjoying ourselves." He nibbled her neck, his wet hair tickling her nose, filling her senses with his freshly scrubbed scent.

She splayed her hands on the tile, refused to give in to the urge to touch him. "It's not that simple."

"Why?"

"I won't be your challenge *du jour*."

He nipped the base of her throat. She shivered in reply, couldn't help herself.

"You're wrong about me," he said.

"Did Miss Q trick you into coming here?"

"No."

"No?"

Lifting his gaze, he peered at her with eyes that let her see into his soul. "My feelings for you haven't changed."

Then, why hadn't he been willing to compromise? Why had he just let her go?

Asking those questions meant letting him see into *her* soul.

He went to work on her mouth this time, his lips tracing hers with soft half kisses that made her want to sigh. "There are no hard and fast rules in love," he whispered. "Let it be simple, let *us* be simple. We're right together."

"You can't know that."

Another brush of his lips, light, sweet. "But I do. Last night only proved it."

"Proved what?" She tilted her face upward to avoid his lips, hated that she sounded slightly hysterical. "That we can make total asses of ourselves."

That got his attention. He straightened, arching a dark brow as he stared down at her. She'd always equated this wry look with sardonic romance heroes who pursued their heroines with possessive charm and demanding seduction.

"What are you talking about? You've lost me."

She couldn't possibly be talking about him. Looking like an ass clearly wasn't part of his daily routine. Inhaling deeply, she took advantage of the distance to clear her thoughts. "We were due in the gallery at seven and didn't show up." The thought made her wince. "Everyone's going to know what we were doing."

Christopher grinned. "So what?"

"My authors will talk, which will start rumors among perfect strangers. I'm Miss Q's guest..." *Although she's on my list of people to confront about this not-so-little shenanigan.*

"...and I'm playing a sleuth in this mystery. You, too, I assume. I hope we haven't ruined anything important. Thank goodness the media isn't covering this grand opening. That would have been a nightmare. I can just hear the sound bite. 'The Senator's daughter was mysteriously absent from the events along with the VP of sales from Global Alliance.'"

She breathed deeply to dispel a chill.

"We've only missed the introduction." He sounded so damn calm. "We can get up to speed this morning. Our absence won't affect the game."

"But I'm never going to hear the end of this."

"You're probably right. Miss Q lives for this sort of thing." Those eyes flashed. "Last night was worth it."

"I'm surprised to hear you say that. Where was the challenge?" She didn't bother to check the irony in her voice. "You never even had to leave the suite to find a date. You never even had to dry off from your shower."

"You're a challenge, love, I'll grant you," he said in a voice so grim that she actually blinked. "But not a game.

There's a difference. I figured getting married would take care of your damn rules so we could be together."

"You and me getting married is *crazy*," she managed to say. "It's impulsive. Can you imagine what people would say?"

"They'd think it was love at first sight."

"They'd think I lost my mind."

"Well, who cares about *those* people?"

Ellen did. Although Christopher had survived the rigorous requirements that routinely intimidated most men she dated and had passed the tests with flying colors, he obviously hadn't been around long enough to appreciate the full responsibility of being a Senator's daughter. High-visibility translated into living life by rules that allowed no room for impulsiveness.

Slipups resulted in negative media attention. Negative media attention resulted in scandal. Scandal resulted in unwanted publicity for the Senator, which in turn resulted in being forced to deal with *the handlers.*

Ellen had had brushes with scandal before, and knew of nothing worse than dealing with her mother's media handlers, less fondly known as the spin doctors. These people turned devastating mistakes into endearing foibles for the public's benefit, swayed opinion from condemnation to approval with their polished presentation and skilled maneuvers.

They coached her on what to say, how to act and what to wear to present just the right image and minimize the effects of careless decisions. The power they wielded was nothing short of scary, and Ellen's few unfortunate encounters with them through the years had taught her to avoid them at all costs.

But even worse than dealing with the media handlers was facing that she'd strayed off course again. She hated feeling unfocused and chaotic in a family of very focused people.

Although her parents had never even hinted that she was a disappointment—they loved her, after all—there was no getting around the fact that their views of her choices always went hand-in-hand with a good deal of worry.

You need to step back and look at your options, Ellen, her mom was fond of saying. *You should always look before you leap.*

"Leaping into a marriage after three months of dating is not in the rule book," she explained. "A private inquiry into your background before I can date is one of the rules. Months of casual dating before I can have sex with you is another."

She'd only lasted three months with Christopher, which was definitely on the light end of acceptable, but not too shabby considering that every time they kissed, one of them had wound up shedding some piece of clothing....

"Marriage is a minimum of two years down the road."

"Says whom?"

"Me." And she meant it.

"Why two years?"

"To see if you can deal with the constant pressure of living under public scrutiny."

That gaze seared into her. "You've got to be kidding."

Ellen shook her head. She would never again let any man into her world unless he was able to shoulder the responsibility. Every choice and action had a consequence. Impulsiveness had absolutely no place around the Talbot family.

"I've never been more serious."

"Fine, then while I've got your undivided attention for the next few days, I'll show you how good we can be together."

Maybe it was the gravity of his expression or the somber promise, but Ellen didn't doubt that he meant what he said.

She also knew if his idea of showing her how good they were together even remotely resembled last night's assault on her senses, she'd never survive. Not and still be able to walk away from him on Monday.

"You don't have to show me anything, Christopher. There's no point. I enjoyed dating you. I enjoyed last night. That's it. There's no place to go from here."

"We can have a future."

"What makes you think you know my mind better than I know my own, arrogant man?"

"Not your mind, love, your heart. Tell me you've felt this way about anyone else and I'll back off."

She opened her mouth to tell him he wasn't the only man on the planet who'd made her lose her head, but the only other time she'd ever even come close to feeling this way had been as a teen. She hadn't looked before she'd leaped and the situation had almost wound up in disaster.

She had no intention of sharing that still-painful memory, though, and it didn't matter, anyway, because Christopher's dimples flickered, just enough to let her know that he wouldn't believe a word she said.

"Oh, what's the point?"

"The point is, I'm the only man who makes you feel this way. You're the only woman who makes me feel this way, too."

His gaze caressed her, promising the world with his eyes, and that damnable honesty threw her off balance again....

"Let me sweep you off your feet, love. Let me show you how to make the rules work for us. I got past your defenses last night and you're right, there are consequences. But I think making love to you was worth any price we'll pay this morning.''

Was he right?

An isolated plantation in a city outside her mother's constituency. Friends and acquaintances. A private training session. No media. The circumstances didn't get more perfect than if they'd been tailored to suit her specific needs. The consequences of facing Miss Q were minor, comparatively speaking.

Rule number two for survival: *Tackle problems head-on.*

Glancing up into the dashingly handsome face of the man who'd been plaguing her thoughts for too long, Ellen recognized a problem when she saw one.

Slipping her hand between them, she wrapped her fingers around a promising erection. Christopher hissed, clearly not expecting her move, and his body went rigid. She gave a leisurely stroke and was rewarded when he swelled in response.

"I don't deny the effect you have on me, Christopher." There was no denying that he made her lose her head all too easily. "I just don't believe we can have a future together."

"We can."

"I'll walk away on Monday."

"We'll see."

Rule number two of sound business strategies: *Understand your limitations and work around them.*

She had a craving for this man that needed to be satisfied. "Why don't we just enjoy the weekend?"

He exhaled a sigh and arched his hips toward her hands. "You won't be sorry, love. I promise."

Was there a threat in there?

Ellen didn't know. At the moment she didn't care. She

steeled herself mentally to accept the challenge ahead—getting this man out of her system once and for all. And since he seemed content to lean back against the tile and give over to her attention, she stepped into the spray, reached for the soap and set about satisfying her craving.

5

CHRISTOPHER STARED DOWN at the top of Ellen's head, wet hair fringing around her nape, brushing her shoulders. Her soapy hands kneaded his chest, the deep strokes of a massage that would have eased tension from his muscles had he felt tense.

He only felt replete, and very pleased Ellen hadn't packed her bags and called a taxi. She'd risen to the challenge, instead, which meant he stood a chance.

With her chin high and her mouth pursed, she avoided his gaze with what appeared from his vantage point to be iron-willed determination not to be swayed from her task. She intended to keep the upper hand, and Christopher wouldn't resist.

Inhaling deeply, he paced himself, amazed yet again at her ability to play with his heart rate with nothing more than her hands and a smile. He'd gone a little nuts last night, hadn't anticipated how seeing her would test his restraint.

He was a damn fool where Ellen was concerned and he only had this training session to figure out exactly what it would take to show her how great they were together and turn a long weekend into a chance at forever.

The clock was ticking—almost as quickly as his heart was pounding when Ellen sank to her knees, water slicing across her shoulders to create a waterfall over her gently swaying breasts.

As much as he was tempted to close his eyes and enjoy her attention, Christopher found himself riveted to the sight of her kneeling before him, a visual feast he'd been denied too long. He'd barely had a chance to become acquainted with her beautiful body before she'd dumped him. And now, every creamy inch of her glimmered in a sheen of mist and droplets, her slim waist curving into her hips, that heart-shaped bottom.

Her dark head level with his erection.

She shielded him from the spray of water, her breath coming in warm bursts against his skin, taunting him, making him jump toward her lips like a heat-seeking missile.

Though he couldn't see her face, he suspected she was smiling. She was comfortable with power, lashing out at her own vulnerability by assuming control. And she was clearly happy in control now, because she slipped her hands around him, coaxed her fingers beneath his scrotum and gave a squeeze to remind him who was in charge....

Then she moved on, lathering his thighs, his knees and down, down, working muscles that were still feeling the effects of Tuesday night's hockey game and giving him a chance to suck in a needed breath.

He couldn't feel anything but the heat of his own sky-rocketing body temperature, even though, judging by the goose bumps spraying over Ellen's arms, they'd tested the limits of the water heater.

But she still kept going, kneeling at his feet, fingertips working along his calves, his ankles, between his toes. Then she motioned him to turn around. Placing his hands on the tile, he braced his legs apart to shield her from the cooling spray that didn't bother him in the least.

She started a new game on her way back up his body, driving him slowly crazy when she brushed her nipples against the backs of his knees, pressed her breasts against his thighs, taunted him with the feel of their soapy fullness. She tested his ability to keep his hands flat on the tile, when he wanted to drag her against him, sink deep inside her.

The silence thickened with expectation, and he wondered if she was paying him back for last night.

We haven't spoken in three months and all you can say is "Don't go"?

What else had there been to say? He hadn't wanted her to go. Not three months ago. Not last night. Not now.

Especially not now.

Slipping her fingers between his thighs, Ellen played with him from behind, making his erection jump and his hips buck. She laughed, a soft sound in the waterlogged quiet, but a sound that spiked his appetite as though he hadn't just spent all night feeding his hunger.

She read his responses easily enough, because suddenly she slithered every inch of her wet skin along his thighs. She molded her body against him, slipping her hands around his hips, lathering, stroking, proving what he'd known all along—that she'd been designed to fit him perfectly.

Why couldn't Ellen see that?

She'd started to move, riding the length of his body with smooth, wet strokes. Her curves molded him, made his blood pump double-time. She slipped her fingers around his erection, a solid grip that made him press into her hands. He wanted to turn around, wrap her legs around his waist and sink inside her, but they were back to that power thing again. She was going to make him come. Payback for last night.

Christopher just closed his eyes.

Her hands started up a mind-blowing rhythm. Each stroke lifting him to an urgent place—the promise of explosive orgasms had made him seduce a woman who said she didn't want to be seduced. All because he needed to feel her hands on him, needed to know what they shared was real.

She pressed kisses along his back, and every time she nipped his skin with her teeth, he bucked hard. Only Ellen had ever made him lose control this way, left him gasping for breath, straining in her hands as he exploded in one of those unbelievable orgasms.

Bracing himself against the wall, he hoped his legs didn't buckle. "Damn."

Suddenly she was up on tiptoes, her face in his periphery, her chin propped against his shoulder. She smiled that bewitching smile and pressed a kiss to his cheek.

"Since we're going to make the most of this reunion…one good turn and all that, y'know."

Christopher could only grunt in reply. Looked like staying in control around Ellen for the next four days was going to be another one of those challenges he supposedly thrived on.

IN A VAIN ATTEMPT TO FASTEN the buttons on her gown, Ellen performed contortions she'd had no idea her body was capable of. She eyed Christopher enviously as he emerged from the closet, shrugging on a buff-colored frock coat *without* calisthenics.

He'd already donned his costume; dark brown trousers, silk brocade vest and a bow tie neatly tied at his throat, looking as if he'd just stepped off the cover of a romance novel. Not flashy and absurd like Mr. Muscle-Butt in his cape at the convention last week, but scrumptious and too handsome to be real.

"You'd need four arms and eyes in the back of your

head to fasten all those buttons without help,'' he said, accurately assessing her situation in a glance.

Striding across the suite, he brushed aside her hands and met her gaze in the mirror. ''I'm your partner for this event, which means—''

''I know what it means.'' She lifted her chin a notch.

''Then, let me help. It's only fair since I undressed you.'' He pressed a kiss to the top of her head.

''You're the horniest man I know.''

''You do have that effect on me, love.''

''Blame me for *your* lack of self-control, why don't you.'' She huffed. ''Now if you're going to help, please do.''

''My pleasure.''

Ellen folded her arms across her chest and steeled herself against his touch as he turned his attention to the row of tiny pearl-shaped buttons. The skimpy chemise she wore didn't offer her much protection against his hands, so close to her skin.

Every nerve in her body went on alert and this wasn't just a result of all the intimacies they'd recently shared. This was another of those phenomena she'd conveniently forgotten in an effort to put Christopher behind her.

But her memory was working just fine now. That absurd breathlessness that constricted her breathing. Those trembly little shivers that made her shoulders rise and fall enough for him to notice. And a flash of dimples indicated that he had indeed noticed.

Of course, she wouldn't have been shivering at all if he wasn't brushing his fingertips against her neck, her shoulders, and any other place he could touch her.

''Having fun?'' she asked.

''I am—''

The arrogant man didn't sound the least bit repentant.

"Have you figured out what plausible excuse you're giving Miss Q, or will you trust me to handle the situation?"

"I'm still in denial," she said.

He glanced up and his laser-blue stare caught hers in the mirror, no less potent as a reflection.

"I'll be heroic and come to your rescue."

"Really? Exactly how will you do that?"

"I'll tell Miss Q that I held you captive so I could make love to you all night. She won't hold you accountable. She knows you couldn't possibly resist me."

Ellen wouldn't even dignify that with a reply.

"Don't like that one? Well, how about I tell her that you took me hostage in the shower? No self-respecting romance hero would have turned you away. Especially while getting the best hand job of his life."

Pulling back, Ellen tipped her face up to his, unable to bear her reflection when her cheeks suddenly glowed red. She refused to blush. And if she was blushing, she refused to look. "Since when have you become an authority on what constitutes a decent romance hero?"

"Since I decided to come to Félicie Allée to seduce a romance editor. Seemed opportune to look into the subject."

Premeditated seduction. Well, she couldn't exactly fault him for doing his homework.

Rule number three of sound business strategies: *Always take the time to research and prepare.*

Shaking her head, she turned back around. "I'll handle the explanations myself, thank you."

He finished the last few buttons and said, "All done."

She chanced a glance to find him surveying her with a slight smile, not enough of one to start up the whole dimple thing again, but enough to let Ellen know he liked what he saw.

And she twirled around, an absurd impulse she couldn't seem to resist. The lightweight fabric held the shape of the dress without bulky crinolines. Even though she wore a chemise—she'd drawn the line at wearing panty hose—she could still feel the breeze drifting into the suite through the open French doors.

"Miss Q had a local designer create an entire line of Southern Charm Mysteries costumes." He tugged the lapels of his jacket.

"Toni Maxwell." She'd noticed the label. "I've visited her shop with Lennon."

Miss Q obviously hoped to further the seduction by having Toni Maxwell design a lot more than costumes. Ellen assumed that Southern Charm Mysteries didn't provide all its guests with a dresser full of sexy undies that bore about as much resemblance to historical bloomers as Christopher in his frock coat did to Mr. Muscle-Butt in his cape.

Bras padded to lift her breasts so high her nipples popped over the lace. Chemises so transparent she'd have been less exposed naked. The thongs were so skimpy she needed a Brazilian bikini wax to wear them. Garters. Silk hose. Very sexy lingerie. If Christopher had any idea what she was wearing under this gown—or not wearing—they'd likely miss the next event.

"It's a departure from your usual style," he said.

Tailored suits for work. Upscale casual after work. "I don't look ridiculous, do I?"

"Love, you could wrap yourself in a grocery bag and look edible." The dimples made a cameo appearance.

"Thank you. I must say you look rather dashing yourself."

And he did. But he only inclined his head in acknowledgment of her compliment and strode toward the dresser, where he picked up a brush and raked it through his hair. She glanced back in the mirror, arranged a ruffle at her throat to cover the faint discoloration there.

Despite her discovery of a telltale hickey, the moment was a companionable one as they went about the mundane business of grooming in silence. Growing up with three siblings meant privacy had been in short supply. As a result, Ellen preferred not to share her space. She hadn't lived with a roommate since college, typically avoided rooming with anyone at family functions or conventions if she could help it.

But she'd slipped right back into the easy camaraderie she'd once shared with Christopher. How could she have forgotten how well they'd gotten along?

Because it had been less painful to forget.

"All set, partner?"

His deep voice sent a shiver through her, a shiver that had nothing to do with the breeze sweeping up from the bayou. She turned to find him closing the French doors.

"All set."

He extended his arm and she looped hers through. "What do you think of the courtyard? Reminds me of your balcony back home. An oasis."

"On a grand scale," she agreed. "Miss Q must be trying to get on my good side by putting us in this suite. She knows how much I love gardens and she's managed to find one that has all my favorite flowers and plants."

"Is she succeeding?"

"Maybe a little."

"She's only trying to help." He steered her out of the bedroom. "She's convinced we're meant for each other."

"And committed to making us see it, too. Don't get me

wrong, Christopher. I realize her heart's in the right place.''

''Good'' was all he said, before ushering her out of the bedroom.

Collecting her purse on her way through the sitting room, she glanced inside to check the battery on her cell phone, to discover… ''That's odd. My phone's off. I hope the battery didn't die.''

She turned on the power, only to have the phone plucked from her grasp.

''You could leave it off.''

Oh, now she understood. ''Did you turn my phone off?''

''You needed your rest.''

''My parents might have called.''

He frowned down at the phone. ''If your parents had known how much energy you expended in bed last night, they'd have wanted you to get some sleep.''

''Insufferable man. I suppose your phone is off so your office can't reach you.''

The dimples again. ''As a matter of fact it is. I left it and my watch in the bedroom.''

''*And* your watch,'' she said dryly. ''Wow, you're taking a real vacation this week, aren't you.''

''You should take one, too.''

''I am.'' She plucked the phone back out of his hand, pressed the power button on and dropped it into her purse. ''A vacation from work. I won't take one from my family.''

On their way through the suite, Ellen glanced at the antique wall clock, and stopped short. ''Three-fifteen? I've never slept this late in my life,'' she said. ''What did you do, knock me out when I wasn't looking?''

He glanced down at his wrist, frowned. ''That clock's not right. Let me grab my watch.''

"Don't bother." She already had her phone. "Eight forty-five. Oh, thank goodness. Owning up to last night is bad enough without having to explain away a whole day, too."

Miss Q was the least of her worries. Ellen had no doubt the little whirlwind would be delighted if she sacrificed all the sleuthing to stay sequestered in the garden suite making love with Christopher. But Susanna and Tracy were participating in this event, too, and unlike Lennon, neither was privy to the details of her private life.

Maintaining a balance between professional and personal during this event was something Ellen had just assumed she'd manage with no trouble. But she hadn't counted on Christopher being her partner. She didn't want her professional image to suffer as a result, especially when it had already suffered a dent from her recent lack of objectivity regarding heroes.

"I need coffee," she said. "Badly."

Christopher only nodded and led her out the door.

He appeared to have familiarized himself with the plantation, because he led her easily back to the great hall, where a magnificent gothic clock read three-fifteen.

"What's up with this?" Christopher asked. "Two clocks broken at exactly the same time seems strange to me."

Before Ellen had a chance to comment, an accented male voice said, "Definitely not a coincidence."

Turning, they found a dark-skinned, perfectly exotic-looking man emerging from the office. Miss Q's companion, Olaf.

Ellen swallowed back a sigh, grateful that the first person they faced after last night's faux pas was one who wouldn't call them on their poor manners.

While there wasn't anything remarkable about Olaf's

brown suit aside from the proportions, his strapping size and bald head emphasized the elaborately brocaded vest and made his bow tie look like a shoestring tied beneath a bowling ball.

"You intentionally set the clocks for three-fifteen?" she asked. "What for?"

"I get it," Christopher said. "Old Southern custom."

Olaf smiled, a bright flash of white in a face as dark as a savage's. "Whenever the master of a plantation dies, all the clocks are stopped at the time of death. A memorial of sorts."

"Okay. This Yankee isn't familiar with that custom," Ellen said. "But, Olaf, you toured me here last year. Why don't I remember all the clocks set at three-fifteen?"

"Félicie Allée wasn't hosting murder mysteries then."

Christopher held her arm linked close when she tried to pull away. "So the master didn't really die at three-fifteen?"

Olaf shot them an enigmatic stare from beneath coal-black brows. "We've had to bend the rules to fit our mystery. Come on, I'll walk you to the gallery where the others are having breakfast, and tell you what I can."

"See, I'm not the only one who bends rules," Christopher whispered as they followed Olaf down another hall.

Ellen remembered having toured this hall before but today she barely noticed the furnishings.

"There was a body found at three-fifteen," Olaf said. "The body of a young woman who was visiting the plantation with her father, the governor of Louisiana. When the staff went to report her death to the captain, they discovered he'd vanished without a trace. So he did die, in a manner of speaking."

"How'd the governor's daughter die?" Christopher asked.

"Don't know for sure. She was found dead in front of the fireplace in the parlor. She appears to have *fallen* and suffered a fatal blow to the head on the outer hearth."

There was no missing his attempt at drama. "Fallen?"

"Or pushed," he said, clearly pleased she'd taken the bait. "It's assumed the captain murdered her and ran away."

"The captain murdered a young girl and ran away? But he was a pirate." Ellen frowned when both men looked at her blankly.

She'd gone into romance editing because she loved to read romances, stories where good triumphed over evil and ended with happily ever after. From the time she'd been thirteen years old, she'd never been able to resist a knight in shining armor, a dashing highwayman, a royal spy or a charming cowboy.

And pirates…Ellen had a thing for pirates. There was just something about a man tackling the whimsy of the sea, commanding a ship the way he commanded his lady's attention.

"Who wrote this script?" she asked. Clearly the author, and these two obtuse men, didn't understand the fundamental rules for romance heroes. "Murdering a woman is not heroic. If any of my authors wrote a hero who behaved that way, she'd end up revising." And those revisions would not cast doubt on the editor's objectivity.

Ellen glanced up at Christopher in time to see him exchange an amused look with Olaf. Pity revision couldn't whip him into shape, too. As far as she was concerned, the entire male species would do well to read a few romances to get a clue about what women were looking for in a man.

Glancing up at him as he held the door open for her to exit the house, she found him watching her boldly, as though he could somehow pluck the thoughts from her head and know she was measuring him against a real hero. She refused to acknowledge the way her sex gave one poignant throb when she gazed into his thickly fringed eyes.

Maybe he should try reading a few more of those books.

"Is that what this event is all about, Olaf?" he asked. "Finding out why the governor's daughter was murdered? I thought a murder mystery was about *who*dunit?"

"Our murder mystery is a *why*dunit," Olaf explained. "You've got to figure out why the captain murdered the governor's daughter and you're going to have a lot of fun while you do."

Their voices must have carried because no sooner had they rounded the corner of the gallery than Miss Q was on her feet, barely giving Ellen a chance to register who sat at the table that had been erected on the wide verandah.

"Oh, you missed it, dears," she said, getting right to the heart of the matter with an enthusiasm that made Ellen cringe. "We had a body. Well, it wasn't really a body, just an actress pretending to be a body, but she was so talented that Harley went for her gun. Good thing her costume bodice was so fitted that she couldn't wear her holster, or else we might really have had a body."

Ellen assumed that Harley must be one of the other participants.

"And that body would have been Mac's, since he was standing right behind her." Josh Eastman, Lennon's husband, rose to greet her. He looked dapper in a gray frock coat with a black pinstriped waistcoat. "Good morning, Ellen. You look lovely."

Lennon's husband Josh was a very handsome man, another of those too-good-looking-to-be-true men. Though he was as tall as Christopher—nearly as tall as the *really* tall Olaf—his rugged features beneath a shadow of ever-present stubble lent him a dark, rough-and-tumble appearance that was as opposite from Christopher's polished good looks as hers were from Olaf's.

After kissing his cheek in greeting, she glanced at Lennon who sat beside him, lovely in a summery gown of blue gingham, mouthing, *Are you okay?*

Ellen nodded.

Across the table Susanna and Tracy watched the exchange with knowing glances, both equally resplendent in their finery. Their gazes darted from her to Christopher and back again.

"Good morning, everyone," he said cordially, exchanging a handshake with Josh and then sliding out a chair for Ellen.

She opened her mouth to assume control of the introductions, but Tracy beat her to the punch. "Are you a friend of Ellen's?"

Christopher didn't miss a beat. "Christopher Sinclair. You must be one of Ellen's authors."

"Tracy Owens and Susanna St. John," Ellen said quickly, but that was as far as she got. Christopher was already circling the table and charming them with that dashing smile.

"I'm an old friend of Ellen's," he said. "We haven't seen each other in a long time, so I commandeered her to catch up." He turned to Miss Q. "You have me to blame for missing the body last night. How do we get up to speed?"

Well, would you look at that? He actually came to my rescue without doing something outrageous. No one at the table believed him, of course, but the gesture was sweet, nevertheless.

"Is there a video to watch or a transcript to read?" she asked, lending her efforts to the cause.

Miss Q darted her baby blues from one to the other, looking smug. "I'll fill you in myself, dears. But you'll have to play catch-up. You've lost a *whole night*." She dragged out each syllable so everyone had a chance to dwell on what they might have been doing on the night in question.

Thank you, Miss Q.

"I'm afraid playing catch-up will have to wait," Lennon said, tossing her napkin onto the table and standing. "I need to powder my nose. So does Ellen."

She didn't have to ask twice. Christopher arched a brow her way, but Ellen would have sacrificed a lot more than a cup of much-needed coffee to escape this bunch.

"Well, then, go powder your noses, dears." Miss Q waved them off before reaching for her teacup. "But come enjoy this delicious breakfast before I take Ellen and Christopher for a walk in the garden to bring them up to speed."

Ignoring Christopher's gaze, Ellen followed Lennon back into the house and to a small half bath off a narrow corridor.

"Where are we?" she asked, as Lennon herded her into the small but elegantly appointed room.

"Staff bathroom off the kitchen." She flipped a light switch and Ellen maneuvered back against the toilet to make way for her. "I had no idea Christopher would be here."

"I guessed as much. Although I confess to a moment of thinking you'd set me up with Mr. Muscle-Butt."

"I would never," Lennon said, aghast. "You must know that, Ellen. We're friends."

"Trust me, if I'd thought for one minute you'd colluded with your great-aunt on these little shenanigans, you'd be rewriting a lot more than your hero in that manuscript you've got sitting on my desk.''

"I do hope you're joking.''

Ellen paused for effect before admitting, ''I am. But I'm simply not believing your great-aunt. You should be really grateful chutzpah isn't a genetic thing.''

Ellen's proximity to Christopher seemed to have had a direct bearing on her ability to think clearly, because now that she wasn't under the direct influence of those lethal eyes, she could dwell on the reality of the situation in a way she hadn't had a chance to yet.

"It's only Thursday. I've still got to survive until Monday with *him*.''

"Auntie Q didn't trick Christopher into coming.'' Lennon grabbed her hands. ''He knew you were going to be here. She swore to me, although I'm not sure I believe her.''

"He said as much.''

"Are you okay? Do you want to bag on the training? Josh will understand.'' Lennon's gaze zeroed in on her throat and her eyes grew wide. ''You've got a love bite.''

"I decided to avail myself of the opportunity at hand,'' Ellen said lightly, ignoring Lennon's frown. ''Well, as I don't usually discuss my sex life…suffice to say you were right about Christopher being amazing in bed. Just don't tell your great-aunt, or the next time I come to town I'll find myself showing up at a wedding where I'm the guest of honor.''

"Ellen, are you sure about this? I know you think Christopher isn't serious about you, but I disagree. He'd never have asked you to marry him if he wasn't.''

"Worried I'll break his heart?''

Lennon either didn't get the joke or didn't find it funny. ''I'm not worried about *Christopher's* heart.''

"Trust me. I've got it under control. Please don't add yourself to the list of people who think they know what I need better than I do myself."

"I hope you're right." She gave a reassuring squeeze and let go. "I'm just so sorry this happened. I honestly never suspected. Auntie Q coerced Josh into using Eastman Investigations to launch Southern Charm Mysteries because she thought it would be good for business—both his and hers. She knows how his investigators have been driving him crazy and figured the team-building training was exactly what they needed."

"Hindsight is twenty-twenty." Ellen fixed her smile in place. "Just tell me there aren't other guests running around with guns. I don't think I can handle much more today."

She shook her head. "Josh hired them so he could work at home more with me, but these two are constantly dragging him into the office. They're polar opposites who clash over everything. We were hoping for a breakthrough this weekend."

"I'll hold a good thought." For herself, too. A breakthrough was exactly what she needed.

"Thank you for being so decent," Lennon said earnestly. "Auntie Q had no right to set you up. All I can say in her defense is that she's well intentioned. She's convinced you and Christopher belong together. She's also obsessed with getting Southern Charm Mysteries off the ground so Olaf has a business to run that interests him."

Something about big brooding Olaf running a corporate training murder-mystery business that relied on actors and role-playing struck her as off-kilter. But Ellen couldn't comment because the door swung open, hitting Lennon in the back.

"Ouch," she said. "Occupied."

"We're here to powder our noses," Susanna shot back.

Tracy elbowed her way in behind her. "Come on, budge up."

The small bathroom had been a tight squeeze for two women in voluminous gowns. Four was akin to riding a subway during Friday-night rush hour. Ellen found herself wedged between the toilet and the wall, her gown twisted around her ankles, her back arched uncomfortably to accommodate a towel rack.

"Guys." She grunted. "Let me out. I can't breathe."

"I'll turn on the fan to circulate the air," Tracy offered.

Susanna stood on tiptoe and peered over Lennon's shoulder. "I'm not going anywhere until I know why you got set up with that positively gorgeous man."

"If I'd known Southern Charm Mysteries provided gorgeous men, I'd never have agreed to be Susanna's partner." Tracy laughed. "And I've already solved one mystery. The mystery of why you two weren't at dinner last night."

"Don't make assumptions." Lennon quickly leaped to Ellen's defense. "This is all Auntie Q's fault. The little meddler is up to her old tricks."

Ellen wasn't much of a sci-fi fan, preferring the fantasy of the past to an unimagined future, but she wished with all her heart that right now she had one of those transporter machines she'd seen on television.

Beam me up, Scotty.

"Christopher and I haven't seen each other in a while and Miss Q didn't mention he was going to be here, to me or to Lennon," she said calmly, resisting the urge to tug up the ruffle at her collar. "There's no problem, though. We discussed the situation last night and we're both content to be partners for the training."

"Did you and Christopher date?" Susanna asked.

"I do hope you didn't waste the entire night *talking*," Tracy added.

Lennon rolled her eyes. "Give her a break."

"You mean like she's given us one lately? I had to reconstruct a perfectly good hero in my last book." Susanna nailed her with a to-the-point non-Hurricane-induced stare. "How could you have dated that gorgeous man and still refuse to believe in heroes? In our books or in real life."

"Did you hear his voice? Who could resist that Deep South drawl?" Tracy, another Yankee, asked while shooting Lennon a knowing glance. "No wonder you married Josh."

A trio of curious gazes cornered Ellen and, short of blowing through them like a snowplow on an icy city street, there was no escape. Schooling her expression, Ellen leveled a stare at her audience and said, "Got it under control, ladies. And I believe in romance heroes as much as I always have."

6

The Garden

CHRISTOPHER LOOPED ARMS with Ellen and Miss Q to escort them down a graveled path that led into the gardens. "We'll head west. The sun's not too high, so we should still be able to catch a breeze off the bayou."

"You'd make a fine master of Félicie Allée." Miss Q smiled. "And I just happen to know the perfect mistress."

Ellen glanced up at him, one dark brow arched.

"She's a very beautiful woman," he agreed, taking in the shiny hair fringing softly around her face.

She leaned around him to peer at Miss Q. "You're just going to town with this madness, aren't you."

"I know grand passion when I see it, dear, and I'd rather risk your friendship than let grand passion pass you by."

"Hmm" was all Ellen said before pursing those sweet lips.

"How could I possibly resist inviting you here?" Miss Q glanced up at him and winked. "Ellen and I visited Félicie Allée after Lennon and Josh's wedding. She fell in love with the place. Didn't you, dear?"

Ellen graciously relented. "Who could possibly resist a plantation set deep in the bayou with a mysterious history and its very own pirate?"

"I certainly couldn't," Miss Q said. "Especially not when I heard the plantation's future was in jeopardy."

Ellen shook her head, sending those glossy dark waves swinging around her face in a way that made Christopher itch to rake his fingers through them.

"I still can't believe anyone would sell an antebellum plantation," she said.

"A tragedy," Miss Q agreed. "But running the plantation as a museum wasn't particularly lucrative since it's entrenched in the bayou outside the city. The original pirate owner of Félicie Allée wasn't even a real pirate, so he can't possibly compete with Jean Lafitte, who had a whole town named after him."

"What do you mean he wasn't a real pirate?" Ellen asked.

"A privateer, dear. Not the cutthroat variety."

"Can't use the cutthroat kind in romances, anyway," Ellen said dismissively. "Heroes have to be noble."

"During the War of 1812, our captain's accomplishments were very noble, and definitely more prestigious than Jean Lafitte's. He just wasn't half the braggart Lafitte was. Alas." She heaved a dramatic sigh. "Lafitte's home is closer to New Orleans. The former owners couldn't make the location work to their benefit."

"They lacked vision and imagination," Christopher said.

"Which is not a problem with the current owners. We're visionaries. And we want to be successful, so both of you be sure to suggest Southern Charm Mysteries to your executive management for your next corporate training."

"I'll keep it in mind the next time the VPs are sending editors to a teamwork training with the marketing department." Ellen rolled her eyes. "Murder sounds about right, but there wouldn't be any mystery to it, I'm afraid."

Miss Q grinned. "You tell your executives we make

corporate training fun, so they won't have real bodies to deal with when the role-playing is over."

"A definite selling point."

Christopher laughed, as pleased with Ellen's reaction as he was by Miss Q's salesmanship. "Let's head into the arbor so you can bring us up to speed on our noble captain and his mystery."

He steered the ladies down a curving walkway toward the bayou, where a light fog still misted off the water. The gardens encompassed ten acres around the house, a wild place where tall cypress trees dripped Spanish moss from low-hanging branches and colorful azaleas and bright wisteria dominated the landscape.

But what pleased Christopher even more than the value of the acreage devoted to the gardens was Ellen's response to them. On one of their very first dates, she'd talked about her tour of his hometown and had waxed poetic about these very gardens. It had been Christopher's first glimpse of the idealistic romanticism Ellen hid deep beneath her cool exterior.

Walking through the gardens at Félicie Allée was like stepping inside a romance novel, she'd said. *The perfect setting for falling in love. The only thing missing was the costumes....*

He would make sure she had every chance to fall in love in her perfect setting before this training session was over.

"So, Miss Q, how about giving us that rundown." After using his handkerchief to ensure Miss Q a dry seat on the bench, he directed Ellen to the bench opposite.

"I'm tremendously sorry you missed the body. I was ever so pleased with the debut performance." Rummaging through the big shoulder bag she'd brought, she withdrew a roll of what appeared to be yellowing parchment paper tied with a red ribbon. "But I can explain everything just as well. First, though, we'll start with your treasure map."

Christopher accepted the map and reluctantly slipped his hand from Ellen's to slide the ribbon away and unroll the parchment. With their heads bowed together, he and Ellen surveyed the finely drawn lines that detailed the plantation's floor plan.

"Well done," he said. "The detail is extraordinary."

Miss Q nodded, clearly pleased by the praise.

"You've planted clues everywhere?" Ellen asked.

The task seemed monumental given the expanse of the plantation.

"Oh, yes." Miss Q leaned toward them, pointed to a room.

"There's your garden suite and here's the arbor. See, we're not far at all."

True enough, the garden suite was situated in the west wing, with the shoreline where they sat not far beyond the walls.

Miss Q's expression brightened and her eyes twinkled. "In a nutshell, Southern Charm Mysteries offers several different styles of corporate team-building events. We do evening and weekend productions as well as conference sessions like this one. I'm sure you're both familiar with those wildly successful murder-mystery games."

"I've heard of them, but never participated," Ellen said before glancing up at him. "Didn't you mention you'd once played with some friends?"

Christopher nodded. "On a ski trip. Had a great time."

"Perfect." Miss Q clapped her hands in delight. "Because that's the premise of our training. We incorporate our team-building into the game and we're debuting with a marvelous script called *Away with the Tide.*"

Ellen bristled beside him.

"What?" he asked.

"That title."

"I believe it was meant to be a play on *Gone with the Wind,*" Miss Q offered.

"I see."

Christopher bit back a smile, suspecting the only thing Ellen saw was that Louisiana wasn't Georgia and that if that title had crossed her desk she'd have filed it in the trash.

Undaunted, Miss Q continued. "*Away with the Tide* tells the story of Captain Julian Lafever, the man who built Félicie Allée in the early eighteen hundreds, after earning a fortune as a privateer in the Caribbean.

"During the War of 1812, the British approached him and Jean Lafitte to use their ships in an attack against New Orleans. Julian convinced Jean to join forces in passing this information along to the U.S. government, instead— for a price, of course," she added with a grin. "They wound up using their ships to defend the city under General Andrew Jackson."

Christopher hooked an elbow over the back of the bench, forced himself to pay attention to Miss Q's story rather than the way Ellen leaned forward intently, clearly fascinated with the history. The overhang of Spanish moss-draped branches filtered the rising sun, filigreed her profile in light and shadow. Her delicate features were bright with interest.

"Sometimes the truth is better than the most clever plot twists," she said with an appreciative nod.

"Absolutely, dear," Miss Q agreed. "And that's the best part of all our scripts—each has been written to blend fact and fiction. These training events aren't only fun— they build team-working skills by forcing our guests to work together toward a common goal.

"*Away with the Tide* features our captain entertaining the governor of Louisiana, who'd come to Félicie Allée along with a group of very influential guests, to honor the captain's service to the government by issuing him a pardon for privateering from President James Madison himself."

"The *why*dunnit is to find out how our captain went from a pardon to murdering the governor's daughter?" Christopher asked.

"That's right, dear." Miss Q reached out and patted him on the knee. "You'll sleuth out what really happened that weekend when he and his sister hosted the governor and his family. The mayor of New Orleans and his family came, too. Got it?"

"Got it, and we've got our map of the crime scene." Christopher tapped the rolled treasure map against his palm.

"And your costumes." Miss Q, looking pleased, swept her eyes over them in their finery before reaching for her shoulder bag again. "I've got your mystery packet right here. It includes details about the murder, a playbill listing the guests, and your very own special secret clue."

"Special secret clue?" Christopher handed the treasure map to Ellen and accepted the thick folder with the Southern Charm Mysteries logo on the cover.

"Each couple has been assigned a special clue to the mystery, your own individual piece of the puzzle. You'll drop that clue to the other couples sometime during the session, and these clues will move you farther along in solving the mystery."

"Drop the clue? How?" Ellen asked.

"That's entirely up to you, dear. As hostess I can make suggestions—you can stage conversations for others to overhear, leave pieces of evidence lying around. How you choose to reveal your special clue is strictly between you and your partner. Be forewarned, though—Olaf and the staff will be watching to make sure you do. Working within the framework of rules and guidelines is also part of the skills we're developing here.

"The whole point of the training is for each couple to work together as a team to compete against the other couples. Friendships are to be disregarded, alliances abandoned and survival your only motivation."

"Sounds rather cutthroat," Christopher commented.

"Your favorite type of game." Miss Q winked. "The higher the stakes, the better."

Glancing at Ellen, he took in her cool expression, her utterly controlled demeanor that revealed itself in squared shoulders and a reserved set to that kissable mouth.

As if the stakes weren't already high enough.

"The best things in life are worth working for."

"I agree entirely." She handed Ellen a hardbound notebook also bearing the company logo. "Here's a journal in which to record your progress. We've got clues and red herrings planted, so you'll want to take good notes. Every night at seven, we'll assemble as a group for dinner. You'll have a chance to assess how far the others have gotten in their investigations. You'll also have access to the staff, who may very well drop clues when you least expect them, so listen carefully to everything they say. Servants are always privy to what's going on."

She stood, smoothed her skirt and smiled down at them. "Familiarize yourselves with your materials. In addition to the playbill and information about the players, you'll find checklists for the training goals we're trying to meet here. Remember, everything you could possibly want to know about the mystery is hidden somewhere in this plantation. You just have to be clever enough to figure out where.''

Retrieving her purse, she slipped it over her shoulder. ''Solving the mystery will require you to be flexible and to work cooperatively in cross-functional teams, sometimes in areas you might be unfamiliar with. You'll be challenged to use some very innovative problem-solving strategies. Skills business people need. Any questions?''

Christopher shook his head, glanced down at Ellen. ''Can you think of anything, love?''

''You've pretty much covered it all, Miss Q. Looks like the real work is up to us now.'' Her gaze slipped between the map she held and the folder and notebook on his lap.

''Well, then, I'll be off, dears. I'll be around if you need me. Olaf, too.''

Christopher placed the folder on the bench, intending to escort her back to the plantation, but Miss Q waved him off. ''Stay put and work on your packet. I'll head back myself.''

''You're sure?'' The house wasn't far, but...

She patted his cheek and smiled reassuringly. ''Get to work, and *have fun*.'' With that she lifted her skirts and disappeared down the gravel path the way they'd come.

''How much did she tell you?'' Ellen asked once Miss Q was beyond earshot.

''About what?''

''About her plans to set us up this weekend. Lennon didn't have a clue.''

Ellen had turned toward him, and Christopher took advantage of their sudden solitude to hook an elbow over the back of the bench and run his knuckles along her cheek.

She met his gaze, her own expression unchanging, but Christopher recognized the way the golden lights in her eyes flickered. He'd become very proficient at reading the subtle signs of Ellen's moods, and intended to become even more proficient by the conclusion of this event. She might be able to school her expression and hide her reactions, but her eyes were thoroughly readable if he paid close attention.

Her eyes were the key. They masked her emotions behind a cool green stare. Or darkened to shadow when she was angry. Or melted, warm liquid gold with desire.

Right now, they hovered somewhere between green and gold, which told him she wasn't nearly as unaffected by his touch as she'd have him believe. So he trailed his thumb along her jaw, aimed for that full bottom lip.

And being Ellen, she stubbornly refused to pull away.

"Miss Q just told me that you'd be here," he said.

"She didn't tell you she'd be playing Cupid and installing us in the same suite?"

He shook his head. Miss Q hadn't told him she'd be playing Cupid because he'd requested the service, so technically he was telling the truth. Giving in to the urge to trace the lines bracketing Ellen's mouth, he watched her reaction in the way the golden lights shimmered deep in her eyes.

Then he let his gaze slip down to the folder. "So, what have we got here?"

It took a moment for Christopher's question to register, another for Ellen to realize he'd neatly changed the subject. Leaning back against the bench, she just as neatly withdrew from his roaming hands.

Flipping through the contents, she was more than willing to move past all talk of their relationship and this setup.

Rule number four of sound business strategies: *Stay focused on the goal.* In this case, sex.

"Looks like our mystery gear. We've got lists and charts and our map." She slipped out the character biographies, a sheath of papers several pages thick. "We really need to spread all this stuff out."

"Come on. I know just the place."

Christopher led her along a path that followed the shoreline where the branches of oaks, cypress and tupelos sifted the sunlight over the bayou into a lazy golden haze. The water appeared almost black from fallen leaves, and the surface rippled softly as ducks flew low. Some sort of wildlife rustled nearby in the underbrush, crackling twigs and dry leaves.

"There's this whole untamed thing going on." Ellen inhaled deeply, caught a whiff of the southern breeze, heavy with the smell of the sea.

"That's the part that fascinates me."

"What?"

"That a woman so comfortable in the urban jungle enjoys a place where time stands still. What's the attraction? I mean, besides the ducks."

The dimples flashed and she felt a tingle at his reminder of their many visits to Central Park, where she enjoyed sitting on the grassy knoll beside the lake with her bag of corn, making friends with the wildlife.

"Oh, no, I just come for the ducks."

He laughed, a compelling sound that rippled on the lazy morning breeze and filtered through her. "Right."

"What's that?" She pointed to a white spire peeking out of a copse of trees on a tiny island.

"An island gazebo. A lot like the one we just left."

"I'd love to go visit. Maybe we could make the time?"

"I thought you were scared of gators."

"There aren't any alligators here. Look at all these ducks."

He arched one brow doubtfully, but she didn't want to

hear an alligator might happen by, not with all these ducks around.

"I think it's the fact that time does stand still," she said. "There's a sense of peace here. Time's going to move along at its own pace, no matter what I do. Makes it easy to put things in perspective. To forget life and work and the million things I should be doing."

"A place where you can be yourself. No pressures, or worries, or expectations."

"Yeah." She glanced up at him, surprised at how well he articulated her meaning.

But Christopher wasn't looking at her, his gaze fixed on a patch of blue sky that shone through a break in the trees, where seagulls cavorted.

He finally brought her to the edge of a grassy bank sheltered by a bright pink azalea hedge, an overlook encompassing a gorgeous spread of blooming azaleas and what appeared to be a meeting place for ducks of many varieties.

"Hold this." After handing her the treasure map, he took off up the slope toward a small utility shed, returned with a blanket and a bag of cracked corn.

"Corn, Christopher? Do most plantations stock a supply like the grain feeders at the zoo?"

"You don't even need a pocketful of quarters. Convenient." He set the bag down, then shook the blanket out and spread it over the grass. "Here, come sit." He waited patiently while she arranged her skirts and got comfortable. "When I saw the ducks, I asked Olaf to have some brought here, just in case we had the chance to come back."

"Oh. Well, thank you."

He grinned in reply, so Ellen spread their mystery gear around her, mulling the way he easily admitted to making thoughtful arrangements he'd clearly hoped would please her.

And he had. Opening the bag of corn, she withdrew a handful and tossed it toward the shoreline, catching the interest of the flock. Domesticated ducks waddled right up to the offering, helping themselves, while the wilder breeds danced around, observing before chancing closer.

She tossed out several more handfuls, caught sight of Christopher shrugging off his frock coat, an impressive display of grace and strength that brought to mind the way those broad shoulders had felt beneath her hands and her lips when they'd made love.

Loosing his bow tie, Christopher flipped open his collar to reveal a discoloration on his throat, an echo of a bruise that appeared striking against his white collar. A hickey to match hers. Reaching into the bag, she grabbed another handful of corn. Funny, but she couldn't exactly remember when she'd done the deed, with so many nibbles and tastes crowding her memory.

He sank down to the blanket, an awesome show of contracting muscle and powerful male grace, and sat across from her with his legs crossed.

They perused the literature in silence, organizing the various categories with corresponding glossy photos of Félicie Allée's rooms, fingers occasionally brushing, knees sometimes bumping as one or the other reached for another leaflet.

She threw out more corn whenever the ducks' supply ran low, and eventually the flock tucked their heads beneath their wings for a nap or waded back into the water for a drink.

Corn for the ducks. Who'd have guessed? Bowing her head under the pretense of inspecting the treasure map, Ellen considered his thoughtful gesture.

If Christopher had wanted to prove how great they were together, why had he waited three months after she'd ended their relationship? And he hadn't said a word about compromising—not that she'd consider a compromise now that she knew he wasn't *the one*.

She didn't get a chance to consider the answer further because footsteps crunched on the gravel path. Christopher had glanced up at the sound, and together they watched a couple round the path, a man and woman she didn't recognize, though their costumes labeled them as either other guests or staff.

"That's the stupidest idea I've ever heard," the woman was saying. "Where'd you study your investigative technique, a mail correspondence course?"

"Harvard," the man said matter-of-factly.

"Josh's investigators?" Ellen asked in a whisper.

Christopher nodded. "Mac and Harley."

Harley was the type of woman who exuded a tough intensity completely at odds with her feminine appearance. She wasn't tall but lithe, which added to an illusion of height. Incredible wavy red hair framed somber features and gave Ellen the impression the woman wouldn't have much patience for people who confused her appearance with her competency.

Mac, on the other hand, might have been cast from the same mold as Christopher or Josh. He had that same larger-than-life maleness about him, and his simply delivered "Harvard" suggested he might have shared their Garden District upbringing.

The two clearly hadn't noticed their audience, unsurprising given the slope of the bank and the lush hedge of azalea blocking a clear view of the water from the path.

"Hiding Brigitte's diary in the library doesn't seem ridiculously obvious to you?" Mac asked.

"Obvious is the whole point." Harley shook her head, sending red hair tumbling over her shoulders. "Try to think like a criminal for a second. Can you actually do that with all your blue blood? If you place the emphasis on *hiding,* the diary will be easy to find because everyone will be looking. We want the emphasis on *overlooking* the diary."

"I'm sure everyone will overlook a book in a library." Mac gave a snort of obvious disgust.

"If you think about it for just a minute it makes sense."

"It explains why prisons are overflowing."

"Well, then, come up with a better idea, and hiding the diary in the bathroom was not a better idea."

"Do you ever do anything but argue?"

"I'm not arguing."

"Shut up, Harley," Mac said, the frustration in his voice obvious even to Ellen, a total stranger. He reached out, grabbed Harley's arms and dragged her against him. "Just shut up."

Then he lowered his head…and engaged her in what appeared to be a very heated kiss.

Harley was so still at first that Ellen couldn't tell if the woman had been shocked into compliance, but when her arms slipped up around Mac's neck, Ellen had her answer.

Their bodies came together as though fused, and for one surreal moment, Harley and Mac looked like lovers off the cover of a romance novel, dressed in their period costumes and framed by azaleas, Spanish moss and filtered sunlight.

Ellen's heart did a silly flip-flop and she refused to look at Christopher. Something about this couple's kiss suggested such longing, such a powerlessness to resist their chemistry. It struck a chord in her, reminded her of how she'd reacted to Christopher last night.

She was suddenly aware of how his knee pressed against

hers and how his big body shaded the sun pouring through the trees. The way her nipples tingled when she heard him laugh softly.

Then a very familiar electronic melody jangled.

Ducks scattered. Harley and Mac sprang apart, both looking breathless and staggered. Ellen couldn't tell which one seemed more surprised, but Harley recovered first and stormed back in the direction they'd come.

Ellen dove into her purse for her cell phone, flipped it open and glanced at the display. "Hi, Dad."

"Hi, honey. Are you enjoying your vacation?"

"Sure am."

"How's the whole murder-mystery thing coming?"

"So far, so good. It's been…*interesting.*" To say the least. She couldn't help glancing at Christopher. He was scowling, so she shifted her gaze back to the ducks.

"Good, I'm glad. It sounds interesting." Her dad chuckled on the other end. "No lounging around on a beach for my girl."

No, indeed. Lounging around on a beach would have been considered a normal vacation pastime. The idea had never even occurred to her. "So what's up, Dad?"

"Your mother has just been announced as a nominee for the President's Goodwill award."

"Wow, she must be thrilled." Ellen schooled her voice and continued to ignore Christopher. "Timing's great, too, since she just arrived back from Bosnia. Kiss her for me and tell her congratulations."

"I will. If she wins, she'll want all of us with her when she accepts."

"When?"

"Saturday night."

Ellen didn't want Christopher to sense trouble. "Of course. Just let me know as soon as you know."

"I will. Until then, you relax and enjoy yourself. This will work out the way it's meant to. You might not have to cut your vacation short. We'll see."

"All right. Love you, Dad."

"Love you, too, honey."

Ellen disconnected the phone, returned it to her purse, and all the while Talbot family rule number one echoed in her head: *All Talbots must be accessible any time, any place.*

To Christopher's credit, he didn't ask. He didn't point out that her call had chased off Harley and Mac before they might have overheard more clues. All he said was "Do you think they'll still put the diary in the library? Let's log it so we don't forget to check."

Mechanically reaching for the notebook, Ellen hoped Miss Q had thought to include a pen in the mystery package. She was happy to escape into denial at the moment. After all, like her father said, if her mother didn't win the award, she wouldn't have to cut her vacation short.

She could hope.

"Lennon only said Harley and Mac were having difficulty getting along at work," she said. "I didn't realize it was...well, like *that* between them."

The tightness to Christopher's jaw didn't ease up. Not one bit. "I don't think they realized it, either. Josh is expecting a lot from this training. Unless those two are another of Miss Q's pet passion projects."

"Good luck to her, then."

He arched a brow. "You actually think she stands a chance?"

Ellen shrugged, not willing to speculate after witnessing that kind of raging passion firsthand. Is that what Miss Q saw with her and Christopher?

*I know grand passion when I see it and I'd rather risk
your friendship than let grand passion pass you by.*

Wise words spoken by a wise woman, or sheer madness? Ellen wouldn't speculate. Not when her breath was
shallow and she felt so aware of the man sitting beside
her. Not when she was fighting back this ridiculous feeling
that she'd somehow disappointed him. He may not know
the details of her conversation, but that tight set to his jaw
revealed he knew full well that duty had just called.

And why on earth should she feel guilty for living up
to her family responsibility? She could feel guilty if she
was forced to abandon the training—although she hoped
by Saturday they'd be far enough into the game that her
departure wouldn't create any big problems. She could feel
guilty that she might diminish Christopher's chances of
winning, if they hadn't solved enough of the mystery by
then.

She shouldn't feel guilty for disappointing him.

She shouldn't care whether he approved or disapproved
of her commitment to her family—although, in all fairness
to Christopher, he'd made it clear long ago that he didn't
disapprove of her commitment, but rather the fact she
placed her family's needs above her own without question.

So why was she sitting here avoiding his gaze and full
of angst about what he thought?

The man was bloody great sex, damn it. That was all.

She'd recognized those sparks between Harley and Mac
because she experienced them with Christopher. Her body
still tingled with the effects of that sort of debilitating passion.

All he had to do was *look* at her and she went to pieces.
He touched her and she forgot time, obligation, *everything*
but the passion she experienced in his arms. That was the
only reason she cared what he thought. And she had four

days—or maybe only three, if her mother won the award—
to get over *him*. She refused to spend her life suffering the
kind of out-of-control longing she'd just witnessed between two mismatched private investigators.

Pining for a man who wasn't *the one*.

Powerless to resist him whenever he glanced her way.
Worried what he thought about her choices.

No, thank you.

7

The Library

ELLEN ESCORTED CHRISTOPHER into the library, where he spread out their mystery gear on a marble-topped table. They'd discovered their special clue to be a society column from a New Orleans newspaper that reported on guests at a Mardi Gras ball. Since the article didn't mention the captain or his sister, neither she nor Christopher could guess what it might mean to their investigation. They'd decided to search for Harley and Mac's diary, instead.

Ellen couldn't imagine what the replica of a nearly two-hundred-year-old diary might look like, but one glance at the walls of overstuffed shelves convinced her that one could be easily hidden in this room, refuting Mac's concerns about the transparency of hiding a diary in the library.

"I'm glad no one's here," Christopher said.

"Just what do you think we'll be doing that precludes an audience?"

Dimples flashed. "I'd like to do any number of things in here with you, love. *All* of them preclude an audience."

Ellen wouldn't dignify that with a response. Tugging up her ruffled collar in what had become a constant effort to hide her hickey, Ellen peered around for a place to begin her search.

Situated on the west side of the plantation, the library

boasted an entire wall of stained glass. Two walls of book-shelves overflowed with clever reproductions of first editions and literary fare from a vast variety of genres. Scanning the shelves at eye level, browsing the spines for curious titles, she decided against attempting the ladder while wearing enough ruffles to make climbing a feat worthy of a stunt double.

Not too much time had passed before he said, "Look at this, love. What do you make of the inscription?"

Ellen crossed the room to find him inspecting a Bible that had belonged to the captain's father. Inside was an inscription written to his son in boldly scrawled words that read,

> *My beloved son Julian,*
> *May these passages guide and comfort you through your life as they have me, and my father, and all the generations of men who bore the great name of La-fever.*

The inscription itself wasn't noteworthy until Christopher flipped the book shut to show her the engraving on the front cover. Ellen understood the significance immediately.

"*Comte* d'Archand? The captain's father was a nobleman? I don't recall any mention of the captain being nobility in his biography, do you?"

"Not a word, but I'll check again." Handing her the Bible, he strode back to the table. "I assumed he became a privateer to make his fortune."

"Which makes you wonder why a nobleman would need to make his fortune running goods out of the Caribbean."

"Exactly."

Ellen followed, depositing the Bible in front of Christopher. He didn't glance up and she continued past, heading back toward a set of shelves by the door. Surveying the titles at eye level, she searched for one she'd noted earlier.

"I was right," Christopher said. "The biography doesn't mention a thing about the captain's title."

She was only half listening. Ah, there it was. Plucking the book from the shelf, she peered down at the cover.

Lafever Holdings

She flipped through the leatherbound reproduction of a book with handwritten entries, stopped at the last entry. "Listen to this, Christopher. 'The Comte d'Archand, Charles Lafever, held his land from the Duc, as did his fathers for twelve generations. He answered his annual obligations, including military service, until his arrest in 1794.' Bless the feudal system and its detailed record keeping."

"You're the history authority. I'll take your word for it."

Whether she edited stories like those Susanna wrote, which were a rich blend of historical fact and fiction, or Tracy's costume pieces that only skimmed social customs for color, Ellen had learned enough about various historical traditions to justify Christopher's opinion. Which got her to thinking...

"You know, if the captain's noble birth is a clue, we really need to know more about him before we can even guess at his motive for murdering the governor's daughter."

"Come sit," Christopher said. "Tell me what you're talking about."

Ellen tucked the book beneath her arm, lifted her skirts and joined him. "Everything you said before about establishing means, opportunity and motive makes sense to solve the mystery, but this is more than a mystery, it's an unfolding story.''

The tiny furrow between Christopher's brows deepened but Ellen didn't give him a chance to ask questions.

''Felicity Clayton was a guest at Félicie Allée along with her parents and the mayor's family, so we already have means and opportunity for the captain to murder her. You said we need to focus on determining motive, which makes perfect sense. But if we don't know anything about his goals, how can we understand why he did the things he did—''

''Or guess what he might do?''

''Exactly, which means we have to find out everything we can about the captain. Conduct an in-depth character study of the man. We need to know his likes, dislikes and his desires. We need to know how far he's willing to go to get what he wants. Once we know these things, we'll be able to guess at what our society column might have meant to him.''

It wasn't until she paused that Ellen realized while they'd been speaking in hushed whispers they'd gravitated toward each other over the table. She was suddenly staring him full in the face. And he looked pleased, *very* pleased.

''You're brilliant, love,'' he said.

And then he kissed her. One solid buss on the lips before he shot her a dimpled grin that was more than enthusiasm for the game. That grin told her he admired her cleverness and was glad she was his partner. That grin made her stomach flip-flop so hard her breath hitched. That grin made Ellen acknowledge just how much she liked to make him grin. And kiss her.

That craving again.

Leaning across the table, she kissed him back.

Christopher's reaction time was much more impressive than hers had been, because she never got a chance to back away before he'd driven his fingers into her hair, locking her against him so he could kiss her back. A real kiss.

His tongue plunged into her mouth, stealing her breath. Her insides swooped again and her thighs tingled— whether from the memory of last night's lovemaking or a brand-new response to this heated moment, Ellen couldn't say. The only thing she could say was that kissing him back sparked her craving as if she'd tossed a lighted match into a puddle of gas.

Their tongues tangled with an urgency that might have been justified had they not just spent a whole night indulging their needs. She grew dizzier and giddier as the tabletop cut into her rib cage. Or perhaps it was only his kiss that crushed the breath from her lungs. Either way, Ellen had to force herself to pull away, before she reached up, threaded her fingers into his hair and gave into this growing ache that should have been at least a little satisfied after last night.

"So," she said, not a little shakily. "I suppose we need to know why the captain's father was arrested. It may explain why he left France for the Caribbean."

"It may." His grin never wavered.

But the damage was already done. Chemistry had become a part of their search. She wondered if they shouldn't just go back to the suite to indulge themselves, so they could get on with their work. Tension mounted to the point where she searched right alongside him just to bask in that crazy glow she got whenever he glanced up from a book to gaze warmly at her.

Until her brain finally took a giant leap out of the gutter. "Christopher! 1794."

He glanced her way yet again, his gaze caressing her

face from her chin to her lips to her nose, until finally meeting hers. "What about it?"

"The French Revolution."

"What about it?" he repeated.

"Honestly," she said, with an exasperation that had more to do with her own breathlessness than his obtuseness. "What did you do when you toured France? Obviously you weren't paying attention to the history."

"Uh, not usually."

"I'm shocked," she said wryly. "What was it that time—bungee-jumping from the Eiffel Tower or swimming the Channel to visit the Queen of England?"

He shot her an equally wry look. "A hot-air balloon."

"While you were on that balloon, did you hear anything about trouble between the nobles and the peasants? Does the word *guillotine* ring any bells?"

"I studied the French Revolution. So shall we get busy looking for something to tie it to the Lafever family?"

With a "Humph!" Ellen hiked up her skirts and retreated to a bookcase on the opposite side of the room. Insufferable man.

But it wasn't long before Christopher dragged her right back to his side again.

"Pay dirt." He held up a fabric-covered notebook. "The captain's mother's journal. And it's loaded with information about their estate and the family." He bent over the shelf again. "There must be a dozen here. Help me look through them."

Ellen hurried over, and didn't have a chance to comment before he motioned her to the floor.

"Sit. I'll hand them to you."

She'd barely spread her skirts when he started handing her books. Organizing them according to date, she started reading the earliest entry.

The journals proved to be a gold mine of information, as the captain's mother, Allienor, had begun writing as soon as she became a bride. Ellen tallied the dated entries against her memory. "Allienor Lafever came to her husband's barony right before the start of the Revolution."

When Christopher didn't reply, Ellen turned her attention to piecing together a picture of the captain's early years.

Working side-by-side in the companionable silence that came so easy to them, she acquainted herself with a young noblewoman who was madly in love with her husband and joyous at the long-awaited birth of a healthy son, after several miscarriages.

Christopher added other pieces to the puzzle—the building strife in France, the start of the Revolution and how the captain's father smuggled his young wife and son out of the country shortly before his arrest.

"I wonder what happened to him," Ellen said. "I hope he wasn't beheaded."

Christopher didn't look hopeful, and she supposed the fact that the captain became a privateer spoke for itself. "We need to find out, though, because Julian had a sister. If the captain's father didn't emigrate with his family, Brigitte may have been a half or even a stepsister."

"Maybe his mother was pregnant when she left." Ellen could hope, anyway, because the thought of the head-over-heels in love Allienor becoming a widow didn't appeal in the least.

Though some impugned the romance genre for its requisite happy endings, Ellen believed that love-conquers-all was the only ending worth reading. She could pick up any newspaper to read far too many stories that ended in tragedy.

"What about those journals?" She pointed to a few at

the bottom of the pile. "They're dated much later than the others. Let's look at them."

They settled in to unearth the resolution of the tale, and Ellen supposed later that it had all begun innocently enough—her skimming through one journal, Christopher through another. Her back started to ache from prolonged sitting on the floor, where even a thick carpet couldn't protect her from the hardwood below. When Christopher pulled her against him, she didn't resist. His firmly muscled chest was preferable to the sofa back, which was stiff and prickly with antique upholstery.

Sandwiched as they were on the floor between the sofa and a freestanding bookshelf, they were hidden in a private little niche in an otherwise roomy library.

Which is why, she supposed, Christopher considered it perfectly acceptable to start idly thumbing her nipple.

She only let him because it felt so good.

The steady *flick, flick, flick* of his thumb brushing across the tip created just the right amount of friction between the fabric and sensitive skin below, skin that had been pleasured so thoroughly last night that her senses leapt at his attention.

A heated languor began to flow through her, running downward from his casual touch, through limbs tight from her awkward seat on the floor, through muscles achy from a night indulging in serious sex. It was such an oozy, pleasant sensation that emphasized the power of his body curled around her, the weight of his arm draped over her shoulders. A sensation that reminded her of those drowsy spells between closing her eyes and falling asleep. A warm, weightless place where her thoughts slowed with her breathing and her mind gave way to her body's command.

Ellen couldn't resist, though being felt up in a library where anyone could have walked in wasn't exactly proper.

In fact, if she thought about her behavior at all, she would have agreed it wasn't even remotely acceptable.

But she was having a hard time concentrating on the journal's passages much less devoting energy to do anything else. Though the plantation had been upgraded with the modern conveniences of central air, a shoofly still hung from the ceiling, and the gentle waving motion and soft whooshing sound only added to the pleasure drifting over her in their idyll.

And when she really got down to it, her gown's flounces covered most of Christopher's hand.

She was content to sit in his arms like this.

Unfortunately, Christopher wasn't.

Soon his thumb became a hand. His fingers molded the curve of her breast, exploring her in a way that made the blood slug through her veins, a lazy heat reminiscent of the Louisiana sun burning the morning mist off the bayou.

And those fingers soon began fondling, kneading her in a way that engaged so much more of her body than just breasts, which suddenly felt too full and heavy. The muscles in her most intimate places awakened, building in tempo to wanting squeezes that radiated through her belly and halfway down her thighs.

Her insides went all mushy, and the journal's entry kept fading in and out of focus. Just holding the book became an effort and she found herself relaxing back against Christopher, just sinking into every curve of his hard body.

She let her lashes flutter closed.

Christopher must have sensed her surrender, because his hand was suddenly trailing down her ribs, skimming across her hips, gathering up wads and wads of fabric along the way.

And when he slipped his fingers beneath her skirt toward

that needy ache between her legs, Ellen didn't question, she didn't protest, she just let her thighs drift apart.

She might not even have bothered wearing the thong-that-wasn't, for he easily brushed it aside. She had the vague thought that she should drop by Toni Maxwell's shop before leaving town, to thank her for designing this line of ready-for-anything clothing—but Christopher's forefinger found her most intimate place and Ellen stopped thinking at all.

With deliberate thoroughness, he rolled that nub round and round and round. The pressure just enough to make her yearn with a delirious ache that spread inside, until her breathing grew shallow and her legs felt like lead.

She felt Christopher shift slightly, heard a sound that might have been him placing the journal on the floor. Ellen wasn't sure. She didn't really care. As long as he didn't stop that steady, exquisite motion.

Round and round and round.

Her sex grew wet with a creamy heat. The thong strap wedged between her thighs. Her inner muscles gathered tight in time with those slow steady circles, deep yearning clenches she was sure Christopher could feel.

He didn't say a word.

He just propped his chin on the top of her head, curled his body around hers and dipped his finger deep into her heat.

She sighed.

He stroked.

She trembled with the strength of her approaching climax. His every push magnified the sensation, played her like he had last night, stealing her reason, until all she could do was ride his hand and let him lead her down the path to exploding senses.

And explode they did.

Time drew to a complete stop, and only slowly did Ellen come back to herself, recognizing the noises that had faded beneath the rush of blood in her ears. The steady *whoosh, whoosh, whoosh* of the shoofly. The deep inhalation of Christopher's breathing.

Ellen couldn't think. She couldn't marvel at how her body responded to this man, how she seemed primed and ready for his slightest touch. She couldn't have moved if her life depended on it. Her sex still clutched him with greedy squeezes that were slowly lessening in frequency.

"Make love to me." His breath was warm against her ear, his voice gravelly in a way that revealed how watching her climax had aroused him, too.

"Here?"

"I'm so hard I won't make it back to the suite. I don't think I can walk." His laughter came easily.

"What if someone walks in on us?"

"Your gown will cover anything that might be showing." He nipped her earlobe with his teeth, sent a frisson skittering straight down to her toes. "Be a little daring, love. I'll be worth the effort. Trust me."

Trust him?

"You're impulsive."

"You play it too safe."

Play it too safe? Said whom? She was lying here with his hand wedged between her thighs, recovering from another of those debilitating orgasms. "I prefer to avoid situations that might result in profound embarrassment."

Another nip. Another corresponding arrow of pleasure.

"I won't let you be embarrassed."

She wanted to argue that he'd already failed in that department by distracting her from the introductory events, by distracting her from work so she'd had to face her authors and admit her objectivity was lacking.

But she couldn't form the words, not when he was wiggling that devilish finger inside her to convince her otherwise.

One part of her, a very daring part, urged her to give in, to give excitement a try. Christopher had just pleasured her so incredibly, and one good turn deserved another....

But he'd touched upon a conflict so deeply ingrained that even longing couldn't bridge it. Ellen was strong-willed and usually grateful for the trait that allowed her to discipline herself enough to follow the rules. She didn't act unless she was willing to live with the consequences of her actions.

Except, of course, when she was with Christopher.

He was the only one who tested her limits, but even so, she wasn't willing to have someone walk into this library and catch her in mid-thrust on top of him. She'd made this mistake before and had learned the hard way not to get caught in compromising positions.

No matter how much she ached.

His breath gusted softly against her cheek. His finger applied just enough pressure to let her know he was still intimately inside her.

But he didn't say anything else. He just waited.

In that instant, Ellen's whole life whittled down to her willingness to take a chance. Could she let go of her firmly held limits and make love to this man right here, right now? Could she allow herself to be swept up in the moment, to chance that someone may walk in?

She couldn't see Christopher's face, but there was a tenseness about him that made her feel as if her entire life had boiled down to overcoming past mistakes.

There was a part of her that wanted to give in so much. And couldn't.

"Let's go back to our suite," she said.

"I don't mind waiting until we finish up here, love," he said easily. "You're worth the wait."

He pressed a kiss to the top of her head. His finger slipped away, leaving her aware of just how wet she was, how much she wanted him.

Maybe it was this sudden emptiness that made her question herself. Or perhaps it was that Christopher seemed okay with her refusal, as though he'd expected her answer. Either way, Ellen wondered now what it would feel like to take a chance, to lift her skirt and straddle him, take him inside her and go for it.

Rule number three for survival: *When in doubt, don't.*

Christopher was exactly the man she didn't need—a man who made her second-guess herself. She'd had her whole world nice and orderly and manageable until he'd come along. Now he was shooting her emotions all out of control, pushing her limits.

Normal people didn't get touchy-feely in potentially embarrassing situations. Except for Christopher. Like the time at the art museum when he'd cornered her next to the Chagall. Or the time she'd dropped by his office for lunch and he'd swept the contents of his desk onto the floor and invited her to be the main course. The man was simply outrageous, impulsive.

Sure, one part of her wanted to give in, but another, louder part resented that he would ask this of her. She'd just let him bring her to orgasm on an antique carpet, for goodness' sake. Didn't that count for something?

Didn't he understand what it had taken for her to sacrifice her biggest and most firmly held relationship rule last night?

Relationship rule number one: *Senators' daughters do not get caught sneaking out of anyone's bed the morning after.*

Maybe they hadn't been caught, but she'd certainly awakened the morning after with him. And here he was, still pushing her, still wanting more. Who did this man think he was?

And why did she care so much about whether she met his expectations?

8

The Dining Room

CHRISTOPHER GRABBED the breadbasket under the pretense of taking another dinner roll, although one already sat untouched on his plate. The breadbasket put him within range of Ellen, who was currently engaged in a whispering session with Lennon.

"What's Susanna doing?" He heard her ask. "Is she looking for something?"

"She's moon-pieing at Olaf," Lennon said, and Christopher had to strain to hear her because she was seated on Ellen's right.

"She'll be lying in her plate if she leans over any more."

"At least she'll get his attention. You should have seen her during the introduction last night. Olaf walked into the room and she hasn't been right since. She thinks he's cute."

"Olaf?" Ellen shook her head, her disbelieving gaze riveted on the head of the table, where the host in question had paused in his address to accommodate the arrival of the sommelier. "He's a very striking man, I'll grant you, just not what I'd have envisioned Susanna going for. You know her heroes. They're all medieval knights with manes of tawny hair."

Lennon nodded. "I think this is another side effect of

Joey going off to college. Mom has just realized that less laundry means more time to have fun.''

Christopher sat back, placed the roll on his plate and reached for his wineglass. Casting his gaze around the table, he noted how the guests settled into conversation to fill the sudden quiet. Tracy was whispering excitedly to Susanna, while casting not-so-covert glances Olaf's way. Miss Q sat at the opposite end of the table with a smile on her face, not missing a thing with her big blue eyes. Even Mac and Harley seemed to be communicating without strife—or kissing—for the moment.

Only Josh, who, like himself, had been excluded from the analysis of Susanna's romantic interest, directed his attention to his plate.

Christopher wasn't interested in speculating on a potential romance between Olaf and Susanna, although Ellen and Lennon seemed fascinated with the subject. He'd rather expend his energy assessing his own progress with Ellen.

And it needed major assessment, because their encounter in the library had taken a wrong turn. He hadn't meant to push her into doing something she found uncomfortable. She'd simply been so relaxed and so irresistible that he couldn't keep his hands off her.

This wasn't the first time that Ellen had had this crazy effect on him. She aroused him, made him feel excited by everything around him. She accused him of being a daredevil, but Christopher had never before wanted to make love to a woman so much he'd been willing to risk being caught in the act. He'd been tempted often with Ellen. He'd wanted her to want him so much that she'd lose herself in the moment, forget all her rules and trust him to keep her safe.

He'd overplayed his hand—*again*.

She'd retreated. A subtle retreat, nothing more than a contemplative silence when they'd returned to their suite to change for dinner and a withdrawal into the bathroom for privacy, but like any distance between them, one closed door had effectively shut him out.

After taking another swallow of cabernet, he set the glass back on the table for a refill, and found that Ellen and Lennon had concluded their analysis of their friend's behavior.

"Enjoying dinner?" he asked.

She nodded, sending waves of dark hair bouncing softly around her cheeks. Lips moistened from the wine she'd just sipped tipped upward in a smile. "The filet mignon is unbelievable. As good as Kevin's."

High praise, indeed. Kevin was a chef back in New York, whose upscale eatery they'd discovered and frequented during the time they had dated. He couldn't help but wonder if her reference to a place they'd considered "theirs" meant she might be moving past their encounter in the library.

He also wondered if she had been back to the restaurant since the last time they'd visited together. He would have asked her, but Olaf chose that moment to continue his address.

"I'm suggesting a game to play after dinner," he said. "Southern Charm Mysteries calls it 'Giving Away the Farm.' The goal is to assess your competitors' progress in solving the mystery, and the rules are simple—each couple chooses to share a piece of information they've discovered today, and each of the other couples gets to ask a question. The clues can be big or small. Either way, you'll be required to exercise critical thinking skills under pressure."

He raised his wineglass in salute. "So take this time to

finish your meals and discuss with your partners what you can reveal without *giving away the farm*.''

Christopher thought the game a clever way to aid everyone in working toward the mystery's resolution. Sharing clues would foster cooperation between the teams—and just might foster a little between him and Ellen.

''What clue do you think we should share?'' he asked her.

With her fork poised in midair, Ellen leaned close enough to gift him with a waft of her delicate floral fragrance, which he hadn't noticed earlier.

''What about our secret clue? Maybe everyone's questions will help us figure it out.''

''That could work, but I don't want to share our ace in the hole until we have at least an idea of what it means.'' She must have applied the fragrance while she'd dressed in the bathroom—in a button-front gown that hadn't required his assistance to fasten. ''What about the captain's title?''

''That'll invite questions about his upbringing and why he left France, which just may send the others looking backward instead of forward if they don't already know about it.''

''You're sharp, love. Have I mentioned lately how much I admire that about you?''

Clearly surprised, Ellen inhaled deeply, her chest rising and falling and making him decide that she looked more edible than the filet in her scarlet gown. The design was simple in comparison to the ruffles she'd worn earlier, but the shiny satin molded her every curve, drew his gaze to the creamy cleavage swelling above the neckline, capturing his imagination with the memory of the sweet-tasting skin below.

She shook her head, and the golden lights flickering in her eyes convinced him she'd been pleased by his praise.

"So you think we should reveal the title?"

"I think the journals would be overkill, don't you?"

"Definitely. The journals would raise questions about what happened *after* they left France. We shouldn't go there."

"Agreed."

The journals had revealed a decent amount of information about the family's journey to the Caribbean. The captain's father had indeed been executed and all the Lafever holdings lost to the new regime. Mother and son had survived some tough years, but Christopher and Ellen hadn't uncovered any specifics about the sister—or *half* sister, as they now believed her to be, from a letter they'd discovered folded between the pages of a journal.

"I know what we should do," Christopher said, casting a surreptitious look around the table.

The other couples were engaged in similar conversations. Josh and Lennon whispered to each other while sipping from the same wineglass with a freedom that Christopher envied.

Across the table, Mac and Harley had squared off again, their strained voices drawing an annoyed glance from Tracy. Susanna, by comparison, appeared preoccupied with Olaf, who sat upright and handed her a linen napkin, apparently having retrieved it from the floor.

"What?" Ellen asked.

"The letter. Let's tell them about the signature."

Ellen's mouth tipped upward in the most delectable grin. "Ooh, you are just too sneaky."

"*Good.* I prefer to think of myself as *good.*"

That gorgeous mouth widened a bit more, prompting a grin of his own. "No argument. The signature is a legitimate clue, but it doesn't give away anything we discovered. Maybe the questions will help us fill in the blanks about the captain's sister.''

Ellen's smile gave Christopher hope that he just might overcome her latest retreat, too. And as the meal wound down, she seemed to bridge the distance, locking him in a debate about the best way to present their clue.

By the time the plates had been cleared away and the coffee served, they'd honed their strategy and Christopher's adrenaline pumped. Not for the game, but for some alone time with Ellen.

He was glad when Olaf finally stood. ''Who's brave enough to volunteer sharing their clue first?''

''Shall we?'' Christopher leaned close to whisper into Ellen's ear.

Before she could reply, Tracy was already sliding her chair back from the table, commanding everyone's attention. ''Susanna and I will. We discovered that the captain's sister was fifteen years younger than he was. This is a great clue, so fire away with your questions, folks.''

Ellen's knee bumped his under the table as if to say, *definitely a half sister.*

''Who fathered her?'' Josh asked, revealing he already knew about the execution, which didn't surprise Christopher in the least, considering Josh solved mysteries professionally. Mac and Harley would probably prove equally tough competitors.

''A man the captain's mom had known from her youth,'' Susanna explained. ''He was the youngest son of a minor baron who left France to seek out his fortune on the sea.''

''His family thought he was a black sheep and disowned him,'' Tracy added.

Bingo. He and Ellen had come across a letter tucked

neatly between the pages of a journal. It had been addressed to *My Dearest Love* and signed *Your Loving Allie* and very obviously had been written between lovers. But the date revealed that the letter couldn't have been written to the captain's father.

Christopher took a turn nudging Ellen's knee under the table. "Now we know who Allienor wrote the letter to."

"They're giving away the farm," she whispered under her breath in a singsong voice that made him smile.

"Lucky us."

And Christopher guessed Josh must be equally pleased with the amount of information his question had yielded, even though he only inclined his head in polite acknowledgment.

Mac tossed his napkin onto the table and glanced up at Tracy, but before he could say anything, Harley cut him off. "Did the black sheep marry the captain's mother?"

Mac shot her a dark look. And he wasn't the only one. Josh was watching the two of them with a narrowed stare.

"A good question." Tracy smiled a slow, dramatic smile. "We're guessing not, since Brigitte went by the name of Lafever."

"We need to know why," Ellen whispered. "How come his mother didn't move to New Orleans with her children? Did she stay behind to be with this guy?"

"Agreed. But that's three questions."

Ellen gazed up at him from beneath thick lashes, a sexy, exasperated look that made his blood descend straight to his crotch. "Help me synopsize it, then."

"Ask if his mother went to New Orleans with them."

"But we already know she didn't—"

"But do Tracy and Susanna know? They've been giving away the farm. I'll bet Tracy gives us more than we ask for."

"That's a gamble."

One that didn't pay off, because Tracy and Susanna didn't have the information.

But Mac and Harley did.

They explained that the captain had earned enough wealth to formally educate his sister, which swung the conversation back around to New Orleans again—the captain's mother hadn't accompanied her children to New Orleans because she and her lover had died when their daughter was just two years old.

This revelation sent every romance writer, and one gorgeous romance editor, at the table into throes of melodrama.

"They *died?*" Tracy splayed her hand across her heart. "Their ship sank in a hurricane?"

"The captain wound up rearing his sister," Susanna added. "How tragic. How noble."

"You'd have rejected that manuscript, Ellen," Lennon said. "Who wants to read about tragedy? The captain's mother loses her first husband to the guillotine, endures all sorts of hardships, and finally finds love again—only to drown." She shivered, and Josh seized the opportunity to touch his wife, slipping an arm around her shoulders and leaning close to whisper in her ear.

"Not my cup of tea," Ellen agreed. "Angst is fine for a little while. Readers want a happy ending and so do I."

Ah, there she was…that idealist who hid beneath fiercely checked emotions. A woman who challenged him to slip past her defenses—not just for a day but for a lifetime.

"Dessert, sir?" an unfamiliar voice asked, and Christopher glanced up as a waiter motioned to a dessert cart.

He chose tiramisu, while Ellen declined dessert in favor of a cappuccino.

"You're sure?" Christopher eyed her skeptically. "I thought tiramisu was your favorite."

"It's very good, ma'am," the waiter said. "Captain Lafever used to have the cream whipped fresh whenever his sister, Miss Brigitte, came home from her fancy school in New Orleans."

Ellen's gaze locked on to his, hazel lights sparkling. *A clue.* "Did he? How often did Brigitte come home?"

"On all her school holidays," he replied.

"Did she ever bring friends with her?" Christopher asked.

"I don't think Miss Brigitte had many friends."

"Did she have her own suite? I didn't see one on the map."

"Miss Brigitte loved Félicie Allée so much that she decorated all the guest bedrooms and took turns staying in them when she was home. She didn't care much for being in one place. She had the wanderlust from her early years on the sea with Captain Julian." He smiled fondly, as though remembering the young woman and her whimsical habits. "The master indulged her. Well, if not the tiramisu, ma'am, would you care to try the ladyfingers? They're light."

Ellen declined, and Christopher said, "She'll share mine."

With a polite nod, the waiter moved on.

"Were those the clues I think they were?" Ellen whispered.

He speared a small bite of the dessert on to his spoon. "But what was he telling us, besides the fact the captain doted on his sister?"

She eyed the spoon with a wary frown. "I'm stuffed. I was hoping the caffeine would revive me."

"Sugar will help."

He'd been hoping to feed her himself, but wasn't surprised when she plucked the spoon from his grasp. She brought it to her lips just as Josh and Lennon took their turn in the hot seat.

The other couples had yielded a gold mine of information in comparison to the Eastmans. Together, Lennon and Josh managed to reveal next to nothing about the family whose land bordered Félicie Allée except that they hadn't been happy to become the Lafevers' neighbors.

"Who were they?" Christopher asked.

"We don't know any more than that they were an influential New Orleans family who also kept a mansion in the city."

He and Ellen tried to be equally evasive when they took their turn.

"We've discovered that the captain's mother went by the nickname Allie," Ellen explained. "So we're speculating that he named the plantation after her. Félicie Allée. We're not sure of the translation, since neither of us remembers much from high school French class."

"There's always significance to the names in my books," Lennon said.

Tracy and Susanna both agreed, which began a rousing dialogue about the translation of Félicie Allée and neatly directed the questions along this vein. Of course, no one else remembered much from French class, either, except to guess that *félicie* sounded like a variation of *happy*. The conversation ultimately wound around to Lennon, whose mother currently made her home in Monte Carlo and spoke the language fluently.

She agreed to make a call for an accurate translation, but as her mother was out, she wound up leaving a message.

The night was getting on and even Christopher had begun feeling the effects of their largely sleepless night. "Tired?"

"A bit." Ellen set the cup back onto its saucer.

A dab of foam remained on the corner of her lip and he smudged the fleck away with his thumb, resisting the urge to trace her pouty lower lip.

But his one small touch introduced an intimacy to the moment that Ellen clearly hadn't expected. Her gaze darted around the table to see if anyone had noticed, and the relief he saw in her expression was way out of balance with what he'd perceived as a very casual gesture.

In the blink of an eye, it was over. She dabbed at her lip with a napkin, her profile set in creamy lines, her expression so schooled he might have imagined her reaction.

He hadn't.

Her upbringing had conditioned her to keep up appearances. Christopher understood that. He also understood that she felt compelled to maintain her professionalism with Susanna and Tracy during this event. But her response had been so automatic, so reflexive that he couldn't help but wonder why someone familiar with the spotlight would be so unsure of herself.

It was a question that needed an answer. Part of his initial attraction to Ellen had been the challenge of slipping past her barriers to get to know the real woman. The more progress he made, the more fascinating he found her. He had gotten to know the intelligent woman beneath that polished veneer and had fallen in love.

But he had already learned the hard way that love didn't give him an advantage. Nor would simply asking the question yield a straight answer.

Which meant Christopher had some sleuthing of his own to do.

9

The Garden Suite

ELLEN DEPARTED THE BATHROOM with what felt like great ceremony. Hair combed. Face scrubbed. Teeth minty fresh. Her attire...well, her choices had been a comfortable but unsexy cotton shorts set or another Toni Maxwell original. She'd gone with the Toni Maxwell, which meant she was practically naked. Whatever body parts were covered could still be seen through the transparent eggshell lace.

Just perfect for climbing into Mr. *Not-the-One*'s bed.

Ellen hung the red satin gown back in the closet, placed the low-heeled shoes in the rack. Christopher was nowhere to be seen, which meant he was either outside enjoying the sultry bayou night or in the sitting room poring over their notes. Either way, she appreciated the privacy. A chance to make peace with this course and rally her determination to see it through.

Which meant climbing into that bed, knowing she wouldn't climb back out again until dawn. It was one thing to share a suite and flirt with Christopher all day long, but sharing a bed represented an intimacy and permanence that she didn't want to think about.

As far as beds went, this was a perfectly good one. Given last night's sexy surprises, she understandably hadn't fully appreciated it. The antique tester had carved posts with sheer side curtains draped softly to match the white comforter. A special bed that had been crafted for a pirate hero long ago and had endured the test of time. A bed worthy of laying aside her hard-and-fast relationship rule.

Pulling down the comforter, Ellen climbed the matching rosewood steps and slipped between the sheets with what also felt like great ceremony. She propped the pillows behind her. Flipped on the bedside lamp. Retrieved the notebook and pen from the night table. Inhaled deeply.

There, she was all set.

Let the night begin.

Almost as if he'd been waiting for his cue to enter, Christopher strolled in from the courtyard, stopping short in the doorway when he saw her.

The moment took on a strangely surreal quality as his gaze cut the distance between them, taking in everything in a glance.

"You're amused," she said. Not a question.

"I'm honored."

"You don't have to seduce me into another coma to get me to sleep with you. I agreed to be your partner and I'll live up to my end of the deal."

Christopher inclined his head slowly, and she could tell by the slight narrowing of his eyes that he was considering her statement, looking at all the angles. "I see."

And something about his calmly voiced statement suggested he did. Right through her. Ellen might look composed. She might sound composed. But that didn't change the fact that when Christopher stared at her with that lightning gaze, her insides melted into a giant puddle of conflicting emotions and sensations.

He didn't utter another word, just crossed the room, unbuttoning his shirt as he headed toward the closet.

Ellen flipped open the notebook, stared down at the

notes she'd taken earlier. With sheer stubborn will she focused on the words, kept her gaze averted from the sight of him stripping off his shirt in an eye-catching display of bunching muscle.

She managed to focus, which was a feat in itself, but she wasn't comprehending a thing she read. How could she, when he shifted his hips around to slide his slacks over a certain *protruding* body part and down those long, strong legs? How could she be expected to concentrate on anything other than the sight of him standing there in briefs that molded his butt to white cotton perfection?

She snapped the notebook shut.

Glancing up, Christopher caught her folding her hands primly on the cover. He arched a dark brow as if to ask "Is there a problem?"

"I'd rather enjoy the show."

Not looking the least bit chagrined, he hooked his thumbs into the waistband in a confident move designed to make the show worth her while. Sliding the briefs down his hips, he exposed a male body part that appeared to be enjoying his audience. That very same part bobbled suggestively as he shimmied the briefs down his legs and kicked them off his feet.

Ellen admired the display with a casual expression that felt frozen onto her face—another huge feat given the way her breath was suddenly skittering through her windpipe.

On the upside, she had a moment to catch her breath when he disappeared into the bathroom. She heard running water before he reappeared, only to disappear again, this time into the sitting room. Then he returned with the remainder of their mystery gear.

On a not-so-upside, Ellen's breathing troubles resumed in force when Christopher hopped onto the bed, lying fulllength beside her, comfortable with his nudity in a way that was so uniquely male. His skin, though not tanned, seemed striking against the white comforter, a display of sculpted muscle that could have been at home in any museum for its sheer masculine grace.

He propped himself up on an elbow, and Ellen noticed that his face was damp. She'd be willing to bet if he leaned close enough she'd catch a whiff of breath as minty fresh as hers.

Well, here they were, all ready to start their night.

Her heartbeat did a ridiculous little hop-skip. She cleared her throat. "Listen, Christopher. I want to say something about what happened this afternoon in the library."

The dimples faded. "I was out of line. I'm sorry."

There was something so earnest in his expression, something so gallant about him accepting all the responsibility when she'd been the one in the wrong, that her heart gave another queer twist. "*I'm* sorry. I overreacted."

His eyes widened just enough to let her know her admission surprised him, a reaction that rankled. But could she honestly expect him to respond any differently? Opening up and sharing her feelings wasn't one of her strengths—not with Christopher. Not with anyone, if she were truthful.

And the moment demanded she be truthful. With only a few inches of comforter between them and a night together looming before them, watching Christopher play the hero demanded she be equally honest, and gallant.

"What you suggested wasn't so outrageous. Definitely not worthy of a subculture Web site." At his frown, she had to take a deep breath to get the rest of the words out.

"It wasn't really about you. I sometimes…talk myself out of doing things because I worry about the consequences."

For one bizarre instant, her admission hung in the air between them, leaving her exposed. It was a strange feeling, one that reminded her why she chose to avoid it whenever possible. Fortunately Ellen only had to endure a split second of waiting, of feeling *vulnerable,* before Christopher reacted.

With insight she'd have expected from a hero in a book rather than a real-live man in the flesh, he understood that she wouldn't welcome questions or comments. He simply slipped warm fingers over hers where she held them clasped on the notebook cover. It was the perfect reply.

Awareness sizzled through her like the beams from the bayou sun, filtered through her slowly, emphasizing the intensity of his gaze, the richness of the silence between them.

"I didn't want to get caught, either, love. I got carried away. You have that effect on me."

Another easy, honest admission. She marveled that he didn't look as though he felt remotely exposed or vulnerable. And even though she did, Ellen couldn't help notice that his strong grip on her hand made the feeling tolerable.

She wasn't sure what else to say—what *could* she possibly say? She'd charged him with being a daredevil when he'd simply been as caught up in the moment as she'd been. After spreading her legs and allowing him to bring her to orgasm, who was she to fault him for wanting to do the same?

That question invited a few others—hard questions, and necessary questions. Like why had she freaked? Gotten angry?

The only answer she could come up with was that Christopher pushed her past her comfort zone, introduced risks that conflicted with the way she chose to conduct her life.

Risks that made her question whether she wanted to continue conducting her life business as usual.

A *really* hard question.

Following Christopher's lead, she squeezed his hand.

He squeezed back.

And then he simply slipped out the notebook, flipped it open and moved them on to the work ahead. "So what have we got?"

"A lot of information to pull together."

"Brainstorming sounds like our best bet."

Ellen nodded. "I'll sort through our notes and you make the lists, or vice versa?"

"I'd rather sort. I think better on my feet."

Ellen didn't point out that he was lying down, stretched out in such a gorgeous display of nudity that her mouth was dry. "Works for me. I think better on paper."

"What a team."

That was the bloody irony of it. But she didn't say that to him, just smiled, and was soon occupied with recording his swift recap of the day's discoveries.

Captain Julian Lafever—dispossessed nobleman forced to make his living as a privateer.

Father executed; mother died tragically.

Fifteen years older than his half sister; responsible for her from the time she was two.

And so on... Ellen's hand rarely paused in her efforts, as Christopher flipped through the notebook, summarizing passages in his hint-of-the-Deep-South voice, a voice that seemed fashioned to complement the wild bayou night deepening beyond the French doors. A voice designed to sound just right when two people were lying in bed, one nude, the other practically nude, talking in hushed whispers.

Nudity aside, Ellen caught glimpses of what Christopher must look like at work—intense, focused and so confident in his manner and presentation, the gears working in his sharp mind before he opened his mouth to speak a word.

A high-powered individual, he was a man comfortable with responsibility and action, as comfortable working in his upscale Manhattan office wearing a several-thousand-dollar custom-made business suit as he was lying naked in a bed.

And he was a natural leader, she realized suddenly, because he'd convinced her that bed was the perfect place to work, too. *She,* who was so very private and particular about what she did in a bed. Beds were reserved for sleeping, or reading manuscripts before falling asleep, or for making love to a man she had no intention of sleeping with.

Yet here she was working side-by-side with the one man who'd driven her crazy since the moment they'd met. Comfortably, companionably, as if working with him anywhere was perfectly normal. Christopher had promised to prove they were compatible, and if he'd meant to convince her they made a great team in and out of bed, he was succeeding.

The thought brought to mind Susanna—pull-no-punches Susanna!—who'd been drooling over Olaf tonight. Ellen thought about how she must feel facing an empty house for the first time in so many years. Perhaps similar to the way Ellen felt arriving home late to her quiet apartment, where no one ever noticed whether she was late or on time. Except for her cat, who never commented.

Alone. A feeling she knew intimately.

How would Susanna, who was barely forty, successful

and deserving of someone special in her life, make the transition? Ellen hoped she wasn't so rattled by the idea of being alone that she'd chase after the first guy who happened down the pike.

Not that there was anything wrong with Olaf. He was an absolute doll. Not conventional romance-hero material, true, but very striking with his ethnic features and grizzly-bear size. Could he be *the one* for Susanna? Ellen didn't have a clue.

And that was also a feeling she was well acquainted with.

"I'm just not seeing the significance of this newspaper article," he said, dragging Ellen from her introspection and making her realize she'd missed whatever he'd been saying. "The only thing this newspaper article tells me is that the Lafevers weren't present at a Mardi Gras ball that other influential society people attended."

The Lafevers weren't present at the Mardi Gras ball. She scribbled into the notebook, then stared at the words, barely able to read her writing…but something about what she saw was enough to jolt her thoughts back into gear.

The Lafevers weren't present at the Mardi Gras ball.

"Why weren't they at the ball?" she asked, drawing Christopher's gaze. "Look at the date on the newspaper. The captain's sister would certainly have been old enough to attend. About the only thing Josh told us tonight was that Brigitte was a pupil in the same young ladies finishing academy as all those other families the column mentions. Doesn't it strike you as odd that she wouldn't be at the biggest ball of the season?"

Christopher only nodded, apparently recognizing she was on a roll and encouraging her to follow the thread.

"We need to think this through. The captain brought Brigitte to New Orleans. This is significant, so we need to know why. For some reason he felt it was important to expose her to society. To have her educated at the same exclusive young ladies academy other influential socialites attended.''

Pausing, she collected her thoughts. "Okay, we've got to remember this was the early eighteen hundreds. There might have been a dozen of these schools around the country, and only for the very wealthy. So why would the captain relocate his business and spend a fortune to educate his sister?''

"Obvious. Dispossessed or not, the man was still a nobleman. He would have had certain expectations for his sister's situation and would have provided her with the means to live that type of life. It was his obligation.''

"Makes sense. Especially given he was so much older than she was. He'd been her guardian most of his adult life. At his age, he'd be looking to secure her future, which would mean—''

"Getting her off the high seas and establishing a place for her in society,'' Christopher said.

"Right.''

"So why didn't they attend the biggest ball of the season? Come on, love. There's a reason, and once we figure out what it is we'll understand our clue.''

She stared down at him, recognized the excitement in his gaze, the determined set to his jaw. He wasn't just challenged to answer a question. Christopher was caught up in solving the mystery, in the thrill of the chase.

And his flashing blue gaze urged her to get caught up in the chase, too.

For one startling instant, Ellen felt as if she were standing too close to the edge of a precipice—she had to jump, or retreat to where she felt safe.

I talk myself out of doing things because I worry about the consequences.

Because she never felt like she measured up and because she had made mistakes, she'd reined herself in and limited her choices. Fresh in her mind was the choice she'd made in the library earlier.

"We need the diary," he said. "If Brigitte was anything like her mother, she'd have written about her life."

"We'll make that a priority tomorrow."

He nodded. "But until then, we've got to speculate on how a man who apparently cared a great deal about his sister wound up murdering another girl the same age."

His comment filtered through her...*clicked.*

"You're right, Christopher." Ellen jumped off the cliff, practically feeling the wind sting her cheeks and rush through her hair when he lifted those too-blue eyes to hers.

Excitement bubbled inside, a physical sensation that made her scoot back against the headboard, draw her knees up. "Think back to what Susanna said tonight about the captain raising his sister. Not only was he a nobleman with a title, he was a *noble* man. Nothing we've learned about him so far indicates he would ever murder anyone, least of all a young girl. He became a privateer, a *businessman.* All right, maybe privateering meant smuggling, too, which wasn't exactly legal, but he wasn't a cutthroat pirate who preyed on the open seas. So what could have made a *noble* man murder a young girl?"

"You're back to motive. We don't have enough information."

"I agree, but we have enough to play the *what if* game."

He arched a silky dark brow.

"The *what if* game. I play it with my authors all the time to brainstorm new storylines. We test out possibilities until one feels right. Let's try it with what we already know. *What if* Julian was suddenly responsible for rearing his little sister?''

"He'd take to the high seas as a privateer to earn a fortune to support her."

She wasn't surprised that he caught on so quickly, and nodded her approval. "*What if* he finally had enough money to create a life for them? What kind of life would he create?"

"One that would place them in society, preferably a society that knew very little about their pasts."

"What makes you say that?"

Christopher shrugged. "By all rights, the captain could have headed back to France. The Revolution was over. He might have made a place in the new regime."

"So you did absorb some history when you were there."

"Just happened to have a chatty hot-air balloon guide." His mouth curved in a half grin.

"Right. So, why do you think the captain wanted to hide his past? Loads of nobles emigrated during the Revolution."

"His sister."

"What about her?"

"He couldn't exactly take her back to France. His father had been executed, so people would have known she wasn't really a Lafever. I don't think presenting her as a long-lost grandchild to her father's family was a good idea, either. Brigitte's father was a black sheep who never married their mother."

"Ohmigosh, you're right." Ellen stared at him, mind racing. "I totally overlooked Brigitte's illegitimacy. Nowadays it's a nonissue, but back then...that's not something the captain would have broadcast. It makes perfect sense that he'd bring her to New Orleans, a place where he could rear her in society without exposing her to ridicule.''

"*What if* the secret of her illegitimacy got out?" Christopher asked. "*What if* society wouldn't accept his sister? Or him, for that matter?''

"Remember what Miss Q said about Jean Lafitte. *What if* people didn't make the distinction between pirate and privateer? A privateer with an illegitimate sister probably wouldn't have been on the guest list to the biggest ball of the year.''

For a breathless instant her comment hung in the air. Then their gazes locked and the pieces fell into place.

"Revenge!" they both said at the same time.

It was an incredible moment. Her heart pounded. Her breaths came shallow. And she couldn't seem to stop smiling.

Neither could Christopher. "We have possible motive.''

"Absolutely. Despite her illegitimacy, Brigitte was a blue blood. If the captain wanted her to be accepted into that world and she wasn't, he might resent that.''

"Enough to murder Felicity Clayton? What did she do…steal one of Brigitte's boyfriends?''

Ellen shrugged. "Maybe she knew about Brigitte's illegitimacy and gossiped at school.''

"Doesn't sound like much of a reason to commit murder.''

"No, it doesn't, does it. But that waiter told us the captain doted on his sister and that she didn't have many friends. Do you think he was so possessive he'd commit murder to stop someone from hurting her?''

Christopher sat up in a display of toned muscle that drew her appreciative gaze. "We need to know more about what was happening in their lives.''

"I'll bet local newspapers will have something in them. There were stacks in the library."

"You up to taking a look through them now?"

"You want to go down to the library?"

"I don't want you to move a muscle, love. You're in my bed and I like you here." Brushing his fingertips across her cheek, he smiled when her breath caught audibly. "I'll go get them. It's late. Chances are, no one will notice we've got them."

He swung his long legs over the side of the bed, another distracting exhibition of rippling muscle and supple skin that made her sorry he was leaving.

She organized the various notebooks and brochures they'd strewn over the bed, while he pulled on a pair of shorts.

"What do you think about putting our special clue in with the rest of the newspapers when we return them?" he asked.

"That's a good idea. I think Harley was right about hiding the clue someplace it will be overlooked. Someone will have to be paying very close attention to see the significance of one newspaper article in a stack of newspapers."

After zipping his fly, Christopher reached for a shirt. "I don't think they meant for anyone to overhear them earlier. Did you get the impression they knew we were there?"

Judging by the way they'd bolted when her phone rang, Ellen didn't think they'd staged the conversation, or the kiss. "No."

"Me, neither." He tugged a polo shirt over his head and reemerged with his hair ruffled. He stepped into his Top-Siders and covered the distance between the closet and bed in two long strides. "Save my place, love. I won't be long."

Before Ellen had a chance to reply, he leaned over and smothered the sound in an unexpected and very steamy kiss. His tongue invaded her mouth, warm velvet, and his kiss sucked the breath right from her lungs. A wave of heat arrowed downward from the point of contact to breasts suddenly aching with awareness, nipples growing so tight they tested the sheer lace of her Toni Maxwell original.

Then, as quickly as he'd kissed her, he was gone. She was left trying to catch her breath and staring at his back as he strode out of the bedroom...*whistling?*

Yes, whistling. Some nameless, upbeat ditty that faded as he moved through the suite, silenced as he closed the door behind him.

Ellen sucked in another deep breath to steady her pulse and marveled at the irony of the situation. Here she was in a man's bed with every intention of spending the night, and he was on his way to the library. Silly man.

Silly Ellen. She sat there staring at that empty doorway for a long time, conscious of the lace against her skin, the cool sheets against her legs and the realization that she hadn't wanted him to go.

Not even to the library.

10

The Gallery

ALTHOUGH CHRISTOPHER HAD GONE round-trip in less than ten minutes, he arrived back in the suite to find Ellen fast asleep. She'd burrowed into the pillows, neither sitting nor lying down, her hair wisping around her face, deep sable strands striking against her creamy skin.

He stared down at her, lashes creating silky half-moons on her cheeks, kissable lips slightly parted, breasts rising and falling softly beneath their lacy confinement.

He wanted her. With an intensity and conviction he'd never known before—not in all the years since his first date. He wanted Ellen, in his bed, in his life, by his side.

Something as simple as watching her sleep suddenly seemed a perfectly worthy use of his time. And for a man who made a living in a business that routinely tested the limits of his ambition and resourcefulness, Christopher couldn't deny the power of this feeling.

What was it about this woman that touched him, that made him ache, that made him weigh everything he did and said against her wants and needs?

While he couldn't claim to have given much thought to whether or not he believed in love at first sight, he did believe in trusting his instincts, and his gut told him Ellen was his match, his equal, the woman meant to share his life.

What would it take to convince her?

She sighed, turning just enough so he could watch her in profile, hear another soft sigh slip from her lips. He ached to climb in bed beside her, to awaken her with a kiss…but something so serene, almost innocent about her in sleep kept him standing where he was.

Completely defenseless. That cool composure she showed the world had faded away, the walls she kept between them were nothing more than piles of rubble at his feet. This was the Ellen he wanted to make love to—the woman who trusted him enough to reveal her emotions, to let her guard down, to believe he'd love her for who she was.

It was this woman he had to seduce this weekend.

Scooping the treasure map off the bed, he scanned the floor plan of the plantation, then reached for the lamp beside the bed. Christopher flipped it off, threw the room into a darkness broken only by the moonlight streaming through the open French doors. Turning on his heel, he headed out through the private entrance in the courtyard and out into the night.

Moonlight paved a silver trail over the grounds. A mist had begun to rise off the water, layering the grass, the bushes and the trees with a sheen that clung to his skin and muted the sounds of frogs and other wildlife.

Christopher circled the building, hoping to complete his task and be back before the fog thickened. Ellen was asleep in his bed, of her own volition. If that alone wasn't enough to lure him back, he wanted to wake her up with his mouth and make love to her while she was still half asleep, a fantasy of his since the first night they'd made love.

But now he had a clue to follow up, one that had nothing to do with Captain Lafever or the governor's daughter.

He stopped in front of the west wing, glancing up to

survey the third floor above the gallery. Pleased to discover he had a clear shot to the set of windows he was looking for, he cast around for some pebbles, aimed and sent the first one sailing toward the glass.

As a kid growing up in the Garden District, Christopher had been part of a tight-knit group who had shared privileged upbringings. Along with the privilege came some very serious expectations, and an equally serious need to cut loose from the constant pressure. Christopher and his friends had been known to sneak out in the wee hours to hit the French Quarter long before they'd been of a legal age to buy a drink. The person he wanted to talk to had been one of that gang.

He sent the second pebble soaring up. Perhaps he could have just knocked on the door…but it was late and Christopher was feeling nostalgic. Not to mention that he'd rather not awaken, or interrupt, newlyweds who might already be in bed.

If Lennon heard the signal, she'd know he was there and come to the window. He sent the third pebble flying.

The fourth did the trick.

The window slid up, but instead of the blond head he'd expected, Christopher found himself staring up at Josh.

"Problem with the door?" he asked.

"Uh, no. Not exactly."

Then the blond head popped out. Lennon waved. "Hi, Christopher. I told Josh it would be either you or Mac. He wanted to check first to protect me."

Josh only shook his head. "I missed this little ritual."

"You got that right, old man," Christopher called up.

"What do you want, Sinclair?" Josh asked. "It's after midnight. And, no, she can't go partying on Bourbon Street."

"I just want to borrow your wife for a few minutes."

"She's busy."

"Here I come, Christopher. Meet me around front." Lennon disappeared from the window.

"Return her in one piece," Josh charged him before backing into the room and sliding the window shut.

Christopher appreciated the sentiment and headed around the building to wait for Lennon, who emerged through the front door a few minutes later.

"Listen, before I forget," she said, "tell Ellen that my mom called back. She has never heard the word *félicie*. She doesn't know the translation and is sure it doesn't mean 'happy.' But *allée* means path. So what's up?"

Interesting. Not even close to what he and Ellen had interpreted the plantation's name to mean. Motioning Lennon down to the gallery steps where they could sit beneath the glow of the security lights, he said, "I wanted to talk about Ellen."

"Shoot. I trust you won't ask me to betray her confidence."

Christopher was certainly glad that someone trusted him around here. "Of course not, but you're close with her, and her family, too. It's really them I want to know about."

"You've met them, haven't you?"

"I've been invited to a few events the Senator hosted. Even made the cut to her birthday party. And I've played golf a few times with her dad and brothers. But I haven't made it through the front door of the family home yet." Unless he could sell himself to Ellen this weekend, he never would. "Do her brothers and sister struggle as hard as she does to have a life?"

Lennon shrugged. "I don't know. One of her brothers is married with kids and her sister's engaged to a very nice man who works for the district attorney's office." She hesitated, golden brows dipping in a frown. "Are you asking me if she'll ever put her relationship with you before her family?"

Leaning back on his elbows, Christopher met her gaze. He'd known Lennon a long time and wouldn't pull any punches. "Yes. And no. I don't have a problem with her family. I understand what their situation demands. But Ellen worries about living up to their expectations, and I'm not sure the expectations aren't hers more than theirs. She's so careful about everything she does that she never relaxes her guard. She's 'on' all the time."

Except when he seduced his way past her defenses.

"That's the truth, bless her heart. I honestly believe she doesn't know how to be any different. Before her mother became Senator, her father was the Secretary of Commerce. Her life has always been about appearances and making the kinds of choices that won't come back to haunt her."

"I get the feeling that some of her choices have come back to bite her. Why else would she want to prove herself? She's an intelligent, accomplished woman. I only interacted with her family for a few months, but they seemed like nice people who love her."

"They do. Very much." Lennon fell silent, and Christopher got the sense that he'd reached one of the limits Lennon trusted him not to cross. Then she asked, "Why don't you wait out the requisite amount of time and marry her?"

"Waiting won't solve the problem." Hell, he'd endured three months of ritual dating and formal screening just to get her into bed. He'd wait *years* if that's what it took to get her to open up and believe in him, in *them*. His gut told him there was a bigger problem here. But if he didn't know what it was, he couldn't address it.

"Then, what will?"

"I originally thought *I* was the problem. That I pushed too fast and too hard. But it's more than me, Lennon. I'll wait, if that's what she wants, but waiting isn't going to make her open up and believe we can work. She's looking for perfect, and you know as well as I do that it doesn't exist. I think Ellen knows it, too. In fact, I think she's counting on it."

"For what it's worth, I agree—"

She squeezed his knee this time, a gesture of reassurance that wasn't doing the trick, although he appreciated her effort.

"I'm very concerned about Ellen. I want to see her happy and she hasn't been since she ended things with you. But you can't force her to believe in you, or in herself for that matter. You know that, don't you, Christopher? She's strong-willed. I admire that a great deal about her. It had to take a lot of strength to stand up to her family and tell them she wasn't going into law or politics. It's also the reason I disagree with Auntie Q pulling this stunt. She can't force Ellen to do anything, either."

Christopher didn't mention that he'd been behind her great-aunt's stunt. He didn't have to. Lennon got to the heart of the matter. "And you can't, either. Ellen has to choose to let her guard down. She has to find her own way to happiness, and because we care about her, we need to help her, not judge her or push her. She's the only one who can choose what she wants from life."

Which drove home the fact that even though he'd gambled everything on this time together with Ellen, he still might not be able to convince her she wanted to be with him.

"I'll put in a good word if I can."

Lennon smiled thoughtfully, a smile that told him she understood just how much he had riding on the outcome of this training session.

MINDFUL THAT DROWSY WAVES of sensation were lifting her through the layers of consciousness, Ellen stubbornly clung to slumber, refusing to wake up from this all-too-delicious dream. Her muscles glowed with a slow-burning warmth that began between her thighs and flared outward with her sluggish pulse.

Her body felt disconnected, her legs weighted with this languid heat, her arms strangely disassociated, though every inch of her skin tingled. A vibration began low in her belly, creeping upward until her breasts grew tight and her drowsy brain decided she wanted to be touched there. She wanted to feel Christopher's fingers stroking her, creating those sensations that stole her breath and made her sex tighten in achy spasms.

Which was exactly what was happening now. She felt wet and hot and ready…not for action, surely. She couldn't have moved, even if she'd had the strength to try. She didn't. All she could do was try to assimilate this sensory assault, identify the feelings and savor the pleasure each created.

All beginning and ending in that most intimate place right between her thighs.

A steady stroking, a rolling sort of motion that created the most incredible friction, a friction that made her burn…she felt a tickling on the insides of her thighs. Realized she was lying on her back.

But she couldn't make sense of what was happening because, at that moment, the rising tide inside her decided to overflow the banks and flood her with a wave of heat that dragged her body out of control and her mind to full consciousness.

Christopher.

She felt his shoulders wedged between her thighs and he was lavishing the most exquisite attention on her most sensitive places. Slowly. Seductively. His tongue speared inside, made her muscles clench to hold him in, made her yearn for more.

She managed to lift heavy eyelids. The room was dark. The Toni Maxwell original had been brushed aside to provide Christopher entry, and he took advantage of that access....

His tongue rasped up to the tiny knot of nerve endings, swirling lazily, rolling that bud so skillfully that another moan slipped from her lips as heat continued to build inside...and then his lips were there, nibbling, sucking, drawing out the sweetest longing.

She shivered, a sensation that rippled from her head to her toes. Her thighs quavered involuntarily, sandwiched his head between them so he wouldn't slip away. Even in this groggy, half-conscious state, Ellen knew she didn't want him to stop. Not now. Not when she felt like this. Not when he was the only one who'd ever made her feel this way.

He must have realized that she'd awakened—if she could truly call this dreamy state ''awake''—recognized that she had no intention of resisting, because his hands suddenly skimmed her thighs, a featherlight touch that sprayed goose bumps over her skin, made her shiver again.

And then his fingers trailed into the juncture of her thighs. Suddenly he was curling those strong fingers in her wetness, separating her skin the way his tongue had, probing just enough to make her arch into his touch.

He let her set the rhythm, and Ellen sank back into the pillows, aware only of the way she felt each time she rolled her hips, tried to fill the emptiness inside that suddenly seemed cavernous. His devilish fingers curled and stroked and probed, never sinking all the way into her heat, but only tasting, teasing and tempting her beyond reason.

And all the while, that wave inside swelled, gaining momentum, making her lever her bottom against his face, where his mouth coaxed the most incredible responses....

Ellen slipped her hands over his dark head and down his neck. Sank her fingers into his shoulders to urge him up, needing to feel him warm and strong on top of her, feel his heat filling this emptiness inside.

"Love me, Christopher."

The words were just there on her lips, a rusty whisper Ellen had no idea she'd had the strength or coherence to utter. But those words filled the hushed darkness, echoing her need, underscoring her vulnerability.

Suddenly his hard body was sliding against hers, and his mouth brushed her ear. "I do."

And then he pushed that hot length inside her, sinking in all the way to the hilt, until she felt filled—not just her body, but her senses. She could smell his familiar male scent with every breath, feel the strength of muscle beneath skin that sealed them together in a thin sheen of sweat.

He was inside her, outside her, blocking her view of the world with his big body, crowding out her thoughts with each silken stroke. Long hot strokes that filled her, lifted her...

His arms slipped under hers, locked her against him to add leverage to his movements. Somehow she found enough energy to arch her hips to meet his powerful thrusts, abandoned herself to the building climax that took over her body. Took over his, too, because she could feel his muscles gathering, knew he was being swept away right along with her.

She sensed he was about to come a second before he

did. Maybe it was the way his body pressed into hers, rigid for a breathtaking instant, or perhaps it was the way his breathing suddenly stopped, a tight hiss between them—but she knew. She dragged her hands down his back, sank her fingers into his butt and thrust up to meet him.

His low growl burst against her ear. His body drove hard into hers, again and then again, as if he'd lost control. Ellen went with him, unable to think of anything but the way her orgasm cascaded through her, a huge rush of sensation that left her knowing that Christopher had been right.

Sleeping all night in his bed was a rule worth bending, no matter what the consequences.

11

The Garden Suite

"GOOD MORNING, LOVE." The sound of Christopher's voice dragged Ellen through the groggy layers of sleep.

"I've brought coffee and beignets. I decided we'd skip breakfast on the gallery and go through these newspapers."

The man sounded more chipper than anyone had a right to, given the amount of sleep they'd sacrificed during the night.

Ellen didn't bother opening her eyes, just rolled over and nestled against the warm pillow. She still wore the Toni Maxwell original, though the lace was all bunched up around her rib cage and she could feel a breast had popped out of the bodice. The rest of her was naked, and deliciously achy from being made love to so thoroughly.

"Time to get up. It's almost nine o'clock."

"All right."

Forcing an eyelid open—just one, because two would have required lifting her head from the pillow—she found Christopher smiling down at her, apparently very entertained.

He also seemed unfazed by her inability to move, and smiled wider as he slipped a hand beneath her arm and urged her to sit.

She forced herself into motion and he propped pillows behind her.

"There, are you comfortable?"

She was upright. That was saying a bunch. "I had no idea you were a morning person."

He waited while she straightened the bodice of the Toni Maxwell, then handed her a cup from a tray on the bedside table. She accepted it and took a grateful swallow. The coffee scalded all the way down, strong and supercharged with caffeine. She gave an appreciative sigh.

"I had no idea you weren't," he said genially. "Hasn't come up in conversation, has it. It's one of those intimate quirks we had to spend the night together to discover."

He was obviously trying to convince her of the merits of her foray into rule breaking, but it was far too early for analysis. Her head was fuzzy and her body still felt too sated from his steamy attention to even attempt any sort of objectivity or analysis, which brought her back to…

Rule number two of sound business strategies: *Understand your limitations and work around them.*

Coherent thinking when she'd just opened her eyes was *not* one of her strengths.

Taking a bite of a beignet, Christopher chewed and poured himself a cup of coffee before he sat down beside her.

She took another sip. "This is wonderful—coffee and beignets waiting for me when I open my eyes. Thank you."

"Just think, you could wake up every day like this if you married me."

"You are just amazing. See how you jump right to the end, skipping all the steps in between."

"That's where we differ in philosophies, love." He

lifted his cup in salute. "You're thinking of marriage as the end. I'm thinking of it as the beginning."

"Another reminder of exactly how opposite we are."

"On the contrary, a reminder of how well we compliment each other. We cover all the bases together."

She couldn't exactly argue that point, so she savored another long draw of turbocharged coffee, instead. It was too early for debate, and just how could she sway a man who'd already made up his mind, anyway?

But Christopher clearly didn't intend to be ignored.

Brushing wisps of hair from her neck, he gazed down at her thoughtfully and said, "Tell me something. Did you like being over? Were you happy without me?"

She paused with the cup at her lips and stared at him over the rim, realizing he'd sucked her into one of his emotionally honest moments. All she could claim was that her still-groggy brain cells hadn't consumed enough caffeine to see it coming.

When she didn't answer, he said, "I wasn't happy without you, love."

He was so bloody honest! He lay his heart there between them, for her to cherish or crush. It was a huge responsibility, one that forced her to think hard about her reply.

For a moment she felt cornered, trapped into dealing with something straight on, that she wasn't ready for and would much rather avoid. But there was no sidestepping his expression, which revealed her answer would mean the world to him.

That honesty disarmed her again.

He was willing to trust her with his heart. Even though she'd kicked him out of her life. Even though she'd buried her feelings deep inside and hadn't given him so much as a backward glance or a reason for her behavior in three months.

Christopher hadn't chased her, or fawned, or clung. He'd simply cornered her and taken advantage of a chance to argue his case. She couldn't help but admire his resourcefulness and respect him for having the courage to open up to her.

"No," she said simply, not a little amazed the admission didn't come with more difficulty. "I wasn't happy being over."

Again, proving himself the insightful person he claimed to be, Christopher backed off. He'd made his point and didn't push for any more emotional honesty. Setting his cup on the tray, he took another bite of beignet and appeared to savor a lot more than the taste of the New Orleans treat.

Until the telephone rang, at least. The sound made her jump, but even her fuzzy brain comprehended that if her father were calling with news of her mother's win, he'd call on her cell phone.

But Christopher frowned and shot her an accusing look. Slipping from the bed, he brushed powdered sugar from his fingers and grabbed the phone.

"Hello." After a moment, he gave a decidedly sheepish grin, which she assumed meant the call was for him.

As she watched him cradle the phone against his ear, Ellen witnessed a transformation from a chipper morning person to a very focused businessman.

"Put him through," Christopher said into the receiver, before hanging up the phone and turning to her. "Forgive me, love. It's my office. That Canadian ski resort deal I've spent the past six months trying to pull together has finally gone to the table. I need to take this call, but I'll take it on the other phone so I won't disturb you."

Ellen only nodded, thinking that no apology was necessary. She understood the way he worked. Months, even years sometimes, spent negotiating multimillion-dollar deals for commercial properties that could come together or fall apart in a minute. She wouldn't dream of interfering with a call. She just thought it ironic that he'd felt the need to apologize to *her*—the woman who never turned her phone off. Which made her consider how he'd turned his off with such important deals pending. An action that spoke volumes about his ability to balance work with his personal life.

When Christopher finally returned half an hour later, Ellen was showered, dressed and in the process of styling her hair. She didn't ask how his call had gone because he beelined for her, spun her toward him and gathered her into his arms.

His smile said it all.

"Closed your deal, did you?" she asked.

"You brought me good luck." He brushed a kiss on the top of her half-wet head. "Now I can relax and get on with our search. I've done my good deed for the day."

Ellen congratulated him on his success, but later, while Christopher was showering and she was sipping the last of the coffee, she couldn't help but think about that phone call.

Christopher, one of the most ambitious, driven men she'd ever known, had turned off his cell phone and had even taken off his watch to make rest and relaxation his priority during the training. He'd trusted that his office would track him down if something urgent came up, and they had.

There was a lesson here, Ellen decided. Not only about balancing work with pleasure, but also about Christopher. A man who could patiently construct a deal over so many months and then put it out of his head to enjoy himself didn't strike her as impulsive, but rather very clear on what he wanted.

SEARCHING THROUGH THE newspapers revealed much about life in New Orleans during the war, a place where people were faced with supply shortages and other daily reminders of struggle, yet tried to live with some sense of normalcy.

While Christopher enjoyed spending a good deal of the morning in bed with Ellen, discussing the possible interpretations of various articles, only one item seemed of particular interest.

Governor Clayton's Daughter Lost at Sea

The headline had caught Ellen's eye and they had learned that Felicity Clayton's body had been lost en route to New Orleans for burial, when the boat carrying her had crashed into a lock. All efforts to recover her body had failed.

How this information might factor into their revenge theory was a question he and Ellen could only debate.

"We can safely pass our society column along now." Christopher set their article on top of the stack at the foot of the bed.

"We should make a copy of it, just in case."

"Good idea," he said. "We'll make a pit stop in the office before we return the newspapers to the library. I'm sure Olaf won't mind."

Ellen only replied with a vague "Hmm," as her attention was fixed in the dresser mirror where she applied makeup, a ritual he found rather fascinating, although he couldn't remember any other woman he'd dated raising a similar interest with her grooming habits.

Not so with Ellen. He noticed everything about her, from the way she'd tucked her hair behind her ears this morning in a sassy look that showed off her face to the way she'd dressed in a simple gown of blue and green checks with puffy sleeves. Even better, the accompanying long yellow apron had extended him the pleasure of fastening not one, but two sets of buttons.

He'd opted for much more casual attire, as well, wearing comfortable trousers held up with suspenders and knee-high boots that lent themselves to searching the nooks and crannies of the guest bedrooms for the diary.

And that was how they began their day. After stopping by the office to make the copy Ellen had suggested, they headed straight to the second floor.

"If Mac convinced Harley not to leave the diary in the library, then I'm voting for one of these bedrooms. Young girls are notorious for hiding diaries under their pillows. Keeping them handy to jot down their dreams."

She sounded so matter-of-fact, but he found the idea of a young Ellen penning private fantasies charming. "Did you keep your diary under your pillow, love?"

She paused in the doorway of the sunrise bedroom, slim fingers curving around the doorjamb as she turned to glance up at him. "Um, well, I suppose so. For a while." A thoughtful frown settled between her brows. "A very little while. I didn't really have much time for that sort of thing."

She'd missed too many opportunities for fun, in his opinion. An oversight he'd take great pleasure helping her correct. Hooking a knuckle beneath her chin, he tipped her head toward him and dropped a kiss on those kissable lips. "If I buy you a diary, will you write your dreams about me in it?"

She took a step backward and laughed lightly. "The whole point is privacy, Christopher. If you knew about my diary, you could read all about my deepest secrets."

"That's also the point. I'd like to see you make time to indulge that fanciful streak you try so hard to hide."

She stared down her nose at him, a look that implied he didn't know what he was talking about. Christopher let her retreat to a comfortable distance, but didn't buy her denial for an instant. Ellen was a romantic at heart. He knew it. She knew *he* knew it, which is why, he suspected, she worked so hard to present herself otherwise.

Unlike the plantation's spacious suites, the guest bedrooms were spread along the second floor in the east and west wings, each area offering a different view of the grounds. The east wing boasted the manicured oak alley leading to Félicie Allée; the west, the lush gardens leading to the bayou.

Charting the bedrooms with the map revealed a great deal about Brigitte's personality that Ellen found significant. "The waiter told us she decorated all these bedrooms to accommodate her different moods. Look at the names, Christopher. Summer, sunrise, vineyard, pearl, rose, forest. Brigitte must have had a very whimsical side to her personality to come up with names like these."

"I'll bet she named the garden and sky suites, too."

Ellen nodded, sending a lock of sable hair onto her cheek before sweeping it back behind her ear. "Even more important, she wasn't afraid to indulge herself."

"What gives you that idea?"

"The fact that she didn't take one of the suites her brother offered her. She commandeered his whole house, instead."

"Makes sense," Christopher said. "And reinforces that the captain indulged her. I don't know what that means to us."

"Maybe we will if we can find that diary."

Pleased to see Ellen enjoying herself, Christopher

helped her search the sunrise bedroom, a decidedly feminine room decorated in pastel shades of pink and gold,
with cypress furnishings and rush-bottom chairs from the
period.

Ellen dug through a dresser, armoire and desk, while he
went through the closet and the sea chest at the foot of the
bed. Though they turned up nothing significant there, or
in the nearby pearl and forest rooms, Christopher couldn't
be more pleased.

Today Ellen seemed to have taken a huge step forward
in allowing herself to be swept up in the fantasy of the
game, taking charge of their investigation and dragging
him from room to room in their search. Christopher let her
take the lead, enjoying a glimpse of a very focused Ellen
who was clearly comfortable in charge. An Ellen who
seemed to be opening up to share her thoughts and discuss
her theories more readily than she had the previous day.

He guessed this new closeness between them was a result of their lovemaking of the previous night. They'd
overcome the hurdle of sleeping together, and the press
hadn't arrived to plaster news of the event in the papers
to publicly humiliate her and her family.

Now if he could just keep the ground he'd gained until
he put the next hurdle behind them...

He focused on seizing small opportunities to encourage
her to talk. He liked that breathy quality to her voice when
she came across something that peaked her interest, enjoyed watching her eyes light up when some revelation
clicked in her brain.

While he searched through an antique rosewood buffet
in the vineyard room—a room featuring delicate hand-
painted vines on the green walls—Lennon's comment
about the Talbot family's reaction to Ellen's career choice
caught in his brain and wouldn't let go.

Personally, I don't think a one of them has a clue why she chose that career, but it was what Ellen wanted, so they rallied behind her.

The point wasn't that her family had supported her, but that Ellen had felt strongly enough about her career to buck the Talbot family's preference for law and politics. This was a significant piece of the puzzle—much more of an advance in solving the mystery of Ellen than solving the mystery of the diary's whereabouts.

"I'm beginning to think we may be off base," he admitted.

Ellen sat back and exhaled hard, blowing wisps of hair from her brow. "Where else would Mac and Harley hide the diary?"

"The bathroom?" he suggested, remembering the derisive comment they'd overheard Harley make in the garden yesterday.

Ellen shrugged. "What do we have to lose? But let's go through the summer room and the parlor first. They're the only two rooms left in this wing that we haven't searched. We could split up to cover more ground."

"I'd rather we search fast together."

He didn't want to split up and risk losing the easy camaraderie they'd spent the morning sharing. But his plan wasn't meant to be. They hadn't made it through the doorway of the summer bedroom before Ellen stopped short, causing him to bump into her. Peering over her head to see the trouble, he discovered a couple, also garbed in historical costumes, sitting on the floor in front of a sea chest, locked in a very passionate embrace.

Lennon and Josh.

They sprang apart at the intrusion. Lennon looked surprised, but Josh scowled.

"You again, Sinclair? What's with you interrupting me and my wife lately?"

"Oops, sorry, guys." Ellen glanced between them with a frown, clearly not understanding Josh's reference, before she sidestepped him and left the room.

Lennon only laughed. "Bye, you two. Go have fun."

Christopher retreated and caught up with Ellen in the hallway, immediately noticing the heightened color in her cheeks. Two thoughts struck him simultaneously. The first was the similarity to his and Ellen's encounter in the library yesterday—an encounter she was surely remembering, given her blush.

The second was that neither Lennon nor Josh had been remotely embarrassed to be caught kissing. Public affection was clearly their right—not only by marriage, but because they held their love up for everyone to see.

That thought brought to mind Lennon's warning of the previous night.

Ellen has to choose to let her guard down.

And though Christopher had managed not to dwell on that thought all morning, he knew Lennon was right. But he still had time to convince Ellen.

He linked his arm through hers and forced a smile. "I'd say there are definite advantages to marriage, don't you think?"

She only lifted that cool hazel gaze. Color still rode in her cheeks, but her expression otherwise might have been sculpted from porcelain.

"I suppose so. Although I'm not sure even a wedding ring and vows can smooth over being caught *in flagrante delicto.*"

"They were kissing," he scoffed, curbing his impulse to demonstrate the differences. First he'd wrap his arms around her...engage that sweet mouth in a hello kiss...then proceed to work his way down the tasty skin of her throat. The love seat in front of the window looked promising, although if he sat her on that table she'd be the perfect height to wrap her legs around his waist....

Damn if propriety wasn't the better part of valor today.

"Rule number three of the Talbot family code of conduct: *Public displays of affection invite public comment and speculation.*" Ellen shook her head, sending her hair swaying around those rosy cheeks. "Nasty business."

"Don't you think that a married couple so obviously in love sets a good example?"

She frowned. "I suppose."

"You suppose? I thought tax breaks for married couples was part of your mother's platform." He forged on. "Isn't marriage also a part of the Talbot family code of conduct?"

"*After* a reasonable engagement."

"A decent romance hero should be able to sweep you off your feet without worrying about reasonable terms of engagement."

"Ooh, you weren't kidding when you said you've been boning up on heroes."

Lifting her chin with his finger, he tipped her pretty face up. "I never kid when it comes to my feelings for you."

"This is real life, Christopher. Not one of my authors' stories." She took a step back and broke contact.

Curtailing another impulse to pull her against him and wipe away that disdainful look with a kiss, Christopher simply said, "Come on. Let's go search the parlor."

They didn't wind up in the parlor, but back in the vineyard bedroom.

"It should be that room." Christopher glanced down at the map.

Ellen sighed. "Turn the map around, hero. See, it's here, *across* the hall."

Christopher rolled the map up, instead. He'd take her word. But they hadn't crossed the hall before Ellen came to a standstill and peered up at the wall.

He followed her gaze. "Like it?"

"It's a Pinabel."

Augustin Pinabel was a French artist who'd made a career of accepting commissions to paint the South's great plantations in the early part of the eighteen hundreds. Christopher and Ellen had first come across the artist while visiting Miss Q's erotic art gallery here in New Orleans. While Christopher had enjoyed the display, Ellen had been charmed by the watercolors depicting long-ago life in the Deep South.

When an exhibition of Pinabel's work had come to the Metropolitan Museum of Art, Christopher had finagled tickets from a client to opening night.

"I believe you're right."

"I know I'm right. Look, here's his signature." She was studying the piece intently. "This looks like Bayou Doré, don't you think, Christopher? He must have painted Félicie Allée on a sunny afternoon." She frowned. "But what's this gorgeous watercolor doing hidden away up here on the second floor?"

"It brings the outdoors where there aren't any windows."

"What a lovely idea. I'll bet you're right." Ellen's smile lit up the dim corridor even more than did the sunny Pinabel, and by the time they made it into the parlor, Christopher was suffering the effects of that smile big-time.

The parlor was actually a double parlor—a huge room with dramatic windows bordered by floor-to-ceiling draperies. Christopher didn't see many places to hide a diary, despite the room's size, and they checked out a buffet and several small tables rather quickly before Ellen stepped outside to see if the door to the summer bedroom had opened yet.

She'd no sooner left the room than her phone rang.

Christopher debated ignoring it, but given Ellen's obligation to those in possession of her private number, he didn't think she'd appreciate missing a call. He reached for her purse and picked up on the fourth ring.

"Hello." He recognized the 212 area code on the display—not Ellen's work number—and waited for the Talbot on the other end to identify him or herself.

"Who's this?" a male voice asked.

Ellen's dad. "Christopher Sinclair, Mr. Talbot. How are you, sir?"

There was a beat of silence on the other end. "Fine, Christopher. Thank you. I always enjoy the lull after an election. How about you? I didn't realize you were participating in the training session. Ellen didn't mention it."

He supposed that shouldn't come as a surprise. "Southern Charm Mysteries is run by mutual friends."

Glancing at the door, he hoped to see Ellen walking back through it before her father got around to asking the question that was hanging between them.

What are you doing with my daughter?

She was nowhere to be seen.

"Ellen stepped out of the room for a minute, sir, but I expect her to be right back," Christopher said, deciding a hasty retreat was his best bet. "Would you like to wait, or shall I have her return your call?"

"Just give her a message, Christopher. I'll call back with the details. Tell her the committee voted unanimously and the award is a go. If there's a problem getting a commercial flight out of New Orleans tomorrow, I'll make private arrangements.''

''Got it.''

''Now tell me how work's going. How did that deal you were working on the last time we spoke wind up? What was it—a vacation resort on the Black Sea?''

''Yes, sir. We acquired the property on our terms shortly after you killed me during the last golf game we played.''

Mr. Talbot chuckled. ''It's nice talking to you again, Christopher. Take care.''

''You as well, sir.'' The pleasantry popped out on autopilot, leaving him free to absorb that one more day wasn't nearly enough time to convince Ellen to take a chance on him.

''LENNON AND JOSH are still in there,'' Ellen said upon her return to the parlor. She was *not* going to speculate on what they were doing in the summer bedroom. She only hoped the diary wasn't in there and that her newlywed friends remembered to lock the door this time.

One glimpse of Christopher's face warned her that something wasn't right, and her gaze slipped to the phone he held.

Her phone.

''Your dad called.''

His voice sounded uncharacteristically devoid of emotion, and she knew instantly what her dad had called to say.

''Mom's getting the award?''

''Yes.''

Usually these calls of duty were only inconveniences that required scheduling gyrations and breathless flights here and there. Not today. Exhaling a huge sigh, she dropped into the closest chair and avoided Christopher's gaze.

"Your dad said if there was trouble getting a commercial flight out tomorrow, he'd arrange private transportation. He said he'd call back later."

That was it. Message delivered.

And Christopher didn't have to say another word. His voice had been completely unreadable, any hint of emotion concealed beneath an oddly controlled tone for a man who usually wore his heart on his sleeve.

She had herself to thank for this particular change, knew he only dealt with her the way she was comfortable dealing with him. With distance. With no surplus emotion to confuse the exchange. No emotional honesty. He was playing the hero again by not burdening her with his reaction to this change in plans.

Then again, he didn't have to. Ellen felt his disappointment as though it were rolling off him like a mist from the bayou. He knew she would leave tomorrow.

And he wasn't going to try to change her mind.

He was going to let her go. *Again.*

The thought blindsided her, so staggering that she sucked in a deep breath to dispel the sensation, hoped Christopher didn't notice. Some part of her, a deep-down part she hadn't acknowledged before, wished he would convince her to stay, just like she'd wanted him to come after her three months ago.

I thought you didn't believe romance heroes existed anywhere but in books, Lennon had said. *Sounds like you're looking for one.*

Ellen wanted Christopher to say something, *anything* to give her a reason to shirk off her duty. She wanted him to rescue her like a bloody hero, like a pirate captain sailing in to save his heroine from the evil villain.

She wanted him to guilt her, or seduce her, *something* to bolster her courage to do the unthinkable—blow off the award ceremony. She didn't want to leave Félicie Allée, or stop sleuthing out clues, or give up the only nights she had to sleep safely in Christopher's bed.

But he didn't say a word. He respected her enough to let her make her choices.

Even if it meant letting her board a plane tomorrow.

Even if it had meant letting her go three months ago.

Ellen came face-to-face with the terrible fact that only a coward would need to be pushed into staying. She didn't get a chance to absorb this sudden insight before he dropped the cell phone back into her purse and pushed himself off the love seat.

"Not much more to search in here," he said, not cool or distant, only matter-of-fact and businesslike.

And just like that, they were back to the mystery again.

He went to glance at the mantel of a fireplace, perusing the ornamental miscellany as though the entire world hadn't shifted since she'd left the room.

What had ever made her think this man had no control over his emotions, that he was an emotional powder keg subject to the whim of his impulses and daredevil desires?

She'd been so wrong. This man who contemplated the knickknacks was so distant, so remote that she knew without a doubt he was as in control of his emotions as she'd ever been. Which meant that his living life so openly and honestly, and, yes, adventurously wasn't about succumbing to impulses and whims, but about choices he'd made.

"Look at this, Ellen."

Forcing herself to stand, to move, she closed the space, each step providing a normalcy she clung to, a distraction.

She glanced at the miniature he held, a beautiful young woman with sleek dark hair and big eyes. "Brigitte?"

He flipped the portrait over, and Ellen scanned the name on the back, gazed up in surprise at Christopher.

"Felicity," he said. "What's her portrait doing here?"

She had no idea, though if she'd had enough of a grip on her faculties to play the *what if* game, she could have come up with numerous possibilities.

But Ellen couldn't concentrate on games now. Not when her pulse jumped into action and her breath came in wispy bursts.

He'd called her Ellen, not *love,* an endearment she'd grown accustomed to hearing. An endearment she hadn't even acknowledged she liked until now, when he had retreated behind the formality of her name.

12

The Study

CHRISTOPHER WOULD KEEP his mouth shut if it killed him. He wouldn't try to convince Ellen to stay. He wouldn't wrap his arms around her and tip that sweet mouth toward his and kiss her until she admitted she didn't want to leave.

Ellen has to choose to let her guard down.

Ellen also had to choose how best to balance her obligations and where to fit him into the equation. Without a word, he handed her the miniature portrait, watched her turn it over to study the young girl's image as though it could somehow answer the questions its appearance raised.

"This miniature suggests a personal connection that we hadn't considered," she said softly. "But to which La-fever—Julian or Brigitte?"

She didn't meet his gaze, and her impending departure stood between them like a wall, no less an obstruction for its invisibility. The mystery provided her the perfect place to retreat from the emotion of the moment, from the unasked questions.

"A personal connection might substantiate our revenge theory," he said, letting her slip away, deciding that keeping his mouth shut just might kill him.

But on a gut level Christopher knew that now was not the time to push her. She was too tightly wound, as though she expected him to come at her in a full frontal assault.

She'd promised him the whole session and was reneging on that promise.

But Christopher was nothing if not skilled in personal relations. Pushing her, or seducing her, or even heaping on the guilt would only give her something to react to, something to help her retreat even farther away.

"Most likely Brigitte had known Felicity since they were both young women about the same age," he said, a change of direction. "How do we follow up on that assumption?"

"Let's give some thought to how they might have known each other. The Lafevers obviously didn't swing with the same social set as the rest of upper-crust New Orleans, if we've interpreted our clue correctly."

"Which leaves what else? Church, proximity—"

"School." Ellen finally lifted her gaze to his, clearly willing to let the mystery sweep them from the turbulent emotional place they'd been. "The waiter said Brigitte attended a fancy school in New Orleans. Given the education system of the time, that would mean a finishing school for young women."

"The school's owners probably wouldn't snub a student whose wealthy brother was willing to pay the tuition. Even if the rest of New Orleans's high society did."

Ellen's eyes sparkled, a stunning display of snapping gold fire and jewel-green lights.

"I'll bet Brigitte and Felicity went to school together," she said. "If we could just find the diary, we'd most likely be able to confirm that."

"Julian had to pay tuition."

"His study?"

"Right." Retrieving the treasure map from where he'd left it on the love seat beside her purse, Christopher scanned the floor plan. "It's in the east wing. Let's go."

Gathering up their belongings, he led her out the door, purposely ignoring the fact lunch would be served downstairs in a few minutes. His appetite had gone the way of the morning's good mood since he'd answered her phone. Right now, he had a chance to get her caught back up in the chase. He was going for it.

As much as the parlor was a place where guests of both sexes could be entertained in comfort, the study was clearly the captain's retreat. Mahogany paneling covered the walls and the black walnut furnishings comprised freestanding bookshelves, comfortable chairs and a massive desk that could hold all sorts of clues to Félicie Allée's master.

A man who was apparently a collector...although Christopher couldn't imagine of what practical use that information could be. Nautical navigation equipment of the period had been housed behind glass-fronted shelves, while specimen coins, trophies, maps and even a variety of hunting equipment were displayed in cabinets and huge chests.

He recognized the master's private domain in the tobacco jars, decanters of port and brandy, and business papers scattered around the room. A place to discuss business. And pay bills.

"I'll go through the desk," he said.

"I'll look around and get a feel for our captain. This was his place. It'll reveal a lot about who he was."

Christopher couldn't quite rally a smile at how singlemindedly she pursued her character study of their murderer. Instead, he turned his attention to the drawers and files, seizing the chance to consider how best to bump up his timetable to accommodate this change in plans.

The desk proved jam-packed, and as Christopher waded through stacks of bills and receipts for stone, lumber and glass, he decided the only way to proceed with Ellen was to lower his expectations. He'd meant to go for the gold during this event, but he'd settle for getting her to agree to see him again. He just needed a chance to continue his seduction in New York and convince her he could fit into her life.

Preoccupied with his thoughts, Christopher almost flipped past a bill he might not have noticed but for the red ink marking it in arrears. He slid the bill from the pile to consider it more closely.

"Look at this," he said.

Ellen had been kneeling in front of a sideboard where a globe and a variety of scientific gadgets were displayed. She glanced up at him. "What is it?"

"A bill for a huge lumber purchase that's in arrears."

"Really?" Shoving soft bangs back from her eyes, she frowned. "I thought the captain was fabulously wealthy."

"That's the impression I had, too." Christopher set the bill back inside the folder. "Maybe revenge isn't the only motive. Maybe money factors."

Ellen didn't reply—just sat there with her checked skirts spread around her, looking entirely kissable with a pouty frown.

Then she inhaled sharply. "Christopher, remember what Miss Q said in the garden?"

"What?"

"That the British approached the captain and Jean Lafitte about using their ships to attack New Orleans. Remember what she said—the captain convinced Lafitte to pass this information along to the U.S. government *for a price.*"

"You think he needed the money?"

She nodded. "Assuming he did sell the information, who would pay the bill?"

Christopher sat back in his chair and folded his arms

across his chest. "A public official would be my guess. The governor or the mayor."

"Both of whom were guests at Félicie Allée the weekend Felicity was murdered."

"What if they thought the presidential pardon should have been enough payment?"

She frowned. "That's a big *what if.*"

"*What ifs* are all we've got right now."

And Ellen's game was all Christopher had to breach the distance her father's phone call had created.

"Well, it's a possibility." She relaxed, a visible release of tension that had her sitting back on the carpet, tucking her knees beneath her and looking up at him. "The captain wasn't the only one to leave the bayou. Jean Lafitte had a falling-out shortly after the war that made him relocate to Texas. Following your logic, he might have left because the government issued the pardon but then stiffed him the money."

"How do you know about Jean Lafitte? Did you come across something in the newspapers?"

"No, it's fact. Susanna has a knack for getting history into her stories without making them read like textbooks."

"Clever, love." He smiled, hoping to bridge the distance even more. "Then the governor must have been the one holding out. The mayor had a son who was also here at Félicie Allée."

"That's right. Noah."

"If revenge over money was the motive, it makes sense the captain would kill the governor's daughter and not bother with the mayor's son."

"But Felicity was a young girl and the captain had a sister. I just don't see it."

What she did see, though, was something on the floor that had her scrambling on her knees to pull up the edge of the rug. "Christopher, come help me. I think I've found something."

Kneeling beside her, he lifted the corner of the heavy wool rug she struggled with, to reveal a small trapdoor in the floor.

"Beautiful and brilliant."

She shot him a sidelong glance, eyes glinting, excitement heightening the color in her cheeks. Then she slipped a fingertip into a metal ring in the wood and lifted the door.

A centuries-old safe.

"I wonder what the captain was stashing in his floor-boards?" She opened the top to the rectangular metal box and withdrew several official-looking documents and a stack of envelopes tied together with a silk ribbon.

"Another trick you picked up from Susanna's books?"

"Lennon's, actually," she replied while scooting backward so he could drop the rug into place. "She used a similar device in *Milord Spy,* the book she just won the RAVE Award for."

Christopher crossed the room, locking the door before anyone stumbled upon them and their discovery. As he turned the key in the lock, the irony of the action didn't escape him. He went to sit beside Ellen, remembering his earlier thought about wanting to lock her inside this room.

Be careful what you wish for....

"So, what have you got?" He sat down and accepted the papers she handed him.

"Looks like the deed to Félicie Allée and some other documents about the property."

"What about those?"

She untied the silk ribbon binding the stack of enve-lopes. "They look like love letters."

Content with his business documents, Christopher perused the information, found that in addition to the deed, he held the land surveys, which showed the bordering property.

"The mayor is the neighbor Josh and Lennon were talking about, the one who wasn't happy about the Lafevers moving in," Christopher said. "Which might just tie into our money-revenge motive. Maybe the mayor told the governor to withhold payment to force the captain into losing the plantation. If the captain couldn't pay his bills..."

He trailed off because Ellen clearly wasn't listening to a word he said. She was scanning a letter with an expression of growing amazement.

"What is it?" he asked.

"You're not going to believe this."

"Then, don't make me guess."

Her gaze pierced the distance, sparkling with excitement, and in that instant, Christopher knew he'd never loved this woman more than when she was breathless and animated—a mood he would help her explore if only she'd give him the chance.

She held out the letter. "The captain and Felicity were in love."

THERE WERE FOUR LETTERS proving that Felicity Clayton was a young woman head-over-heels for the socially unacceptable privateer. Ellen insisted they read them all before Christopher unlocked the study door and risked anyone happening upon them. And luckily she did because someone tried to get into the room.

"Shh." Ellen signaled Christopher to silence with a finger on his lips.

It had been an unconscious gesture, but one that introduced an intimacy to the moment she hadn't planned on. Before she even realized what he was about, his lips parted, drawing her finger inside, a suggestive motion that made her gasp.

Those too-blue eyes glittered.

Ellen sat back, tugged her finger away, a withdrawal from his warm velvet mouth and the thousand soft sensations swirling inside, melting the distance between them.

Christopher wouldn't let her.

Nipping her fingertip with his teeth, he halted her retreat, sucked her finger back inside his mouth with a slow pull so suggestive of lovemaking that those soft swirling sensations began to crash in on each other like waves.

Knocking echoed through the room, followed by "Whoever's in there, are you going to be much longer?"

Susanna. One of the last two people on this plantation that Ellen wanted to have find her sequestered behind a locked door with Christopher. She'd probably already been to the summer bedroom and encountered Josh and Lennon.

Christopher held on defiantly, several interminable moments ticking by before he relinquished his grip.

"What was that all about?" she whispered.

"You tasted good." Without another word of explanation, he unfolded the next letter and began to read.

That was it. Christopher wanted and he took. Such a simple explanation to account for this riot of emotion inside her. But an explanation that was quintessential Christopher Sinclair. Though he wasn't guided by impulse as she'd once believed, he'd chosen to take what he wanted from life. Pleasure, fun and excitement were all aims he considered worthy pursuits.

She had to admire a man who took what he wanted. That sort of focus suggested strength of character…

Which Christopher had in spades.

…and a love for life's pleasures that seemed positively liberating to a woman who spent so much time talking herself out of what she wanted because of potential consequences.

Which she did in spades.

An undeniable and sobering little truth. One that was too much to tackle while she sat so close to this man, with their knees bumping, their fingers brushing when he returned the letter, and her insides a jumble of awareness that made his every breath whisper through her like a warm breeze.

Ellen forced herself to focus on her own letter, a letter that gushed with the longing of a young girl for a man more than a decade older. A very noble man, apparently, who wouldn't denigrate their love or risk her reputation.

"This wasn't a crush. It was a love affair that explains so much," she said, grateful—yet again—for the mystery that provided a distraction from the turmoil of self-analysis.

"Explains what?" Christopher glanced up, only this time Ellen was ready to take on those eyes. "I haven't found a clue about why the captain might murder her."

"Not why he would murder her, but why he *wouldn't*. The captain and Felicity were an item, so I think we can safely rule out revenge."

"One of Miss Q's red herrings, do you think?"

Ellen shrugged. "Possibly."

"Lovers' quarrel? Passion killing? An accident?"

"We need to know more about their relationship, because I don't see how these two could have gotten together. Think about it, Christopher. Felicity was the governor's daughter. Society didn't accept the Lafevers, which meant they wouldn't have run into each other at events like the Mardi Gras ball. Unless…" A light bulb went off in her head. "Society wouldn't accept the Lafevers, but *what if* that didn't stop two young girls from becoming friends?''

Christopher smiled. More of a grin, actually, but enough of one that his dimples flashed and told her he was very pleased.

Ellen wasn't going to overanalyze the crazy fluttering response that began low in her belly or why those dimples mattered so much.

''This does explain why the miniature was in the parlor,'' he pointed out. ''Felicity was important to the captain. Brigitte could have been their cover—''

''Doesn't wash. The governor wasn't going to let his daughter visit Félicie Allée on weekends off with her school chum even if the president was issuing a pardon. We're missing a piece here. A big one.''

''Perhaps the money clue isn't a red herring.''

''What if Felicity was in love with the captain and the governor was holding on to the money to…oh, I don't know, *convince* the captain to discourage his daughter's affections?''

''Blackmail makes more sense. We need to find Brigitte's diary. If her best friend and brother were an item, she would have written about that in her diary, don't you think, love?''

Love. The endearment slipped from his lips in a rich burst of sound that spiked those tingles inside her to a new pitch and drove home her earlier realization that she liked being this man's love, no matter how much she told herself that her feelings were about sex and cravings.

Whoa.

Ellen inhaled deeply to dispel the suddenly chilling sensation that wiped away all her yummy feeling of well-being. She was not going to tackle this right now. Absolutely not.

"We need to find Mac and Harley."

"Do you think they're just going to tell us where the diary is if we ask?"

"No. But I'm hoping they'll be so busy bickering that we can get the drop on them and overhear something important."

Christopher only nodded, apparently seeing the logic even if he couldn't understand her sudden need for a distraction. But she couldn't tackle another cold hard truth about how much she felt for this man, not right now. She needed to think, and she couldn't do that under the influence of those eyes.

He lifted the rug so she could return the letters to their hideaway, before leading her from the study.

As it turned out, Ellen found all the distraction she needed without having to search for Harley and Mac at all.

The sound of voices brought her and Christopher to a stop in the foyer off the hall, and just as Ellen slowed to hear who was speaking, a hand lashed out, grabbed her by the arm and pulled her inside a…coat closet?

Grabbing on to Christopher to steady herself, she wound up dragging him backward, too, where he stumbled, stomped on her foot with his size twelves and came up hard against her.

"Ouch—"

"Shh!" Harley and Mac hissed at the same time.

Ellen caught her breath, disbelieving that for the second time in as many days, she'd wound up a party of adults sandwiched in a room no bigger than a shower stall. Only this time, instead of four women in voluminous skirts, she now had to contend with two strapping men well over six feet tall. At least there was no towel rack digging into her ribs.

By comparison, Christopher appeared delighted at the arrangement, taking advantage of the close quarters to snuggle up against her until he molded to her backside like a spoon. She could feel his sex—behaving itself, fortunately—pressed against the small of her back, his body heat penetrating even her gown. She tried vainly not to bestow damaged toes to Harley, who was making an equally valiant effort to keep at least a little breathing space between them.

Mac frowned, but didn't have to issue another reminder to keep quiet, because the sound of laughter filtered through the foyer and they all quieted to listen.

"The training isn't over until Sunday night," Tracy was saying. "That's two whole days."

"I can think of any number of ways to put that time to use, gorgeous, but I don't think Ms. McDarby will look kindly on me fraternizing with her guests. I need this job."

The man's voice wasn't familiar, and Ellen didn't think he was the actor-waiter who had dropped clues at dinner last night.

More laughter, and then Tracy said, "Who says we have to let her know?"

Ellen couldn't say she was surprised. Though her relationship with Tracy was largely professional, she did know Tracy blew through men like Ellen blew through felt-tip markers when revising a manuscript.

Even so, it took another five minutes for Tracy to convince the guy to meet her later that night, which, considering the guy's worries for his job, Ellen thought, was an impressively short time.

Their voices finally faded away and Christopher led the campaign to evacuate the closet. Ellen gulped fresh air, almost stumbling as Christopher swept her aside to make room for Harley, who burst from the closet like she'd been shot from a gun.

"What a waste of time!" she said. "We've been suffocating in that broom closet—"

"*Coat* closet." Mac emerged behind her, straightening his cravat. "It was worth a try. After dinner last night, who knew what we might overhear."

Made sense to Ellen. Tracy had given away the farm last night, but apparently Harley was of another opinion.

"She's trying to eat the guy for dinner. And whose idea was it to dress up in these getups, anyway?" She tugged at her skirt with a huff. "This is the stupidest thing I've ever done. And you're standing on my hem so I can't move."

Mac caught Ellen's gaze and winked. "Forgive me, angel, but I think you look lovely. Who'd have guessed? Have you ever worn a dress before?"

Harley tipped her nose in the air and turned her back on Mac in a pointed gesture. She forced a smile, then lifted her skirt and swept off into the hall.

Mac shrugged. "Hope you all have better luck than we've been having."

He strode off in the same direction.

"Well." Ellen couldn't think of anything else to say.

"Well, right back at you." But Christopher wasn't smiling. "Josh should start looking at severance packages for those two. And Miss Q, too, if that actor takes Tracy up on her offer."

"I don't think the guy stood a chance. You heard how she badgered him. She's into romance, not relationships, which I assume accounts for her propositioning a stranger."

"Doesn't matter."

She didn't disagree and found his attitude another testimony that while Christopher might be proficient at bending the rules, he wasn't the wild man she'd accused him of being. They'd both gotten caught up in the library yesterday, but that didn't make him any more impulsive than she was.

"On the upside, at least we've learned that Mac doesn't think their investigation is going well," he said. "He's a private investigator, so that's got to count for something. But Harley really hates that costume."

Christopher shrugged. "Some people don't get into role-playing."

Before she knew what he was doing, he'd dropped a kiss onto the top of her head.

"But I'm glad that's not a problem you have, love, because you look good enough to eat."

"Christopher." Ellen danced away. After all, they were standing just outside the hall where anyone could walk through. "No, that's not my problem." She had quite a few others at the moment, but fortunately *that* wasn't one of them. "I think the historical costumes are charming."

But Christopher had already known that, she decided, remembering a conversation they had had while dating. She had thought Félicie Allée was the perfect romance novel setting and that the only thing missing was the costumes....

The costumes.

She glanced at Christopher, found him taking the treasure map from his pocket. He smiled absently as he unrolled the parchment, considering where they should go next, now that her idea of following Harley and Mac hadn't yielded anything productive. He looked so handsome in his double-breasted shirt, the suspenders emphasizing the breadth of his chest, the leanness of his waist....

Costumes weren't missing at Félicie Allée this weekend.

Neither was corn for the ducks.

Ellen walked the distance into the hall, needing to extract herself from the confines of the hallway. Christopher followed without comment, clearly absorbed in the map, and Ellen took a deep breath, concentrated on what it was that was bothering her about the costumes.

And whose idea was it to dress in these getups, anyway?

Harley's complaint rang in her head, and then suddenly pieces began falling into place, pieces to another mystery that had been right under her nose...the costumes.

Ellen thought she knew whose idea the costumes had been. The same person who'd filled the suite courtyard with all her favorite flowers.

And the menu with all her favorite foods. Filet. Tiramisu. Beignets. French coffee and espresso.

A Pinabel in the second-floor hall.

Even a vis-à-vis mirror, a piece she'd admired at a museum exhibition with Christopher.

All coincidences?

Ellen didn't think so.

Suddenly there was another mystery that needed to be solved, one far more important than what had driven a noble pirate captain to murder the young woman he loved.

Was Miss Q the only culprit involved in this weekend's setup or had the little matchmaker had a partner in crime?

13

The Drawing Room

"WHERE CAN I FIND Miss Q?" Ellen popped her head inside the office door and caught sight of Olaf, who sat behind the desk, looking the part of an old world plantation owner in his black cutaway jacket.

She'd parted company from Christopher, leaving him in the conservatory on their continued search for the diary.

"Miss Q said she was going to the drawing room to catalog the statuary and other pieces for the insurance company. She's been trying to make time for the past month."

"And you didn't offer to help, Olaf? I'm surprised."

He flashed her a smile that was dazzling against his dark skin. "I offered to do it for her, but she enjoys handling the pieces herself. She's a collector at heart, and getting Southern Charm Mysteries off the ground hasn't left her enough time to fully appreciate the acquisition of the plantation."

"I can only imagine. From what Lennon has said, you've both been working 'round the clock."

"We've been juggling historical restoration contractors with corporate attorneys and an advertising company. And then there was coming up with the scripts and training the actors."

"You're making me tired just listening to all that work." Ellen laughed, her gaze sliding to the full-scale floor plan of the plantation on the wall above Olaf's head. "Christopher has our map. Would you mind pointing out the drawing room for me?"

"Of course."

As Olaf stood behind the desk, she caught sight of a small, framed newspaper item hanging beside the map. Dated in June of 1820, it announced the marriage of a California luxury liner heiress and a successful hotelier. Ellen hadn't realized luxury liners had been around that long ago.

"Here it is." He pointed to another room on the ground floor in the east wing. "Just head straight down the hall. It'll be on your right."

"Thanks, Olaf." She waved and started on her way.

She found Miss Q alone, admiring what appeared to be a small trinket box.

"Hello, dear," she said, glancing up at Ellen's intrusion. "Christopher actually let you out of his sight? I'm surprised."

"Not willingly, trust me."

"Attentiveness is a good quality in a man. It means he's interested. My Joshua was always attentive to me, bless his soul, and Josh Three is the same with Lennon. Look at Christopher's parents. They're the love match of their generation."

Ellen wouldn't argue that point. She'd met Christopher's parents on numerous occasions and they were clearly very comfortable with public displays of affection. Christopher, too—though in all fairness while he'd always been attentive, he was never clingy, which was a quality that drove her crazy.

Miss Q held out the box she had been admiring, and Ellen drew near, realizing there were two companions of different sizes on the table.

"Aren't they lovely?" she asked. "They're Russian lacquer boxes that Julian brought home to Brigitte. I don't know that he actually acquired them in Russia, more likely he met up with some Russian smuggler in his travels."

Ellen traced the mother-of-pearl inlaid swan on the lid. "Seems likely," she said, then got to business. "I was hoping to speak with you alone."

"Certainly, dear. Have a seat." Miss Q motioned to the sofa before replacing the box beside its fellows.

Ellen did as she bade, waited until Miss Q arranged her taffeta skirt and settled beside her. Then she took Ellen's hands in her own and asked, "What can I do for you?"

"I'd like some answers."

"I won't be able to help you much with the mystery. I've told you all I can."

"I'm not asking about *Away with the Tide,* Miss Q. I'm more interested in *The Devil and Ms. Talbot.*"

Her blue eyes twinkled and, in that moment, Ellen couldn't help but compare the little whirlwind with another adventurer whose eyes, albeit a deeper shade of blue, twinkled in a very similar manner whenever he had mischief in mind, or sex. *Those* blue eyes always made her heart beat too fast.

"I want to ask you why you colluded with Christopher to set me up for this training."

Rule number six of sound business strategies: *Always make it appear as if you have more information than you want.*

"I told you, dear. I can spot grand passion a mile off. In your case, all the way across the eastern seaboard. You two are perfect for each other."

"How involved was Christopher in planning for my arrival?"

"Very involved."

"He told you...*things* about me, didn't he. Things that helped you tailor my arrangements."

"Well, of course he did, dear. He wanted Félicie Allée to be a place where you could feel safe and comfortable. He wanted you to relax and have fun while you were here. But he didn't tell me anything too personal. Christopher's a gentleman. You know that."

"He talked to you about the menu?"

She nodded.

"What about the garden in our suite?"

"He mentioned some of the varieties of flowers you like. It was no trouble to include them when the landscapers were laying out the arrangement for the courtyard."

Right. "And the costumes?"

She nodded again, her smile growing.

Ellen wanted to ask about the vis-à-vis mirrors, but found the memory of their reflection while making love snatched the question right from her lips.

"The Pinabel?"

"Isn't it just exquisite?" Miss Q squeezed Ellen's hands tightly. "Can you believe he acquired it?"

"And what...he just *lent* it to you?"

She nodded happily.

Sheesh. Ellen couldn't even imagine what that painting must have cost. And she supposed that answered her question about the mirrors, too.

"You went along with all this, Miss Q. You arranged your grand opening to accommodate me?"

"Of course I did, dear. I care about you and Christopher. He wants to seduce you and that's so very romantic."

She was smiling dreamily, and even though the controlled left side of Ellen's brain shrieked at the absurdity of this entire situation, the too-romantic right side couldn't help but appreciate how much effort he'd put into making her visit to Félicie Allée perfect.

"It's rather heroic, actually."

Miss Q actually giggled. "But of course he's heroic, dear. With a name like Byron, what else could he be?"

That statement stopped Ellen cold. "Excuse me? Did you just say *Byron?*"

"Yes, dear. Byron Christopher. You are familiar with the poet Lord Byron? He was a great romantic. Christopher's just like his namesake."

"Ah, yes, I've read his work. I just didn't realize Christopher's first name was Byron. He never mentioned it."

"Byron after the poet and Christopher after his grandfather. His mother loves Lord Byron's poetry and simply had to name her son after him. And you know how his father dotes on her." Miss Q leaned forward and said in a whisper, "Between you and me, dear, Christopher can't stand the name, though he'd never tell his mother that. Luckily for him, his grandfather couldn't stand the name, either, and refused to use it. From the time Christopher was old enough to talk, he would correct anyone who did." She smiled. "He's always had a mind of his own."

Well, that news certainly came as no surprise, and Ellen had no trouble envisioning a black-haired, blue-eyed little boy informing his entire family that he'd choose his own name, thank you very much.

She'd thought Christopher was impulsive, crazy even, but he was simply a man who knew what he wanted and wasn't timid about making sure he got it. Even when he was two years old.

And now he wanted her. Enough to talk Miss Q into planting gardenia and wisteria and having costumes designed. He'd even purchased a Pinabel.

Christopher possessed all the qualities she admired—on

the written page and in real life. Yet she'd run screaming, telling herself that heroes didn't exist outside of romance novels and that she didn't care for him.

She'd been lying, to Christopher and to herself. She cared that she'd never seen a childhood photo of him, could only guess at the beautiful child he'd been, with that charming smile and those big blue eyes.

She cared that she hadn't known his real name.

No doubt her mother's handlers had known. But she apparently hadn't paid close enough attention to the details of their preliminary report. And she hadn't allowed Christopher close enough to easily share something so little, yet so significant about him.

Why was she so afraid to abandon herself to the way Christopher made her feel? Why couldn't she trust herself to make the right choice?

Glancing down at the paper-thin hands still holding hers, Ellen couldn't help but think that here she was, sitting face-to-face with a woman who'd lived a life filled with passion, a woman who hadn't been afraid to trust herself and take chances.

"How did you know when you'd met *the one,* Miss Q?"

Those withered hands held hers firmly. "I knew when I'd met the man who made me feel more alive when I was with him than without him. Being together became more important than playing life by the rules."

A choice.

Through Lennon, Ellen knew enough about Miss Q's life to know that she'd been forced to make some very hard choices to be with the man she loved. Something in her kindly blue eyes suggested Miss Q wouldn't mind answering another personal question. "Did you ever regret your choice?"

"Not once in fifty-five years. I shared my life with the

man I loved. What greater aspiration is there? I let myself believe it would all work out, and it did.''

Another choice.

''Lennon chose to believe it would work out with Josh.''

''Yes, she did, dear. I don't mind telling you that I despaired she ever would. But she finally found the courage to let go of her silly notions that romance heroes belong in the bedroom. Look how happy she and Josh Three are now.''

Ellen nodded. She was well acquainted with Lennon's views regarding the differences between heroes and husbands. Then Lennon had met Josh, who'd blown all those ideas right out of the water. She'd taken a leap of faith to be with the man she loved and was living the rewards right now.

Ellen only had to look at Lennon and Josh to see they were both happy with their choices. Especially when she compared them to Tracy, who hadn't found a man to believe in yet, who'd taken to propositioning a stranger for a fling on a corporate training weekend so she wouldn't be alone.

Sleeping with a stranger wasn't an option for Ellen, which meant she would wind up alone.

Did she want to live her life alone?

Miss Q smiled thoughtfully. ''So what's stopping you from believing in your romance hero, dear?''

That question arrowed straight to the heart of matters.

I am.

Christopher loved her. He'd colluded with Miss Q to make sure Ellen knew how much he still loved her. No man had ever made her feel the way he did, and it wasn't just about lovemaking. Although there was no denying their sex was awesome.

"I'm stopping myself," she finally said, although her answer sounded beyond pathetic when she voiced it.

Miss Q only squeezed her hands reassuringly and Ellen suddenly understood that for all her outrageous behavior, Miss Q was a woman with more courage than anyone she knew.

I let myself believe it would all work out, and it did.

"You need to get out of your way, dear," Miss Q said honestly. "Why shouldn't you marry the man you love?"

Love. She'd agonized about the way Christopher always made her lose control, about the way he pushed her past her comfort zone, but she'd never had the courage to think about why he was able to do those things. She'd never allowed herself to admit how much he meant to her.

Why?

You'll find many people who would rather deal in denial than face their fears, her mother had once told her. *It's safer.*

Had Ellen been afraid?

She claimed to be a woman who knew what she wanted, but when it came to love, she'd been in serious denial. For three months she'd told herself she was over Christopher, only to have her authors force her to face the truth. For the past two days, she'd told herself she just needed to get him out of her system.

Gazing into Miss Q's knowing blue eyes, she admitted, "I need to take a hard look at what I want for my life." *At whether I have the courage to stop playing it safe.*

Miss Q smiled. "Now you're talking, dear. That's exactly what you need to do. Should I mention that Félicie Allée is the perfect place to puzzle out that particular mystery? After all, we specialize in mysteries here."

"Lucky for me."

She kissed the dear lady on the cheek, thanked her for

her candor and left the drawing room with Miss Q's voice still echoing in her head.

I let myself believe it would all work out, and it did.

Could Ellen find the courage to believe?

She didn't know. But she was determined to find out, because she loved Christopher. She had from the first time he'd shown up at her office during lunch hour with a loaf of freshly baked bread for the ducks.

CHRISTOPHER MANEUVERED THE skiff off the shore and hopped in, smiling when Ellen grabbed the sides as the boat rocked beneath his weight. "I won't let the gators get you."

She drew a deep breath, visibly steeling herself until the boat settled into an easy motion.

"Explain to me again why you think the diary might be out on the island?" he asked. "And why we have to look now."

It was midnight, dark except for a sliver of moon and a thousand stars jeweling the sky with an unearthly glow. Christopher would have preferred to be in their suite right now, in bed, but Ellen had insisted. So he'd aimed to please....

"Two reasons, actually. The first is what Mac said at dinner."

"He wasn't nearly as forthcoming as Tracy last night." Tracy, the woman who'd flirted all through dinner with a certain actor Christopher hoped had better sense than to trade a few hours with a beautiful romance author for his job at Southern Charm Mysteries.

Certain things were against the rules and Christopher understood them. Unfortunately, now was not an opportunity to point out to Ellen that he did occasionally follow rules.

"Mac may not have said as much but he gave us an important piece of the puzzle. He said that Felicity met Brigitte for a midnight meeting on the island while she'd been staying at the mayor's plantation."

"I know. Felicity told her that the governor was forcing her to marry the mayor's son, which means he and Harley know the girls were friends. But I don't recall Miss Q saying that clues would be planted outside the plantation."

"She didn't say they wouldn't be, either."

Christopher shrugged, pleased if for no other reason than that Ellen had allowed herself to get so caught up in the sleuthing that she'd coerced him into a midnight boat ride. A spontaneous action if ever he'd seen one.

"I wonder if Felicity ever met the captain on the island? They would have had to meet in secret and that wouldn't have been easy. It would have been romantic, though."

Especially on a night like this. "You know what's romantic?" When she lifted her gaze, he said, "You are."

And she was, sitting there with the moonlight bathing her creamy skin. She'd thrown on a summery dress and a pair of sandals. She had her legs stretched out before her, sleek, endless legs he couldn't stop thinking about tangled through his in this hazy night heat.

He wasn't going to suggest they find out how romantic the night could be. Not with only hours left to get a shot at the future. He'd reserve the pleasure of sex under the stars for another time. Right now, he needed to get Ellen to the island and then get her back to bed.

Tonight he'd play by the rules.

Rowing smoothly, he listened to the night sounds echoing across the water, unseen wildlife protesting their presence. Christopher remembered the sounds from his youth, from times spent on various family vacations and school trips.

He wondered what Ellen thought about the wild bayou night, but he wouldn't ask, not when he'd much rather know... "So, what's the other reason we're out here tonight?"

"There's something I want to discuss with you."

"Shoot," he said.

"You asked me why I'm so determined to play by the rules and I told you it was because living inside a fishbowl means my whole family lives with the consequences of my choices." Hiking her knee up on the bench, she stared out over the water, a casual stance that Christopher didn't buy for a minute. He didn't say a word, just continued to row, and waited.

"But I've been doing some soul-searching and I think it may be more than that, Christopher. I think I may be afraid of dragging someone into my life because being involved with me comes along with so much baggage."

"I see," he said, searching for a reply that would encourage her to keep talking. "Everyone has baggage, love. I happen to come along with a good bit myself, a job with lots of international travel, parents who act like hormonal teenagers—"

"Your parents aren't baggage. It's wonderful to see two people so much in love. Miss Q's grand passion in action."

He snorted. "If you'd caught your parents making out under the bleachers during a high school football game, you might have a different view."

"Felt like the fifth wheel, did you?"

"Let's just say it took me a while to appreciate the finer points of the situation." He paused, searching for the right words to ask the question that would fit another huge piece of the puzzle into place. "So what makes you doubt you're worth dealing with the baggage?"

"You know, I never realized I did until this weekend," she answered quietly. "I didn't have a clue. And I'm not sure I have an answer—or a complete answer, anyway."

"What have you come up with?"

She hesitated, perhaps searching, as he'd been, for the right words. He didn't push, just rowed in silence, contemplating the way the starlight made her skin glow.

"I guess I don't feel I measure up to my family," she finally said. "I've always been the odd man out, the one who takes a left turn when everyone else takes a right."

"That makes you interesting, not less than your family."

"If you'd been told you weren't the 'proper fit' for your family's alma mater because you were *interesting,* you might take a different view."

Christopher remembered his similar words. "Fair enough."

"When I think about it, I can't ever remember *not* feeling this way. My mother always says I march to the beat of a different drummer."

"Your family accepts your choices."

"Of course they do. They love me."

"None of this explains why you put so much energy into living by the rules, love. Last night you told me you limit your choices because you don't want to slip up. That's very…well, *focused,*" he said for lack of a better word.

Something he said seemed to hit home, because Ellen sat up, a thoughtful smile on her beautiful face. "I think all my slipups over the years have reinforced my feeling like the odd man out. I've gotten to the point where I'm trying to be invisible."

A true tragedy. "Everyone makes mistakes, love."

"But I've made some doozies."

"Nothing you've told me about sounds like a doozy."

"That's because I haven't told you about Steven."

The tone of her voice left no doubt that Steven didn't bring back happy memories. "Who's he?"

"A boy I went to high school with. My first love." Turning away, she gazed out over the water as though reliving memories she found difficult to share.

"So what put Steven in the doozy category?"

"An unfortunate series of choices and events, starting with us not respecting the baggage I come with. We were young and in love, and we wanted to see each other more than we were able to because of my father's job. Lots of nighttime functions. In our infinite sixteen-year-old wisdom, we resolved the problem by sneaking out late at night. Most of the time Steven would come get me in his car and we'd go cruising around. Sometimes we'd park. It was pretty innocuous, really. Or would have been, if my father hadn't held a position on the president's Cabinet."

Christopher watched Ellen in silence, her cool expression warning him that she needed to talk without interruption.

"In a nutshell…Steven's car was in the shop one night so I borrowed my brother's motorcycle, which would have been no problem because I knew how to ride it. But Steven had this guy thing going on, so I let him drive, which wouldn't have been a problem, either, if not for the reporter who'd been tailing us."

Christopher wished she would look at him. He wanted to see her eyes, try to divine what emotions were racing through her that she wouldn't share. But she kept her gaze on the water, kept her tone even. "How long had the reporter been following you?"

"About a week. We had no idea until later, of course. But that night we had the motorcycle, so when he came

up on us in the park, we realized we were being followed."
She sighed. "All I could see was the headline and how
disappointed my parents would be. I freaked. Steven tried
to be my knight in shining armor."

Finally turning back to him, she met his gaze, and
though darkness shadowed her eyes, he could see her regret.

"We took off. The reporter chased us. We wiped out in
a ditch. I was thrown clear, but Steven went with the bike.
Emergency surgery and twelve hours of not knowing
whether he'd wake up or what kind of condition he'd be
in if he did…well, thankfully, he did. And he was fine."

That wasn't the end of the story. Christopher knew it as
surely as he heard the heartache in her voice. "And afterward?"

"My father is a man with a lot of power. His people
swept everything under the rug since we were both minors.
It wasn't easy, but he did. I owe him a great deal. My
mom, too."

He didn't point out that all kids got in over their heads
and that caring, responsible parents usually helped pick up
the pieces. His own parents had come to his rescue while
he'd been growing up, more often than he could recall.
But he didn't want to put her in a position where she felt
the need to defend herself, so he asked, "What happened
to Steven?"

She shrugged. "He didn't want to see me anymore.
Didn't think dating me was worth putting up with all the
complications I came with. I certainly couldn't blame
him."

That casual shrug explained everything. Ellen had been
hurt. Because of the press, she'd lost the boy she'd loved—
almost literally.

He must have let something in his expression slip, because Ellen leaped to reassure him. "We were very young, Christopher. Our relationship wasn't meant to last."

"That doesn't change the fact that the press directly impacted your relationship and your life. That's a heavy load for a sixteen-year-old."

She nodded. "Perhaps even more than I realized. When I look back on so many of the choices I made, I seem to have spent a lot of energy dodging the spotlight."

Suddenly her career choice made sense, as did her willingness to stand up for what she had wanted. She had needed to go into a business that put distance between her and her family and indulge an idealistic side that all too often got buried beneath the rules.

Christopher also understood why Ellen had dragged him out here. Both the night and the boat gave them a distance they could never have while lying together in bed.

"I'm glad you talked to me, love."

And he was. She might be leaving Félicie Allée tomorrow, but now that he understood what he was up against, he stood a chance. If he could convince her to see him again once they got home, he could prove he'd willingly take on her "baggage," and be more than able to handle it.

But he wasn't going to push. Not now. Not until they were in bed and he'd loved his way past her defenses.

"I was long overdue an epiphany." She tipped her face to the sky and stretched out on the bench, soaking up the starlight as though she were tanning. "Thank you."

"You're crediting me? Why do I find that alarming?"

She laughed softly. "It's a good thing, really. You've made me stop and think about what I'm shutting out of my life, what I want for the future."

"You want me."

He hadn't meant literally, but she simply said, "I do."

And before he had a chance to register that she'd just admitted the very thing he'd wanted to hear, she followed up her statement by undoing the top button of her dress....

"Warm?" he asked.

"Mmm-hmm. The temperature hasn't dropped much."

Her fingers worked a second button, and Christopher leaned in for a better look. He may have decided against suggesting sex in the great outdoors tonight, but he was definitely not above enjoying the scenery. And this scenery was awesome. He could just about see the swell of her breasts as her bodice parted.

Then she went for a third button and those full breasts, covered only in a filmy *something,* spilled out.

"You must be really warm," he commented conversationally, not wanting to discourage her from this uncharacteristic display of boldness that was raising his temperature.

"I am. It's so hot tonight," she replied just as conversationally, before lifting a hand to sweep the hair off her neck.

Extending her arm had an amazing effect—both on Ellen's bodice and his rocketing body heat. This little show was intentional, so Christopher sat back, shut up and hoped she wouldn't stop. He'd be more than happy to row them in circles all night for a chance to help Ellen explore this daring side of her personality.

She was right, an epiphany was a good thing.

The fourth button slid free of its hole, then the fifth, sixth and seventh, revealing that the filmy little *something* she wore was so transparent that the stars reflected off her sleek curves.

Shrugging halfway out of her dress, Ellen met his gaze, looking as composed as if she were greeting the president, and asked, "You don't mind, do you?"

"Please, get comfortable."

One of them should be, and it wouldn't be him—not while sitting on this wooden bench with his erection growing stiff enough to use as an oar.

Slipping her arms through the sleeves, she let the dress slither in a puddle around her hips, leaving her upper body clad in nothing more than starlit silk so sheer her nipples smudged into dark sworls. "There, that's much better."

"I agree."

She sighed, tipped her face to the sky and closed her eyes, offering him the opportunity to caress her with his gaze, the way her every curve glistened in the growing mist.

Oh man, the view was just getting better and better.

They sat in silence as Christopher forced the oars through the water with careful strokes designed not to jar this beauty from her star-bathing. Her full breasts rose and fell with every breath and her nipples peaked through that whisper of silk. Her gorgeous body spread out before him, sleek and inviting, spiking his need to touch her and to know just how far she would go with her bold game.

But Ellen drove all questions from his mind when she lifted her bottom and shimmied the dress over her hips. Riveted, he watched as the lightweight fabric rode down those smooth thighs, along shapely calves, finally pooling around her feet. At *his* feet. This boat was not big.

Freeing herself from the circle of fabric, she stretched until her toes wiggled against his shoe.

The contact snapped him out of his daze. "You're not a pod person, are you?"

Ellen chuckled. "I'm not a pod person, Christopher."

"You do realize you're sitting practically naked in the middle of Bayou Doré, don't you?"

Her lashes fluttered open and she speared him with a sparkling gaze. "The real question is, have you noticed?"

"With both eyes and a few body parts."

"A few?"

"Mmm-hmm. My heart's pounding and my mouth is as dry as the sand on that island over there. And there's another body part just straining to make an appearance—"

"Your mouth is dry? I was hoping to make you drool." Letting her thighs drift apart, she aimed a vision of her barely covered sex his way.

With growing amazement Christopher watched her fingers glide slowly down the expanse of her stomach, along the juncture of her thighs, brushing aside the scrap of fabric and zeroing in on… Oh man, every drop of blood plummeted to his crotch so fast he felt dizzy.

When she rolled her fingertips in a suggestive motion that must have felt very good, judging by the way she shivered, Christopher knew he'd rowed them through a tear in the space-time continuum straight into the Twilight Zone. He'd recognized Ellen's potential for passion, but he'd had no idea how she would effect him when she finally let her guard down.

For one split second he relaxed his grip on an oar, accidentally allowed it to slip away with a barely discernible splash. He spared it only a parting glance and tightened his grip on the other oar before it got away, too.

"You asked me what I'd write in my diary about you," Ellen said silkily. "Lennon and I brainstormed a scene for her latest book…it's about a Regency smuggler with a boat. It got me thinking about how sexy it would be to make love outside, beneath the stars. I'm not going to stop myself tonight."

Ellen definitely wasn't playing by the rules right now,

and if she wanted to take a cruise on the wild side, Christopher was happy to row the boat.

"Not scared of the gators, love?"

Reaching behind her, she gifted him with a breathtaking display of toned skin as she dragged something from her purse.

A bag of marshmallows?

She must have recognized his confusion because she explained. "They're for the gators."

"You brought marshmallows for the gators?"

"I read they liked them."

Bayou tour boats let their passengers toss marshmallows overboard, but he suspected she was thinking more along the lines of feeding an alligator as if it were a duck. He refrained from comment, unwilling to burst his urban princess's bubble. Not when he had the perfect opportunity to play her hero.

Pulling in the remaining oar, he scrambled to his knees and palmed her breasts. "I'll wrestle the gators for you, love."

Ellen arched her back and leaned into his touch, with an unfamiliar boldness that made his whole body tense. Although he knew they were far enough from the plantation that not even Lennon and Josh on the third floor could see them through the cover of trees and darkness, he found Ellen's sudden daring more exciting than he could have imagined.

The night was alive around them, filled with echoing sounds and sultry air that caressed them as gently as he caressed her breast with his mouth.

The fine silk of her see-through garment was nothing more than a whisper separating flesh from flesh as he swirled his tongue around a rigid peak, drew her inside his hot mouth.

She sighed, leaned forward enough to kiss the top of his head. It was a simple gesture, but one that conveyed all the tenderness in the world, one that told him he'd made more progress in winning Ellen's heart than he'd dared to hope.

Christopher wanted to drag her into his arms, prove to her through touch that she'd made the right choice, but the logistics were impossible. This seduction could go no farther than steamy kisses and foreplay until he brought them to the shore again.

But steamy kisses and foreplay sounded right just now.

Ellen slipped her hands into his hair, down along his neck and over his shoulders. She sighed, a soft sound that echoed through the night, through him, made him hope she'd finally recognized the truth.

They belonged together. They could find a balance between playing it safe and breaking the rules.

If only she'd let herself believe in them.

He'd use every trick in the book to convince her.

Rolling her nipples between his thumbs and forefingers, he smiled when she squirmed, scooted forward on the bench to press her breasts into his hands. He continued smiling while trailing his mouth upward, tasting, exploring her neck in a way he hadn't thought to when her hair had been long.

He made his way all the way up to her delicate, very sensitive ear...and exhaled. Her breath hitched audibly, her breasts rose and fell beneath his hands.

Then she tipped her face to his, brushed her lips across his. "I love you, Christopher."

Her words filtered through him, blocking out all the night sounds, stunning in their intensity, in their honesty.

She loved him.

He'd known it, but knowing was so different from

knowing she knew it, worlds away from hearing her admit it and having her prove it by stripping in a boat in the middle of the bayou to arouse him.

She loved him.

"I know."

He claimed her mouth in a kiss that proved he'd never doubted her love for an instant. No matter how much she'd denied him, and herself, no matter how far she'd run, no matter how hard she'd fought, he loved her and had believed she loved him.

Christopher kissed her with an urgency he could barely control. She'd thrown caution to the wind—for a little while, at least—and seemed to be testing her limits, their passion. He wanted nothing more than to help her explore.

His hands restlessly kneaded her breasts, itched to coax those soft sighs from her lips. He wanted to plunge deep inside her, prove that what they shared was unique, worth believing in.

But he'd already done a thorough job of exploring what terrain he could.

"Christopher, you've got to get us to the island." Her voice was breathless, just the right combination of urgency and need to make his heartbeat stumble over itself.

With a final flick of his tongue against her kiss-swollen lips, he sat back. "To the island, hmm?"

"Anywhere we can make love will work."

He recognized the desire in her beautiful face, desire she didn't hide. Touched, he lifted his hand to her cheek, was rewarded when her lashes fluttered shut over those incredible eyes and she pressed her cheek into his palm as though she longed for his touch.

She loved him.

"This boat won't work, love?" he said softly. "Afraid

we'll capsize and get eaten by the gators? I thought you brought marshmallows.''

Her eyes opened, her gaze alight with golden sparks, with pleasure. ''I don't think marshmallows will work if we're in the water. I nicked myself in the shower this morning so I'll probably smell like a midnight snack.''

''I'd eat you over a marshmallow any day.''

Her smile made his heart pound harder, and he couldn't help but be amazed by the excitement building between them.

Ellen wasn't holding back. She'd given over to the moment, given over to *him,* and he wasn't about to miss a second of this remarkable transformation.

Unfortunately, the consequences of taking his attention off the boat had translated into their drifting off course. He had to work hard with only one oar to get to the island, but the tender expression on Ellen's face promised he'd be well rewarded.

The gazebo was in a sorry state of disrepair. Though it had been restored periodically throughout its history— even rebuilt once after a hurricane—the previous owners of Félicie Allée hadn't wanted the liability of shuttling guests to and from the island to see a crumbling structure that while historical, wasn't particularly significant.

''This what you had in mind?'' he asked, extending his hand to Ellen to help her climb out of the boat.

She reached for her bag and then swept her gaze over the island that wasn't much larger than Félicie Allée from one shore to the other.

''It'll do,'' she said.

But the wooden steps had rotted in places, and Christopher didn't trust them to support even Ellen's weight.

''Here, let me.'' Grabbing her around the waist, he hoisted her over the steps onto the solid stone foundation.

She reached down, took his hand and helped him launch himself up, too.

"Sure you don't want to put a border of marshmallows around the perimeter so the gators will have something to eat before they get to us?" he suggested.

"Silly man. I think we'll be quite safe up here." But her bravado was exactly that, because she darted a glance around, as if having second thoughts. "Don't you?"

"Very safe. I told you I'd protect you. Trust me."

"I do."

He slid her bag down her shoulder and dropped it onto the ground, moving all evidence of marshmallows and alligators out of sight. Ellen wound her arms around his waist and nuzzled against him, every barely clad inch of her long curves making him long to get naked.

But she clearly had her own agenda for what was going to happen next, because she pulled his shirt up, forced him to lift his arms to help her drag it over his head. It landed on top of her bag. The night air hit his bare skin in a burst of moist heat that was nothing compared to the sight of Ellen dropping down to her knees, taking his shorts along with her.

He barely had time to savor the sight of her dark head poised against his crotch or even to register the fact that she *really* wasn't playing by the rules tonight, before she left his shorts around his ankles and zeroed in on his erection.

She drew him inside her mouth with one long wet pull.

Christopher's hips buck hard. His moan echoed through the night, a strangled sound that frightened whatever wildlife had been slumbering in the branches overhead, judging by the rapid fluttering of wings and rustling leaves that startled the quiet.

Ellen didn't seem to notice, or care. She had a lip-lock

on him that was coiling his muscles so tight that the lightest brush of her soft hair against his thigh made him shake.

Her fingers sliding beneath his balls did a lot more than make him shake. He full-fledged rocked this time, driving his erection into her hot satin mouth.

Ellen was in control of herself, and of him. She weighted him in her palm, fondled him with her gentle fingers, just the right amount of pressure to earn another strangled gasp.

He should stop her, and soon. There was no way in hell he would last long under this sort of determined assault, against the skilled touches of her mouth and fingers that were going to make him explode.

But Christopher's fingers had mutinied against his brain's command because they were suddenly threading through her soft hair, pulling her *toward* him...and his hips were swaying gently...and her tongue was rolling around his deliciously aching flesh and driving him out of his mind.

"Damn, Ellen." Cupping her face in his hands, he forced her to stop the rhythm that would push him right over the edge.

She replied with another long draw that made his knees buckle.

"Damn." He sank back against the decaying header, felt the rough wood scratch his back. When Ellen sank back on her haunches, drawing her mouth away and leaving his wet erection exposed to the air, he groaned.

The sound of her throaty chuckle promised greater things to come, which did much to restore Christopher's equilibrium.

He had Ellen up on her feet before she had time to gasp.

The filmy nothing she wore shimmered over her body in the darkness, but his eyes had long ago adjusted to the lack of light and he could see her every curve, the way her breasts quivered with each rise and fall of her chest. He wanted to bury himself inside her, desperately.

He was going to make love to her. No question. The only question was where?

Urging her around, Christopher came to stand behind her, sliding his hands down the length of her slender arms to guide her toward the railing. "Put your hands here and hang on."

Ellen didn't say a word. She braced herself and pressed her sweet bottom back against him to cradle his erection between her silk-clad cheeks.

Christopher maneuvered aside the wispy silk, wound up ripping apart snaps in his haste. Worked for him. Now there was nothing to stop him from being where he wanted to be....

Taking aim, he found her wet and ready and he sank inside, one hot stroke that dragged a groan from his depths. Her moan filled his ears and for a moment he couldn't move, could only stand there and absorb the feel of her body melting around him.

Standing as they were, he could reach all her intimate places while still protecting her soft skin from the threat of splinters, or worse. He slipped his hands around her, down between her thighs. He rolled that nub with his fingertips, was gratified when she shuddered, a full-bodied shiver that wedged her against him even more.

He dragged his mouth against her neck, infinitely grateful for her new short style that allowed him to access her smooth skin so easily. She tipped her head to the side and suddenly he could catch her mouth with his—the side of her mouth, anyway. But it was enough. Their tongues tangled, warm velvet and tasting of sex, a taste that made him ache to draw out so he could sink inside her again, to thrust

and thrust until he satisfied his need for this woman tha
only grew stronger each time they made love.

But he didn't move until Ellen rolled her hips an
pressed against him, the signal he'd been waiting fo
Christopher pulled back, then plunged inside, all wet he
and softness.

Again, and again.

His body gathered and tightened, built with the amazing
gut-wrenching intensity he felt only with her, each strok
making his control slip a little farther from his grasp.

Ellen's breath clashed with his, her low moans—c
maybe they were his—mingling with their kisses, as sh
levered herself with her arms, raised up on tiptoes to me
his thrusts, her sweet bottom slapping softly against hin
the erotic sound echoing through the misty night. Then he
sex seized up around him as she reached climax. His bod
exploded.

Grasping for the railing, Christopher used his arms t
bracket her before he inadvertently collapsed and ser
them both sprawling to the ground. His heart thudded. Hi
thighs shook. He breathed harder than if he'd swum acros
the bayou, dragging Ellen and the boat behind him.

He'd never felt so damn good.

"Christopher?" Leaning back, she arched her neck unt
they stood cheek to cheek. "Can we see each other agai
after we get home? It's not marriage, but will you let it b
enough?"

He laughed, a broken sound. "It's enough, love."

14

Louis Armstrong Airport

ELLEN HOISTED HER GARMENT BAG over her shoulder, waved goodbye to Olaf.

"Take care." He shot her a dazzling smile and Ellen decided he'd make the perfect hero for Susanna. "You're sure you don't want me to tell you how the mystery wraps up?"

"No, thank you," she said, for the fourth time since they'd left Félicie Allée. "If you do, you'll rob Lennon and me of a perfectly good reason to spend four hours on the telephone."

Christopher and Lennon had both insisted on driving her to the airport, but Ellen had refused their offer, a combination of guilt for making them miss valuable sleuthing time and a need to avoid prolonging the goodbyes. She'd intended to call a taxi, but when Miss Q had pulled rank and offered Olaf's services, she'd had no choice but to accept. The woman simply didn't know the meaning of the words "no, thank you."

With a final wave, she moved with the traffic inside the airport to begin her long wait to the ticketing counter. Her dad had finagled a last-minute commercial flight, and Ellen was almost sorry. Private travel arrangements to Washington, D.C., would have expedited her passage through the airport security process. She'd likely have been in the air in less than half the time.

Which would have given her less time to brood about leaving.

She was brooding all right, big-time. She wasn't ready for her vacation to be over. Not yet. She'd gotten caught up in the mystery and the missing pieces still nagged at her. She and Christopher were so close, she could feel it.

Maybe she should have just let Olaf tell her how the story resolved and put an end to her suspense. But that would have meant accepting that her part in solving the mystery with Christopher was over. She wasn't there yet either.

Denial, a truly amazing thing.

Stepping into the long line at her airline counter, she inclined her head in greeting to the mom with the spiky red hair in front of her, opening a bag filled with coloring books, handheld video games and other items to entertain her two girls during the wait.

Propping her garment bag by her side, Ellen decided the fact that the captain and Felicity weren't getting a happily ever-after only exacerbated her need to solve the mystery. After all, they'd been in love. Those letters…that sort of passion deserved a happily ever after.

She and Christopher deserved it, too.

Maybe that was the real source of her discontent. She'd counted on vacationing until Monday morning, which meant they should still have two full nights to make love before giving up the sort of round-the-clock closeness they'd shared at Félicie Allée. Two nights to prove how much she loved him, before she was back to paying close attention to her comings and goings and how they might be interpreted.

Unless, of course, she married him….

But marriage after six months—three of which they hadn't even spent together? Ellen shook her head. She had to abide by the conventions. Or face the consequences of which her whole family would partake.

She had to play by the rules.

Just like she had to leave today. Her mother was receiving a presidential award, a huge honor…

Mom has received other awards.

…it was understandable that she wanted her family around her…

Would Mom really miss her this once?

…but the press would comment on the missing daughter…

So what? She deserved a life, didn't she?

Yes!

Ellen stared absently through the crowd surrounding her, discontent building as she came face-to-face again with the unpleasant fact that she was the only one holding herself back.

If any of her authors ever put a manuscript on her desk with a heroine who didn't believe in romance heroes and always played it safe, Ellen would have deemed the heroine unworthy of the hero's love, probably unworthy of revisions, too.

Who wanted to read about a heroine who was too scared to take risks? A heroine who let *the one* get away?

Better yet, who wanted to *live* that way?

Okay, technically she wasn't letting Christopher get away. She'd hear from him as soon as he returned to New York. They'd work out some sort of timetable.…

But romances were supposed to have happy endings, damn it.

She didn't want a timetable. She wanted to fall asleep tonight in Christopher's arms. She wanted to wake up to his hot kisses or to him serving espresso and beignets with those dimples flashing.

She wanted a damn happy ending.

I let myself believe it would all work out, and it did.

"Come on, lady. Move it!"

The irritated voice jolted Ellen from her thoughts and she gazed at the scowling man behind her.

He pointed at the ticketing counter. "Your turn."

Ellen issued an automatic apology, which did nothing to erase his scowl, before she moved to the counter. The clerk smiled, a rather pleasant smile, she thought, given the sort of nonstop chaos the tighter airport security measures inspired.

"Your ticket, please."

As she handed over her ticket, the poster above the clerk's head caught her eye.

A sleek white cruise ship cutting through turquoise water.

"Ma'am?" the clerk asked, but Ellen didn't reply.

She was too busy remembering the article about a cruise ship heiress in the office at Félicie Allée.

"Ma'am? Is there a problem?"

No problem at all.

Ellen had just found the missing piece to the mystery.

"I'm sorry," she said, lifting her garment bag from the floor. "I've changed my mind. I won't be making this flight."

The ticketing clerk stared as if she might be a bomb about to detonate, but before she could comment, Ellen slipped away from the counter and headed back toward the drop-off area.

Finding a reasonably quiet corner to hide from the flow of noisy arrivals, she dug through her bag for her cell phone, pressed the speed dial.

Her dad picked up on the second ring. "Hello, honey, what's up? Not a problem with the flight, I hope."

"No, the flight's fine, Dad. But I won't be able to make it home for Mom's award." The declaration came surprisingly easy, which could only mean she'd made the right choice. "Nothing's wrong, so please don't worry. It's just that I'm right in the middle of something important right now. I really can't cut my trip short. Not even for two days."

"What's this all about? You're sure everything's all right?"

"I promise. I'll explain everything when I get back to town. I just have a commitment to fulfill. I hate missing Mom's acceptance, but I hope you'll both understand, and trust me. Everything's fine. It's better than fine, in fact. It's great. Please just kiss Mom, tell her I'm very proud of her and not to worry. I'll be home in two days."

"Does this have something to do with Christopher?"

"Yes."

There was a pause on the other end, then he asked, "Are you happy?"

He was worrying, anyway. She could hear it in his voice. And she loved him for it.

"Yes."

"He's a very good man, honey. You know how we feel. Nothing has changed."

"I do know. Thank you."

"Well, I'll see you at home on Monday," he said. "We'll talk then. In the meantime, enjoy the rest of your trip."

"I love you, Dad."

"I love you, too, honey."

That was it. He'd obviously known she hadn't reached this decision lightly, and while he might not yet understand all that her decision entailed, he trusted her to work things out.

The entire process of placing her needs above her family's had taken less than five minutes from start to finish. Lightning hadn't struck. Her dad still loved her. His main concern had been for her happiness.

All the torment over the past few months suddenly seemed ridiculous and unnecessary. She'd been talking herself out of living, to avoid the conflict of her needs and her duty.

This wasn't what her parents wanted for her.

This wasn't what *she* wanted.

Just because she took the left turn instead of the right didn't mean she'd disappointed the people she loved. Yes, she'd made mistakes, but real strength lay in learning from those mistakes and in learning to forgive herself.

Maybe the torment had been necessary, after all.

Let the spin doctors spin. That was what her mother paid them for. Christopher was worth fighting for.

Ellen returned the phone to her purse and headed outside to hail a taxi. But she'd barely made it to the curb, when the sound of a blaring horn caught her attention. She glanced up to see a sleek gray limousine maneuvering toward the pickup ramp. Unable to contain her smile, she waited while it pulled to a stop directly in front of her. The driver's door opened and Olaf stepped out, looking just like a hero from another century in his cutaway jacket.

"And to what do I owe this pleasure?" she asked.

"Miss Q told me to make a few passes, just in case your travel arrangements changed."

"She did, did she? How very thoughtful." *How very perceptive.*

After circling the limousine, he took her garment bag. "A taxi back to Félicie Allée would cost a small fortune."

One she gladly would have paid.

"Thanks." He opened the door and she slipped inside the cool interior. But before he'd closed the door behind her, inspiration struck.

Ellen took a deep breath and gave in to impulse. "Olaf, would you mind making a pit stop before we head back? I need the services of a good jeweler. I assume you know one around here?"

He shot her a dazzling grin. "I do, indeed."

"Then, if you wouldn't mind..." She sank into the plush seat feeling...*liberated.*

Just a few hours later, Olaf dropped Ellen off in front of Félicie Allée with the promise to return her garment bag to the garden suite. She wasn't worried about her clothing, though. She had a wardrobe filled with costumes, one of which she'd soon be donning to hunt down Christopher and share her surprise.

During the drive back, she'd asked Olaf's permission to search the office, and he'd granted her request with a jauntily delivered "The entire plantation is fair game."

Although he hadn't said anything else, Ellen got the impression he approved her request and that feeling fed her excitement. She entered the hall, considered finding Christopher, but as the hall and the office were both empty, she decided to follow up her idea first.

Ellen headed straight to the wall with the newspaper clipping. It was a brief society piece dated June 1820, a small, innocuous-looking article she was surprised she'd even noticed.

California Cruise Ship Owner Weds
West Coast Hotelier

Bridgett Lovett, well-known owner of Lovett Luxury Sailing Ships, a fleet of vessels offering a variety of cruises along the Californian coastline, married wealthy hotelier Samuel Collins, owner of twelve properties in major West Coast cities.

The bride's brother, fellow Lovett Luxury Sailing Ships owner Jack Lovett, and his wife Félicie, hosted the wedding at the groom's grandest hotel in San Francisco for more than five hundred guests.

Jack and Félicie Lovett.
Julian and Felicity Lafever.
Goose bumps peppered down Ellen's bare arms. It *had* to be them—which meant the captain hadn't murdered Felicity for revenge or money or by accident. He hadn't murdered her at all. He and Felicity had staged her murder, arranged for her corpse to disappear and left Louisiana to live happily ever after.

It fit perfectly. If the captain had approached the governor on that fateful weekend to ask his permission to marry Felicity and was denied…if defending New Orleans in battle and receiving a presidential pardon weren't enough to make the governor accept him what else could the captain possibly have done to prove himself worthy?

If the governor still intended to force his daughter to marry the mayor's son, then the captain would have only had two choices: let the woman he loved marry another man, or stage her death and sweep her off to a new life in California.

A hero would never give up the woman he loved.

Just like Christopher hadn't. Even though she'd been blind. Even though she'd never given him any reason to hope she'd change her mind. He'd believed enough for the two of them.

Ellen laughed aloud. Here she and Christopher had been thinking that Félicie Allée had been named after the captain's mother—some French variation of "happy Allie." But now that she thought about it, naming the plantation after his mother didn't make sense. She'd died long before the captain and Brigitte had relocated to Louisiana. The captain had been building the plantation while falling in love with Felicity.

She glanced up at the article again. Félicie Lovett.

Félicie must have been the captain's nickname for her, and Lennon's mother had said the translation of *allée* meant "path." Félicie's path to the man she loved. A path she hadn't been afraid to take, because she was a heroine worthy of her hero.

Ellen folded her arms across her chest, hugging herself and rocking back on her heels. She had to go find Christopher. He'd know what happened next. Did they present their theory now to Miss Q and Olaf? Or should they wait until the denouement, which wouldn't take place until tomorrow night?

She needed to know because she wanted to take him back to the garden suite and spend the night proving she was very, *very* grateful he'd never given up hope for them.

Ellen glanced back up at the framed article and smiled. Right out in the open for everyone to see. Harley's notion about hiding clues where people would overlook them as obvious had been right on target.

As she circled the desk to leave the office, Ellen glanced down to where scattered papers and a glimpse of familiar handwriting caught her eye. She peered down curiously at a signature she might never have noticed if not for the name that leaped out at her as if it had been lit in flashing neon.

B. Christopher Sinclair.

Byron. Who'd have guessed? She certainly wouldn't have. Not in a million years. Though his mother's love of

Lord Byron's poetry didn't come as any real surprise. Christopher had come by his romantic streak honestly.

And she was counting on his romantic streak right now, because if all went as she hoped, she wouldn't be left out of knowing the intimate details of his life ever again.

With a fingertip, she eased the document from beneath others, curious to see what he'd signed his full name to when he'd never used it while they'd dated. She glanced down at what appeared to be…

An authorization for a work order?

Lifting the document off the desk, Ellen scanned what turned out to be a work order for the repair of the island gazebo where they'd made love last night.

Why would Christopher be signing for repair work?

But his wasn't the only signature. Quinevere McDarby's name was elegantly scrawled below his.

Owners, Southern Charm Mysteries, Inc.

It took one stunning, breathless moment for Ellen to absorb the evidence right before her eyes, to register the impossible fact that Christopher and Miss Q were the co-owners of Southern Charm Mysteries.

"We?" Ellen had asked Miss Q at the start of the training.

"Quite a few of us have been involved in pulling together Southern Charm Mysteries," she'd replied.

B. Christopher Sinclair.

Which meant Christopher must also own some part of Félicie Allée.

"The former owners couldn't make the location work to their benefit," Miss Q had said.

"They lacked vision and imagination," Christopher had agreed.

"Which is not a problem with the current owners. We're visionaries."

Visionaries, indeed.

The blood was rushing so hard in her ears that Ellen never even heard the door open, not until she heard Christopher's voice.

"Olaf said you'd come back."

She glanced up. Their gazes locked over the desk, over the document she held. One look at his face told her he was reeling from her unexpected return. No less than she was reeling. He recovered first, must have recognized her stricken expression because he frowned.

"Ellen, I—"

"You own Southern Charm Mysteries with Miss Q?" she asked.

"Yes."

"And Félicie Allée?"

"My company held the majority shares on the property. When they were going to sell it, I saw an opportunity to put the place to work. I thought it was a chance to turn the plantation into something people would appreciate, rather than leave it down here to rot in the bayou."

Though she recognized the words as her own from a conversation long ago, the reasoning was quintessential Christopher. Sharp business acumen edged with the unexpected. Unorthodox. Like his marriage proposal.

"But why?"

"Because of you, love."

"You bought an antebellum plantation because I liked it. Christopher, that's crazy."

He shrugged. "It's a solid investment. You thought the plantation had potential and I trust your judgment. Félicie Allée is the perfect place to host murder-mystery training sessions. It's also the perfect place to host a seduction. But it took...well, it took me some time to pull it together."

She blinked, had absolutely no idea what to think. Or

what to say. A crazy tightness mushroomed in her chest, made it impossible to breathe, let alone talk.

And she'd thought the Pinabel had been extravagant.

"I got what I came for, love, so I consider the training a success." His too-blue gaze searched her face, a caress that melted away some of her shock, geared her up for... "You'll take my calls once we get back to New York."

She winced at the reminder of her behavior when she'd ended their relationship—behavior that had seemed so logical at the time seemed completely horrible now. Christopher hadn't let her go. He might have compromised if only she had given him a chance.

He'd been *the one* all along.

She'd so misunderstood this man, all because she'd been afraid of pushing past her own limits, of moving outside the comfortable safe boundaries of her life.

But no more. Ellen was through playing it safe.

I let myself believe it would all work out, and it did.

Ellen believed. She'd have to remember to tell Lennon she'd been right about heroes all along.

The work order slipped from her fingers, fluttered back to the desk. "You went through all this effort and expense just so I'd take your phone calls when we got home?"

He folded his arms across his chest and smiled. "Actually, I'd set my sights a lot higher, but given that the session was cut short, I thought it best to reevaluate my objective."

Her heartbeat fluttered wildly as she searched his gaze, recognized the truth she saw in those beautiful eyes.

The time had come to put up or shut up.

"I think you should stick with your original objective."

"Excuse me, love?"

The man obviously didn't get it, and Ellen couldn't blame him, which reminded her of his comment about a pod person invading her body. He had every right to think she'd been invaded. She'd done nothing to let him know how she felt, hadn't even acknowledged the truth to herself.

But that was back when she'd been living life by the rules.

Reaching for her purse, she flipped it open, dug inside. Christopher watched, his deepening frown clearly conveying what he thought was coming.

But she didn't pull out her cell phone, proving that times were indeed changing.

"Will you marry me?" She lifted out a square jeweler's box. "I brought you a ring. I thought it might…you know, make it official."

"You want to marry me?"

"Yes, Christopher, I do. In say…oh, I don't know, two months. Is that enough time to plan a decent wedding?"

He glanced down at the ring, and she felt all fluttery inside, nervous, expectant, *vulnerable*. She needed him to react, but as he really wasn't recovering quickly this go-round, she reached for his hand and slipped the ring on his finger.

A square gold band split into two smaller bands that cradled a gorgeous diamond. A simple, very masculine ring, beautiful on his strong hand, which was exactly what she'd hoped for.

And it was a perfect fit.

Just like they were, together.

"Will you marry me, Christopher?"

Ellen searched his face and something about the way his expression had softened told her she'd touched him, deeply. When he lifted his gaze, she saw all the love she felt mirrored in those gorgeous eyes.

"You're ready to toss out the rule book?"

"Not exactly." She placed his hand on her waist and stepped into the circle of his arms. "I'm making up new rules. The first one is—If I let myself believe it'll all work out, it will."

"And it will." Dimples flashed. "I'll marry you, love."

Then his mouth came down on hers, promising her a future filled with firsts, and Ellen knew what her second rule for happiness would be: Know when to abandon all the other rules.

The Hall

CHRISTOPHER LED ELLEN into the hall to say goodbye to the guests. They were dressed in their twenty-first century street clothes for the trip back to reality, which they'd be making together earlier in the day than expected. Ellen's father had arranged private transportation for their return flight and invited them for dinner at the Talbots' home on Long Island.

The time had come to explain the new game plan and invite his future in-laws to the wedding. And he'd be by Ellen's side to issue that invitation—exactly where he wanted to be.

But until then, they would enjoy the company of their friends and acquaintances, bask in the glow of their win. The denouement was over and they'd claimed the prize. Southern Charm Mysteries' grand opening training session had been a success.

"I think it's significant that we have three private investigators here and not one could solve this mystery," Miss Q said from her perch on a bench.

She'd abandoned her costume, as well, and Christopher was glad they were through the grand opening, because now Olaf would take over the daily operations and free

Miss Q up for her next adventure. She'd gifted Olaf with a business he enjoyed running, and would eventually own once she turned over her shares. Christopher appreciated their partnership, too, knew the business would be in good hands.

All in all, the new owners of Southern Charm Mysteries, Inc. were very pleased.

"Significant?" Josh stared down at Miss Q with a surly expression. "I'd say it's lame."

"Lennon, did you write this script and purposely hold out on Josh so you wouldn't win?" Ellen asked.

Lennon shook her head. "I didn't write the script."

"But there's something so familiar about this story setup." Ellen eyed Susanna and Tracy warily.

"Don't look at me," Susanna said. "I haven't had time to moonlight. I've been rewriting my latest book, remember?"

"Me, too," Tracy chimed in.

Though Christopher could only assume Susanna and Tracy referred to the status of their current projects with Ellen, he did recognize the effect on Ellen. Color rode high in her cheeks, but she smiled, an amused, beautiful smile that underscored her newfound commitment to enjoy the moment.

"No, I don't suppose either of you would have had the time." She laughed and fixed her gaze on Miss Q. "Was it Stephanie?"

"Yes, it was, dear."

"I should have known. If the twist didn't give it away, the awful title should have."

"*Away with the Tide* isn't nearly as bad as *Lord of the Ravished.*" Lennon rolled her eyes.

"Thank goodness."

"Stephanie has a warped sense of humor." Tracy sat

down beside Miss Q. "We came to investigate a murder. How were we supposed to make the leap to romance?"

"There were plenty of clues." Miss Q patted her knee. "Ellen and Christopher found quite a few."

"Actually, Ellen discovered both the clues that turned our investigation around," said Christopher. He wouldn't take credit for her cleverness. Not when he liked the way she smiled at his gallantry. "We were looking for Mac and Harley's diary the whole time, but we never found it."

"How'd you know about the diary?" Mac asked.

"We overheard you and Harley arguing about where to hide it," Ellen explained. "Where did you finally decide on?"

Mac scowled at Harley, charging her with the blame, but Josh was scowling at the two of them even harder.

Harley ignored them both and said lightly, "So you were with the ringing cell phone we heard that day. We decided on a shelf in the summer bedroom."

Ellen shot him a glance that said, *The only bedroom we didn't search.*

"Don't sweat it, though," Harley continued. "You didn't miss much. The diary only corroborated Brigitte and Felicity's friendship."

"Really, the mystery was very simple to figure out, dears," Miss Q said, drawing all their attention. "If you came at it with love as the motive. The captain's father loved his family so he smuggled them to safety before his execution. The beautiful Allienor loved her son, so she reared him to manhood before allowing herself to find love again and give birth to Brigitte. The captain loved his sister so he tried to create a wonderful life for her. It all makes perfect sense."

Christopher wasn't exactly sure how many guests would

think to come at a murder mystery from the love angle, but he supposed that was a plot twist in itself.

"Speaking of love," Ellen said. "Christopher and I would like to invite you back to Félicie Allée on Labor Day weekend for our wedding. We hope you'll all be able to join us."

After a moment of shocked silence, everyone erupted into good wishes. Lennon launched herself at Ellen and they hugged.

Josh shook his hand. "Won't be a dull moment, trust me."

"I'm counting on it," Christopher said.

Miss Q and Olaf hung back with smiles on their faces— they'd been let in on the wedding plans earlier to secure the date for the wedding—and the chorus of congratulations and questions continued until Tracy's voice rang out over the confusion.

"Where's the ring?" she demanded.

Ellen reached for his hand, and Christopher smiled gamely as she displayed his engagement ring.

"Ah, excuse me, Ellen—romance editor who's supposed to know these sorts of details—" Tracy said with a frown. "Are you getting senile in your dotage? Did you somehow miss that *he's* supposed to give *you* the ring?"

"No. I'm not getting senile, Ms. You'll-reach-your-dotage-a-month-behind-me. *I* proposed to *him.*"

"This time." Miss Q chuckled.

"Ellen will have her ring as soon as we get home," Christopher promised.

"Speaking of home—" Miss Q stood "—it's that time, I'm afraid. I want to thank you all for participating in Southern Charm Mysteries' grand opening session and ask you to remember us for all your training needs."

With her words, the group broke up to say individual goodbyes.

Christopher overheard Susanna say to Olaf, "So I guess I'll be back here in September."

"I hope to see you before that." Olaf led her toward the door. "If you don't make it to town to see your son, I've got a supplier in Shreveport I need to visit...."

Christopher looped Ellen's arm through his, tucking her close by his side for the trip back to the real world to greet their future.

With a bright smile, Miss Q followed Olaf and Susanna through the door, and, as she swept past, winked up at them and said, "Ah, *l'amour*."

Epilogue

AFTER REPEATED KNOCKING didn't yield an invitation into Ellen's apartment, Christopher used his key to let himself in. She hadn't been expecting him back in New York until the following day, but as he'd wrapped up negotiations for controlling interest in a Las Vegas hotel, a two-thousand-room property currently an entertainment hot spot and a plum acquisition for his firm, he'd hopped on an earlier flight.

He might have called to tell Ellen he'd be coming over, but he had the element of surprise on his side tonight and had decided to run with it. After all, Ellen had been making a great deal of headway lately in learning to allow herself to enjoy life's unexpected moments. She'd even shown promise in arranging a few surprises of her own.

Like the night he'd arrived home from Germany, where an analysis of a historic site had held him up, to find her draped across his leather coach wearing nothing but high heels and his tie. Who knew his fiancée had such a latent impulsive streak?

Tonight Christopher found her on the small balcony, misting orchids as she inspected the leaves with a thoughtful expression. She was still dressed in a suit, and he suspected she hadn't left her office until late.

Silhouetted in profile against a night sky that blazed

with lights brighter than the stars, he felt his pulse quicken and a smile form on his face. His sense of contentment with the world continued to grow stronger as they neared their wedding day.

"Will you miss your garden, love?"

She paused in mid-spray, darting a surprised gaze his way. Just as quickly, surprise dissolved into pleasure on her beautiful face.

"I'll be sad to let it go, but I'm excited to start another in our new home. We'll have so much room."

"We've been approved by the apartment home owners board?"

She nodded. "We're ready to close whenever we can arrange our schedules to get to the title office."

"Let's make it a priority. I want to use this last month before the wedding to get some work done on the place. I want our home ready when we come back from our honeymoon."

After an intensive search, they'd finally found the perfect apartment on the Upper East Side, a place where they could face whatever life had in store for them.

"I took Mom and Leah by to see it yesterday. They loved it. Said we lucked out big-time."

Christopher set his briefcase on the dining room table. Shrugging off his jacket, he loosened his tie and draped both over a chair. "I only wish we were having as much luck tracking down your engagement ring."

"Not for a lack of searching." She hung her mist bottle on a neatly arranged shelf that contained various gardening supplies. "I did see one yesterday that has potential. I passed the jewelry store on the way to lunch with Mom and Leah."

"Potential, love? I thought we agreed we'd only consider a ring that sent you over the moon."

"I'm beginning to think such a beast doesn't exist. There can't be many jewelry stores left that we haven't visited."

Christopher reached into the change pocket of his jacket. "Such a beast exists."

Something in his voice must have given him away because Ellen narrowed her gaze. "Really?"

"Really." He stepped onto the balcony to join her. With a sense of excitement, and not a little anxiety, he presented her with a blue-velvet jeweler's box and popped open the lid.

For a moment, she eyed the ring inside dubiously. He only allowed himself to breathe again when her beautiful hazel eyes widened and her mouth popped open in kissable astonishment.

"Oh...my...gosh." Her gaze darted up to him and then back to the ring again, before she plucked it from the box for a closer inspection. "Christopher, this is it! How did you...I mean *where*—"

"I had it designed."

The ring held a striking solitaire set in a streamlined swirl of polished gold.

"There's an inscription," he said.

My love, always.

"It's perfect." Her eyes glinted suspiciously.

Taking it from her, he slipped it onto her finger, pleased with the fit. As he'd already asked her to marry him, he thought about asking her to love him, always.

But Ellen had caught her lower lip between her teeth as though she was losing her fight with tears, so he said, instead, "I'm glad you think it's perfect, love. I was beginning to think we'd have grandchildren before finding you an engagement ring."

She lifted that misty gaze, frowned. "What would you have done if I'd hated it?"

"Put it up for auction on eBay, I guess."

"Christopher!"

He laughed. "It never even occurred to me that you'd hate it. Like you said, we've visited nearly every jewelry store in the city. I had a good idea of what you were looking for. I just needed a jeweler to design it for me."

"Who?"

"Miss Q hooked me up with an artist back home who specializes in designing erotic jewelry. She told me you admired several of her pieces on display in the Eastman Gallery."

Ellen extended her hand to survey the ring again, and Christopher savored her tender expression, the contentment that made her every exhalation sound like a sigh.

Then, in the space of a heartbeat, that weepy glow in her eyes took on a hint of playfulness he'd never seen before their return from Félicie Allée and was only now becoming acquainted with.

"So this ring was designed by an erotic artist, hmm?" she said thoughtfully. "Let me see what's so erotic about it. The inscription has definite erotic potential, of course."

Slipping the jacket from her shoulders, she hung it from the gardening shelf before turning her back to him and motioning to the button at the collar of her blouse.

"My love, always," she said softly while he unbuttoned her blouse. "I do, you know."

"I do."

His body temperature began to climb when she pulled the silky blouse over her head and tossed it aside absently. It snagged on the branches of a ficus tree. Ellen either didn't notice or care, because she turned her attention to unzipping her skirt.

"So what else is erotic, do you think?"

Besides the sight of her shimmying that skirt down her long legs? "The design sort of reminds me of a cherry on top of a soft-serve ice-cream cone."

"An ice-cream cone?" She glanced down at the ring as though that thought had never occurred to her, and she wasn't entirely certain she liked the parallel. "What's so erotic about that?"

Cocking a hip against the railing, he feigned a nonchalance he was far from feeling, as she stepped out of her skirt, leaning over in a studied move of sleek curves and feminine grace, a move he knew was intended to make him salivate. And did.

"When I think of ice cream, I think of licking."

"Hmm." She stood up again, tossing her skirt through the open door and not glancing back when it missed the chair she'd presumably been aiming for and landed on the floor. "Are you thinking about licking right now, Christopher?"

"I am, indeed, love."

"Good, because I was thinking that my new beautiful engagement ring might be most erotic..." she trailed off while popping the hook to her bra "...if it was the *only* thing I was wearing."

Her beautiful breasts spilled out, gleaming pale in the moonlight, and he folded his arms across his chest to keep from pulling her against him. Ellen had the floor and he'd decided before ever leaving Félicie Allée to do everything in his power to help her explore this playful, impulsive side of herself.

It was good for her, and, he thought as he watched her breasts plump invitingly when she leaned over to peel away her panty hose, there were obvious benefits for him.

"Out here, love, really? Where the whole city might

see?'' Which wasn't entirely true. Not only was the night dark, but no prying eyes could possibly see through the jungle of plants that comprised Ellen's balcony oasis. "What about rule number three of the Talbot family code of conduct, which states clearly that public displays of affection invite public speculation?"

"Didn't anyone tell you that rules were meant to be broken?" Ellen shrugged, making her breasts jiggle invitingly. "I suppose I'll just have to devote our future to showing you."

"You do that, love." Because from where Christopher stood, the future looked so damn good.

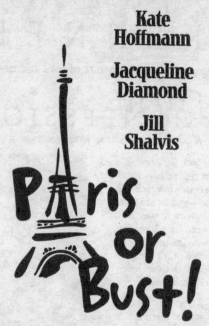

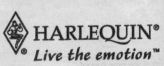

COOPER'S CORNER

Welcome to Cooper's Corner...
a small town with very big surprises!

Coming in April 2003...
JUST ONE LOOK
by Joanna Wayne

Check-in: After a lifetime of teasing, Cooper's Corner postmistress Alison Fairchild finally had the cutest nose ever—thanks to recent plastic surgery! At her friend's wedding, all eyes were on her, except those of the gorgeous stranger in the dark glasses—then she realized he was blind.

Checkout: Ethan Granger wasn't the sightless teacher everyone thought, but an undercover FBI agent. When he met Alison, he was thankful for those dark glasses. If she could see into his eyes, she'd know he was in love....

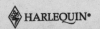

HARLEQUIN

AMERICAN *Romance*®

Celebrate 20 Years
of Home, Heart and Happiness!

Join us for a yearlong anniversary celebration as we
bring you not-to-be-missed miniseries such as:

MILLIONAIRE, MONTANA

A small town wins a huge jackpot in this six-book continuity
(January–June 2003)

THE BABIES OF DOCTORS CIRCLE

Jacqueline Diamond's darling doctor trilogy
(March, May, July 2003)

♛ A ROYAL
TWIST

Victoria Chancellor's witty royal duo
(January and February 2003)

And look for your favorite authors throughout the year, including:

Muriel Jensen's JACKPOT BABY (January 2003)

Judy Christenberry's
SAVED BY A TEXAS-SIZED WEDDING (May 2003)

Cathy Gillen Thacker's brand-new
DEVERAUX LEGACY story (June 2003)

Look for more exciting programs throughout the year
as Harlequin American Romance celebrates its 20th Anniversary!

Available at your favorite retail outlet.

HARLEQUIN®

Makes any time special ®

Visit us at www.eHarlequin.com

HARTAC

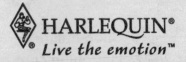